'So you don't see it as an honour to be the King's mistress? Many women would.'

'His Majesty has a new wife,' Ginny said, 'of whom I am fond, sir. I would be shamed, not honoured. You, apparently, see things differently. You stand to gain.'

Sir Jon's reply was not quite what she'd expected 'Believe it or not, mistress, I am not as eager as you seem to think to propel you with all haste into the King's bed. I can manage without his rewards. So tell me,' he continued, 'is there someone else?'

Here was the perfect opportunity, Ginny thought, to invent some mysterious and handsome lover to whom she had given her heart, to show Sir Jon she could play the dalliance game as well as he. But for the life of her she could not do it, and the chance slipped away before she could make the slightest dent in his arrogance.

'No,' she whispered, looking at the gold aglets on his sleeve. 'There's no one.'

He lifted her chin to make her eyes meet his. But the shadows were deep and there was little for him to r   f hostility of

BETRAYED, BETROTHED AND BEDDED

Juliet Landon

Published in Great Britain 2014
by Mills & Boon, an imprint of Harlequin (UK) Limited,
Eton House, 18-24 Paradise Road, Richmond, Surrey, TW9 1SR

© 2014 Juliet Landon

ISBN: 978 0 263 90970 8

Harlequin (UK) Limited's policy is to use papers that are natural, renewable and recyclable products and made from wood grown in sustainable forests. The logging and manufacturing processes conform to the legal environmental regulations of the country of origin.

Printed and bound in Spain
by Blackprint CPI, Barcelona

Juliet Landon's keen interest in art and history, both of which she used to teach, combined with a fertile imagination, make writing historical novels a favourite occupation. She is particularly interested in researching the early medieval and Regency periods, and the problems encountered by women in a man's world. Her heart's home is in her native North Yorkshire, but now she lives happily in a Hampshire village close to her family. Her first books, which were on embroidery and design, were published under her own name of Jan Messent.

Previous novels by the same author:

THE WIDOW'S BARGAIN
THE BOUGHT BRIDE
HIS DUTY, HER DESTINY
THE WARLORD'S MISTRESS
A SCANDALOUS MISTRESS
DISHONOUR AND DESIRE
THE RAKE'S UNCONVENTIONAL MISTRESS
MARRYING THE MISTRESS
SCANDALOUS INNOCENT
  (collaboration with the National Trust)
SLAVE PRINCESS
MISTRESS MASQUERADE

Prologue

1536

There were still days that late autumn when the light was so bright and clear that it almost hurt the eyes. Even in England. On this particular morning, only a month before All Saints, the low sun bounced its rays across fields of stubble and flooded the sky with a cobalt blue that made the party of riders blink and shade their eyes against the glare.

'Over there, see?' said Sir Walter D'Arvall, pointing to a distant mark on the horizon. 'The towers? Still in place, thank God.' His voice held a tone of relief and excitement, for the grand and glorious priory towers and their bells were usually the first to be destroyed in King Henry's purge of religious foundations since his much-publicised rift with his Holiness the pope.

In the small group accompanying Sir Walter, his second daughter, Ginny, had just returned home after living for over four years with a northern family and, having had enough of her mother's attempts to count through the linen cupboard once more, had leaped at her father's invitation to visit Sandrock Priory across the rolling downlands of Hampshire. The prior, Father Spenney, had a good-looking nephew, Ben. He and Ginny had known each other since childhood and, in her absence, they had seen each other only infrequently. There would be some catching up to do. She spurred her horse forwards along the tracks. 'Is Father Spenney expecting us?' she said, meaning, *Is Ben expecting me?* She hoped he had not taken his vows while she'd been away.

'No,' said her father. He did not tell her, as perhaps he ought to have done, that the other person he expected to meet at the priory was another neighbour, Sir Jon Raemon, heir to much of the land adjoining his own, and proprietor, for the past three years, of Lea Magna while his father was incarcerated in a French prison. At twenty-four years old, the responsibility for an estate the size of Lea Magna was considerable, more than most young men would have welcomed, but Sir Jon was the kind of man to make a good son-in-law, eager and competent. Now Ginny was back home, he might, God willing, be on the look-out for a well-bred, well-trained young woman to ease his path through life, and even if the dowry would not have set his heart racing, her looks, Sir Walter thought, might make up for what the dowry lacked. Although they might not, if Sir Jon turned out to be as pragmatic as himself. At well-turned sixteen, Virginia D'Arvall had an exceptional beauty, and Sir Walter had never believed he would have the slightest difficulty in finding a husband for her. So far, his theory had not been put to the test but today…today, it might be.

At Sandrock Priory, Sir Walter and Ginny were escorted into the library, where Father Spenney stood at the top of a ladder handing down books to a team of brown-clad monks. Not being a man of expansive gestures, he merely smiled his pleasure and climbed down, holding out his hands to his friend and neighbour. 'A sorry state you see us in, Sir Walter,' he said sadly. 'I never thought to see such a day. Ah, well!'

'We shall talk,' said Sir Walter. 'Then maybe…who knows…?' He shrugged. 'But you remember Virginia, Father? She was a lass of twelve or thirteen years when you last met. You see a change?'

'Father,' said Ginny, 'we have all changed, except you.' Her eyes searched for Ben amongst those monks who had begun a discreet exit. Finding a pair of adoring brown eyes, she smiled at the change in him, too. The same age as Ginny, Father Spenney's nephew had never been in a position to develop his friendship with Sir Walter's daughter, but as children there had always been an attraction that they knew could, with more contact, grow into something deeper. Now, with the priory about to be dissolved by Act of Parliament, it looked as if Ben and his uncle might be lost to them altogether unless her father offered them a home.

Father Spenney's hand smoothed over the leather-bound volume on top of a pile, his fingertips lingering over the gold tooling and heavy jewelled clasp. 'We're trying to save them,' he said. 'You know what they'll do with these, Sir Walter, if they get their hands on them? They'll sell them to grocers and chandlers for wrapping paper. They're sending books by the shipload to bookbinders for the leather and parchment. They reuse the metal pieces and the pages they'll use as rags.' His voice wavered, balking at the images of destruction. 'Priceless,' he whispered. 'Hundreds of years old. Doesn't he realise what's happening to them?'

A voice from the archway at the far end of the library turned all heads in his direction. 'When the king makes a decree,' the man said, striding forwards, 'it may mean that something suffers in its wake. If he made exceptions for this, that, and the other, there'd be those who would take advantage. It would be chaos, Father.' The man came to stand beside Sir Walter, removing his cap and extending his hand in greeting. 'Sir Walter. Well met, sir. I hope I see you in good health? And your lady wife?' Taller and broader than the two older men, his athletic frame and easy, graceful bearing would have drawn attention in any crowd, for not only was he perfectly dressed in a black fur-lined mantle over a black brocade doublet, but he was also the handsomest man Ginny had ever seen. So good-looking, in fact, that she could hardly take her eyes off the strongly chiselled features and the thick dark hair that showed the imprint of his cap, before he replaced it. The jaw was square and well defined, the neck muscled and frilled by a delicate linen collar edged with blackwork embroidery, with rows of gold aglets to tie all edges together.

His voice matched the figure, Ginny thought,

well modulated and richly dark. And he was working for King Henry VIII to destroy the monasteries. He greeted the prior as though they had already met that morning. 'My assistants are preparing lists, Father,' he said. 'Are you ready for them in here?'

'A few more minutes, Sir Jon, if you will?' said Father Spenney. 'But you recall Mistress D'Arvall, surely?'

Sir Jon swung round to face Ginny and slowly removed his cap again with a graceful flourish and a bow that allowed him to keep his eyes on her until he was upright. 'Mistress D'Arvall? I thought I knew all your family, Sir Walter. Where have you been keeping this one hidden?' He made it sound, Ginny thought, as if she was the last of a litter.

'With the noble Norton family in Northumbria until last week, Sir Jon. Virginia, this is our neighbour, Sir Jon Raemon. I don't believe you ever met, did you?'

'No, Father. Sir Jon,' Ginny said, making her curtsy. Northumbria, her father had said, where she had been introduced to young and not-so-young men by the score, where not one of them had held her interest for more than a day or so, though she'd had to pretend otherwise out of politeness to her hosts. She had learned how to conduct herself in every situation and was now, in theory at least, supposed to be able to handle herself as a lady should. But there were times, she was discovering, when nothing could prepare one for the heart's response to this kind of thing, when it refused to obey commands to settle back into its rhythm, to beat less loudly, to give her her breath back. Her eyes were held by his, dark and probing, as if he could see that something deep inside her was already changing, writing that life change on her heart for ever. If one believed in love at first sight, then this must be it.

'Mistress D'Arvall,' he said, taking in the full picture of her in a pool of bright sunlight. It caught the white-gold mane that fell down her back, lighting up the perfect complexion and the autumn glow in her cheeks and lips. The grey black-rimmed eyes glistened like quartz, incredibly thick lashed. 'I have met your two brothers often at court. The elder one, Master Elion, assists your father, I believe, in the household offices.'

'He does, sir. He aspires to be comptroller of the royal household one day, but he'll have to wait a while.'

Sir Jon smiled. Dead man's shoes, indeed.

'And the younger...Paul, is it? What does he aspire to?'

'To be a gentleman of the king's bedchamber. The king likes him well.'

'Hmph! And you, mistress? You seek a place at court, too?'

There were several pairs of ears listening. This was not the moment to be discussing her future and all those clever responses she'd learnt deserted her. 'No, sir. I am a countrywoman at heart.' What was she saying? He would think her unlettered and dull, domestic, bovine. She could do better than that. 'But these books belonging to the priory, Sir Jon. Is there not a better way of disposing of them? Some safe place, perhaps, where they could be kept until...well... I mean, are *you* not in a position to turn a blind eye to their existence here? Once destroyed, they can never be replaced, can they? As the king's official, do you condone the destruction of such priceless treasures? Will you allow it?'

Sir Jon's eyes widened under the welter of questions, but instead of answering them directly, he spoke to her father. Which she resented. 'What do you have here, Sir Walter? A bookish daughter?'

The quartz eyes glittered hard. 'I am not bookish, Sir Jon,' she replied, 'but I know an irreplaceable item when I see one and there are hundreds here. Individually, they must be worth—'

'Mistress D'Arvall,' said Sir Jon, unused to being lectured by a woman, 'I am aware of their worth. But when the king gives me an order through his secretary, Sir Thomas Cromwell, I tend not to question it unless I want to lose my job. Which I do not. The priory must be emptied, and Father Spenney understands that it must be done efficiently and quickly. We don't have time to find buyers for individual items, however precious. As I have said, if His Majesty were to start making exceptions, we should be here for ever. He needs the funds rather urgently, you see.'

Father Spenney was more resigned. 'I think you may be on a loser here, Mistress D'Arvall. Don't pursue it. It's useless.'

Sir Walter disagreed. 'Does Cromwell know exactly what happens to every item, Sir Jon?' he said. 'If not, then I have a suggestion that might find favour with you and our beloved prior. Would you care to hear it?'

The silence in the room, padded by shelves of books and manuscripts, was almost tangible as Sir Jon absorbed the implications of a scheme as yet unspoken, while the noble head turned to

look at Ginny with a sweeping survey that she
thought he might have used on a piece of prime
bloodstock. It both infuriated and excited her.
Then, ushering his neighbours to one side for
a more personal discussion, he said, 'Shall we
talk about this, Sir Walter? And my lord prior?
What exactly do you…?'

Ginny and Ben remained to draw some comfort from a hurried conversation and a privacy
they had not thought likely to happen. How
would they manage once the priory was closed
down, emptied, sold off, and re-used for secular
purposes? Where would Ben go? What could
he do? How would he earn a living? Her father,
Ginny was sure, would not allow them to be
homeless. Ben would not now be taking vows.
His pleasant face softened as he drew on that
hope, while the thought of seeing more of her
than before would mean more to him than food.
Even so, as plans were tossed to and fro within
Sandrock Priory on that autumn morning, Ben
sensed that something had already happened to
Ginny that she herself would find impossible
either to admit or explain. And although she
spoke oftener and kindlier to Ben than to Sir
Jon, it was the young gallant with the authority over people's livelihoods and the manners of
an arrogant courtier that held her attention on a

knife-edge, as if she would keep every detail of him in her memory to sustain her in the days, weeks, months ahead. His place was at court. Hers, by her own choosing, was at D'Arvall Hall. They were unlikely ever to meet again.

Ben, however, was a known quantity, nearby and adoring, the very antithesis of Sir Jon Raemon with his royal connections and ambitions. Not that she and Ben could ever have become marriage partners: Ben's orphaned state and lack of prospects excluded him completely from her father's list of potential sons-in-law. Her affection for the gentle, scholarly, young novice would never soften her father's heart, nor would it be encouraged.

So when Ben backed away before the approach of Sir Jon, it was with a combination of regret and excitement that Ginny ceased to hear Ben's last few words to her and instead felt the presence of the man who was already forcing an entry into her heart as Ben had never done. Sir Jon glanced briefly at Ben's departure, then at Ginny's wary expression as if to discover the exact depth of the affection remaining in her eyes, a look she felt was too invasive by half. 'We have known each other since we were small,' she said before he could ask. 'I believe he will be a physician one day.'

'Is that so?' Sir Jon replied, without enthusiasm. 'So you have spent some time with the Nortons up in Northumbria, your father tells me. I know that family well. Is that where you learned to have opinions, mistress? Or were you always strong-minded?' His eyes continued to roam at leisure over her, taking in every detail of her face and hair, her slender waist and the hands holding leather gloves, and she wished she had worn her new French hood instead of letting her hair loose like a girl.

'Strong-minded, Sir Jon? Is that what you call it when a woman is able to express herself on matters other than the price of fish? The Nortons, as you should know, encourage the young women in their care to speak for themselves and to contribute to discussions. I thank God I can do more than sew aglets on a man's points, sir.' She saw the flicker of a smile tweak at the corners of his wide mouth and knew that her choice of dress accessories was open to more than one interpretation, his points being the cords that kept his breeches tied to his shirt, amongst other places.

The blush that stole upwards into her cheeks showed him that she was not a young woman, like so many others, who would fall at his feet so easily. Spirited and intelligent, how many hearts had she broken up in the north? he wondered. 'I'm sure you can, mistress,' he said, 'if ever you stay silent for long enough.'

'Long enough to what, Sir Jon?'

'To allow your husband a word in edgeways, mistress.'

'Husbands and their requirements are not on my mind, nor am I yet ready to saddle myself with a life of silent obedience. I'd have gone into a nunnery if I'd wanted that, sir.'

'Then that would have been a great waste, Mistress D'Arvall, after all those years of training. Did they teach you anything else other than how to express yourself, and to sew, and to appreciate books?'

'Many things. Including how to hold on to one's conscience and not to confuse it with duty. 'Tis sometimes difficult to know the difference, Sir Jon. Have you not found it so?'

The twinkle of laughter in his brown eyes disappeared as he detected her disapproval of the work he was doing for his royal master. It was a brave man, these days, who could afford to heed his conscience on every matter. Brave men's heads had rolled, including those of abbots and priors. 'No, I have not. Not yet,' he said softly. 'I am quite clear about which is which.

And if I may offer you a word of advice, Mistress D'Arvall?'

'Certainly. Please do.'

'Then I suggest you confine your opinions to what you understand best. Things are rarely as clear-cut as they seem to be.'

His words of advice were courteously spoken and Ginny had the sense to accept them without taking offence. 'I shall take your advice, Sir Jon,' she said. 'Thank you. I tend to see things from one angle instead of from several.'

'I did, too, at your age.'

Inwardly, Ginny smiled at this as though he exceeded her years by decades instead of a mere eight.

That same evening, at home, Ginny obeyed a summons to her father's room where he and Lady Agnes D'Arvall sat beside a roaring fire, their faces flushed by good food, wine, and warmth. Here they told her that Father Spenney and young Ben had been offered the position of chaplain and assistant with them, since the office had been left vacant for a year after the death of the previous one. He and Ben would live with them as part of the household. Not only would it solve their problem, but it would look good for Sir Walter and Lady Agnes to have a properly staffed chapel once more, with perhaps a choir, too. Such details mattered in society.

Sir Walter had apparently discussed it with his wife, although the decision was his. Lady Agnes had never been required to agree with anything Sir Walter said, except as a formality. The next thing they told her, however, concerned Ginny even more personally than Ben being part of their household. It was to do with Sir Jon Raemon.

'Sir Jon has agreed,' said Sir Walter, 'to consider my offer of your hand in marriage.' He continued before she could make a sound. 'He has also agreed to allow me possession of the priory library, for a considerable sum of money, I might add, so you'll be pleased to hear that the books will be spared from destruction.'

Having one's marriage prospects mixed up with a library of rare books was not something Ginny had ever anticipated, nor could she help wondering which was most important to him. 'Marriage, Father? To Sir Jon? He favours the connection, then?'

'He certainly *favours* it, in principle. Of course, there are things to be decided—property, dowry, jointures, that kind of thing. Financial details. He has promised me a firm answer as soon as he's able. Maybe in a week or so.'

'And me, Father? Shall I give him my answer as soon as I'm able?'

Both parents glared at her, detecting a certain facetiousness instead of the grateful excitement they thought due to them. 'What on earth can you mean, Virginia?' said her mother. 'Sir Jon doesn't need an answer from you. You will do as you're instructed and think yourself fortunate. Your father has had this in mind for some time. You might thank him, instead of arguing.'

That night, Ginny had hardly slept for excitement. Sir Jon wished to make her his wife. It was two weeks before they had a message from Sir Jon to say that his father, a prisoner of war in France for the past three years, had died. It was another month before Ginny was told, almost casually by her father, that the hoped-for marriage would not now be going ahead. Sir Jon would be marrying a very wealthy woman, well known at court. Huge properties. Massive dowry. Beautiful wife with good connections, and older by some three years than an inexperienced sixteen-year-old. Sir Walter was disappointed but philosophical. 'Politics,' he said unhelpfully, in answer to Ginny's question why.

Over the past six weeks, Ginny had existed in an unreal world of make-believe, of elation and fright, of overwhelming emotions and mental preparation in readiness for the dream of all dreams, of being wedded to the only man ever to share her wildest fancies of love and possession, and a good many other things too vaguely intimate to dwell on for long. Brought up to regard herself as a good catch for any man, she had almost taken it as a matter of course that, once negotiations were complete, he would come to claim her in person and make himself just a little less forbidding than he had been at their first meeting when her father had talked to him of deals. But Ginny, in love for the first time and so full of hope, was hurt, insulted, and bitterly resentful to have been rejected for someone older, wealthier and more royally connected than herself. The humiliation would not be forgotten or forgiven, and if those were indeed his best reasons, she hoped his marriage would be a disaster and that his crops would all fail, year after year.

So for the following three years, while Ginny remained at home with her mother, saw her older sister married and bear a child—rather too soon to escape comments about dates—

and heard about the death of Sir Jon's wife in childbirth, her heart ached with a wound that was taking far too long to heal. Had it not been for Ben's adoration and the chaotic housing of Sandrock Priory's library, life might have been dull. And had it not been for her parents' regular attempts to tempt her with possible suitors, much too soon after the first, she might have made more of an effort to recover.

Then the king had come to stay at D'Arvall Hall on a hunting trip and Ginny's contact with the royal court first-hand had begun a chain of events that opened the old wound all over again. In that autumn of 1539, Ginny was six months past her nineteenth birthday, and if she had been considered lovely before, she was now stunningly beautiful and worthy of the king's admiration. For him, the sight of the daughter of his cofferer at D'Arvall Hall seemed to soothe his heart as much as his sight, though at the time, Ginny thought nothing much of his interest. According to her information, the king was equally interested in every young woman at court, and flirting was part of normal court behaviour. She had, however, sadly underestimated the situation.

For reasons that she kept to herself, Ginny did not respond with the expected level of enthusiasm when, just after New Year in 1540, her father sent a message to say that she was to go to court. Immediately. 'But I'd really rather not, Mother,' Ginny said, putting down her basket of herbs on the table. 'You know I have no wish to get involved with that crowd.'

Her mother rarely raised her voice, but this time she could not contain her annoyance. 'For pity's sake, Ginny! Will you but *listen*, for once? The king has a new wife now.'

'Another one? Who is it this time?'

'If you took more interest in your father's news, you'd know. She is the Lady Anna of Cleves…'

'Cleves?' Ginny frowned.

'In Flanders. A small duchy. The king needs an ally in Europe. It's a good match, but the king wishes you to go and help with her wardrobe. She's unfashionable. She needs help with her English, too. She has no music skills. No dancing. No card games. You should be flattered to be asked to help.'

'Commanded, Mother.'

'Whatever. And take that basket off the polished table.'

A week later, Ginny was at Hampton Court Palace, not far from London, with a court that contained Sir Jon Raemon, now aged twenty-seven, widowed, a father, and favourite of King Henry. Favourite of just about everyone except, that was, of Mistress Virginia D'Arvall.

Chapter One

'Yes, Father,' Ginny murmured for the fourth time as Sir Walter D'Arvall checked every buckle and strap of the bay gelding's harness. As the king's cofferer, he lived his life by lists, weights, and proportions, payments, people and accounts, and his new day had begun even before it checked in over the stable roofs of Hampton Court Palace. Watching her father's hands roam over the well-stuffed bags and pouches, Ginny caught the eye of the two young grooms who would be her escort, waiting patiently for the inevitable criticism.

It was levelled at her instead. 'It's all very well you "Yes, Father", my girl,' he said with a last push at the bulging pack behind her saddle. 'If things start to fall off, you'll wish you'd listened to me. Now, don't ride on after nightfall. You two hear me?' he admonished the grooms. 'Not a step. Get as far as Elvetham and stay overnight with Sir Edward Seymour's lady. She'll look after you. You should make D'Arvall Hall by tomorrow midmorning, with an early start. These days are so short. We could have done without the snow, too.' Turning his lined face up to the grey sky, he blinked at the flurry of white settling on his eyelids. 'I don't suppose it will do much.' He delved a hand into the leather pouch hanging from his belt and withdrew a folded parchment, passing it to Ginny with the command, 'Take this to your mother. Keep it safe. In your pouch, close to your person. It's important.' A blob of green wax from the office glistened in the pale light.

'Yes, Father. How important? About the boys, is it?' Sir Walter was ambitious for his offspring. The message would surely be about her brothers.

'Not about the boys, no. She'll tell you. Time to be off, Virginia.'

She wished he might have taken her into his confidence, this once, as he did with Elion and Paul. At almost twenty years old, was it not time he could trust her with a verbal message?

If Lady Agnes could tell her, then why could he not?

Not that she minded being back home for a while. Hampton Court Palace was a fine place to stay, even in winter, but the bewildering intrigues of the royal court demanded all one's skills in diplomacy these days and, even with father and older brothers to lend advice, each day had been a challenge that made her glad of her temporary position. To leave, she had needed only the new queen's permission, and the gentle Anna of Cleves was as easy to please as anyone could wish. What a pity, Ginny thought, that the lady had found so little favour in the eyes of her cantankerous husband, Henry.

At the back of Ginny's mind was another reason for wanting to escape, for she had not been flattered by King Henry's unwanted attentions that, instead of being focused on his fourth wife, were being directed at her in an embarrassing juvenile charade she found difficult to evade. Only a month ago, she had been summoned to go and assist the new Queen Anna, whose taste in the heavy German fashions was fast becoming the source of some comment, not to say amusement and scorn. Unable to see past the costume to the sensitive lady beneath, the king had sent for Ginny to educate and remodel his dowdy twenty-four-year-old bride in the English manner before he himself became a laughing stock. Ginny had found the task much to her liking, forming a friendship with Queen Anna to which their mime language added a piquancy.

But the king had had more than fashion in mind when he'd sent for her, and it was not long before Ginny realised that her father must have been aware of Henry's interest even then, his easily wandering affections, his ruthless pursuit of passable young maids, his need to be surrounded by admiration, as he had once been. Sadly, Sir Walter's personal ambition did not allow him to protect his daughter from the royal lust with the same concern he showed over her journey home in the snow on a February morning.

'Yes, Father. Time to be away,' she agreed, gathering her skirts for her father's lift up into the saddle.

'Allow me, Mistress D'Arvall.' The deep musical voice behind her caused an uncomfortable flutter of annoyance, for she'd hoped to be away without notice, and now here was the man who had not until this moment offered her more than two words at a time, much less his assistance to mount. Her father was looking smug, as if he'd arranged it.

'Thank you, Sir Jon,' she said, taking hold of the stirrup, 'but I can manage well enough with my father's help.'

'You'll manage even better with me,' Sir Jon replied. 'Place your foot on my hands and hold the saddle. There... Up!' In one effortless hoist, he propelled her upwards so fast that, had she not clung to the pommel, she might have gone over the other side.

Gathering the reins, she looked down on him with tight-lipped irritation, her legs half-bared by the impetus of the movement. 'I cannot imagine how I managed before,' she said, suspecting that this impromptu show of interest was more for her father's sake than hers. Yet in her month at court, Sir Jon Raemon had done nothing to make her days more comfortable. A nod, a slight bow, or an impolite stare had been the sum total of his regard for her, though for others it was quite the opposite.

Too late to hide her legs from his gaze, her father drew Ginny's skirts into place while she adjusted the other side, rattled by the man's unwelcome closeness. He had changed since that first meeting when he'd been twenty-four and she a very opinionated sixteen. Now a trim dark beard outlined his square jaw, emulating the king's own device for concealing fleshy jowls, though Sir Jon's muscled neck was clearly visible above the white frill of his shirt collar. From above, she saw how closely his hair was cropped, fitting his head like a black velvet bonnet that joined the narrow beard in front of his ears, and the black brows that could lift with either disdain or mirth were now levelled at her, giving back stare for stare. She knew he was laughing at her discomfort, though the wide mouth gave nothing away.

Her father's smugness had vanished. 'Mend your manners while you're at home, Virginia, if you please,' he said sternly.

That stung. 'There's little wrong with my manners, Father, I thank you. Had it not been for all this baggage, I could have managed by myself. I've been riding since I was three, remember. Sir Jon is confusing me with those of his friends who like to pretend a little maidenly helplessness. Easily done. They're thick on the ground here at court, are they not, sir?'

Her horse threw up its head at Sir Jon's roar of laughter that Ginny usually heard from a safe distance. Close to, she could see the white evenness of his teeth smiling at her prickly retort. 'Correction, Mistress D'Arvall. I could no more confuse you with another woman than forget my name,' he said. 'And that's the most I've heard you speak since you came to court. Even an attempted put-down is better than nothing, I suppose. The manners will come eventually.'

'Then I hope they'll never be as selective as yours, Sir Jon,' she said, easing her mount round to present its wide rump to him. 'Farewell, Father. We cannot waste any more time.'

'Virginia! Do you forget who you're speaking to?' he scolded, holding the bridle. 'Sir Jon is—'

'Yes, I know who Sir Jon is, Father. They're all the same, these gentlemen of the bedchamber. They rate themselves highly. Too highly.' Her words were almost lost beneath the hard clatter of hooves on the cobbled yard as she and the two grooms moved off and Sir Walter let go, sliding his hand over the gelding's back and pulling gently at its tail, fanning it out.

Recently elevated to being one of the king's gentlemen of the bedchamber, Sir Jon was rather higher up the social ladder than Sir Walter, to whom he showed every respect. A great well-built handsome creature of the kind King Henry liked to have about him, his excellence at jousting, hunting, dancing, and music was well known to all at court, and wherever the king was, there also was Sir Jon Raemon in attendance. But although Ginny had never been short of company or admiration, Sir Jon and she had exchanged no pleasantries or conversation since their first tense meeting at Sandrock Priory, not even when they had met in the dance. Other young women she knew would have rectified that situation within days, but Ginny saw no reason to, and many reasons why she should not. The man had plenty of worshippers and she would not be one of them.

Sir Walter shook his head, sighed and turned back to his friend, whose expression was much less serious and far more admiring, his eyes following the trio out of the gates and along the track that ran alongside the River Thames. In the weak light of early morning, Sir Jon could see only Ginny's slender figure swathed in furs, riding astride in the manner made fashionable by the king's second wife. Enclosed by a headdress and hood, her lovely face had been the only part of her visible, except for the brief glimpse of shapely ankles, but he knew from oft-recalled memory how her glorious ash-blonde hair framed her face and could sometimes be seen in a heavy jewelled caul behind her head. He had not exaggerated when he'd said she was impossible to confuse with others. She was, in fact, the most distinctive and desirable woman at court, and if she thought her absence would not be noted, then she was much mistaken.

Well able to understand and even to sympathise with her coldness during her month at court, Sir Jon would entertain no doubts about his ability to bring about a change in her attitude, for their first meeting at Sandrock was still as fresh in his mind as yesterday. She had been caught on the wrong foot even then and had given him back word for word the reproofs he'd offered, just to provoke her, to make her rise to his bait. Sharp-tongued and courageous, she had fenced verbally with him as few women did at court where their flattery and simpering helplessness was, as she had said, thick on the ground. None of them was worth the chase. Since that meeting, however, so much had changed for him, not all of it for the best, and now, although he was sure of her interest while she tried to hide it, the situation would require some careful handling and patience on his part. The lady's strong opinions were deeply rooted in so many misconceptions that it was hard to see how best to proceed. Only time would tell. Perhaps, he thought as he turned away, a certain firmness of manner might be best, in the circumstances.

* * *

After an overnight stay at Elvetham Hall, where Sir Edward Seymour and his lady lived, Ginny and her escorts reached home just as her father had predicted, even to the weather. His estimates were never far out, for the snow had been no more than a warning flurry that covered the rolling fields like a dusting of flour. The gardens of D'Arvall Hall looked like an embellished chessboard, and fine wreaths of smoke from the tall redbrick chimneys showed her that the servants had been up and about for half a day, and the distant clack of an axe on wood called up the image of wide stone fireplaces with blazing logs, warmed ale and her mother's welcoming arms. Riding into the courtyard through the wide arch of the gatehouse, they were met by running grooms, shouts of surprised greeting and the sudden bustle of skirts at the porch as Lady Agnes D'Arvall and her ladies emerged with faces both happy and curious, their breath like clouds in the freezing air, puffing with laughter.

Always content to stay at home rather than at court, Lady Agnes D'Arvall was nevertheless eager to hear from her daughter every detail of the life there, unbiased by the accounts of husband and sons. Politics, rivalries and appointments were far less interesting to her than what the ladies were wearing, doing and saying, information that Ginny was soon happy to supply across a white cloth spread with trenchers of warm bread, cheeses, roast pigeon and wild duck, apple-and-plum pie, spiced wine, nuts, and honeyed pears. Good homely fare, Ginny told her mother, that she'd missed at court.

'What, with all that variety and every day different?' said Lady Agnes. 'I doubt your father and brothers miss it so much. I think that's one of the things that keeps them there.'

From what Ginny had seen and heard in her month of the queen's service, the main attraction of the court for her older brothers had less to do with food than with women—more varied, more attractive and easily obtained. 'You know full well what keeps them there,' Ginny said, closing a hand over her mother's wrist. 'Father believes that, with enough of the D'Arvalls in the king's service, he'll be in line for promotion. Heaven knows, the king puts people down and sets others up so fast these days, I dare say Father could find himself Lord Steward one day.'

Lady Agnes leaned forwards so that one of the long black-velvet lappets of her headdress flapped onto her bosom. 'No, I really don't see that happening. Yes, Sir Walter is ambitious, and I believe the king regards him well, but commoners don't make leaps of that kind, my dear. Well, apart from Thomas Cromwell, of course. Tell me about the king's new wife, Queen Anna. Does he like her any better now?'

'No, Mother. I fear not. He rarely comes near her except at night.'

'After only a month? Poor lady. Then what? Has he taken a mistress?'

Delivered lightly, the question held more interest than Lady Agnes had intended and her daughter's ears were quick to detect it. Since King Henry had first noticed Ginny during his brief stay at D'Arvall Hall late last year, Lady Agnes, as ambitious as her husband, had recognised what might result from his mild flirtation, for that was how he had wooed and won his second and third wives, Anne Boleyn and Jane Seymour. His summons to her daughter, just after the New Year wedding to the Lady Anna of Cleves, had been no great surprise to Sir Walter and Lady Agnes, or indeed their sons, even disguised as a temporary position in his bride's new household. Now the seemingly innocent question about mistresses demanded more than a simple denial when the king's amorous intentions were rarely simple.

'Flirtations, Mother,' Ginny said. 'That's all he can do, I think. Several of Queen Anna's ladies were with Queen Jane before her death, and some go even further back than that. He flirts with most of them. It's almost expected of him. All the men do it.' It was a fact of court life. It meant nothing.

But if Sir Walter was ambitious for his sons, his wife was equally ambitious for her daughters, and any suggestion of interest from Henry would raise her expectations sky-high. 'And you?' said Lady Agnes gently. 'He still flirts with you, does he?'

Ginny turned a shelled walnut over and over in her fingers, studying its contours. 'That's why I'm glad to get away,' she replied, aware that her mother's two ladies were listening to her reply. They had known her since she was a babe. They were also aware of the king's methods in pursuing women he wanted. 'I've grown to admire Queen Anna,' said Ginny after a pause. 'She's a lovely lady.'

'Lovely, dear?' said Lady Agnes. 'I thought they said she was not.'

The elder of the two ladies interrupted. 'Men,' she whispered, angrily. 'They'll say black is white if it suits them. Our Good King Henry will do whatever he pleases to get himself out of a situation he doesn't much like, even slandering a good woman.'

Again, Ginny's hand came to rest and comfort her mother, understanding that this particular reference was not to the king's present dilemma, but to his first wife, whose life was made a misery after his affections had changed. She had been much beloved by everyone, unlike his second. Ginny continued, 'Queen Anna's only fault is that she didn't fit in with Henry's expectations. She's taller than he thought, for one thing, and Master Holbein's painting made her look sweet and demure, which she is. But Master Holbein and she could converse in their native German so he was able to see much more of her inner loveliness, and that was what he portrayed. And then there was that awful fiasco at Rochester when she landed and Henry rushed down to surprise her without any warning. That really was the stupidest thing to do. What woman likes to be seen when she's not looking her best, I ask you?'

'Well,' said her mother, 'I'm pleased to know you like her. So what does Sir Walter think about all this? Is he—?'

'Oh! I almost forgot. I have a letter for you. Wait, Mother, I'll go up and get it from my pouch. He'll tell you what's happening, I expect.'

With a space cleared on the table before her, Lady Agnes smoothed the parchment out, adjusted a pair of fragile spectacles on her nose and frowned at the words underlined by her moving finger, words she had clearly not expected. In summer, perhaps, but not in February. 'He's bringing the king,' she murmured. 'Again. Oh, my lord!'

'Where? Here? Why could he not have told me himself?'

'For two nights, for some hawking. With a few friends, before the court moves to Whitehall.'

'With the queen? Does Queen Anna come, too?'

'Er...no, dear. Not the queen.'

'Hah!' said the lady who'd spoken before. 'What's that all about, then? Not hawking, you can be sure of that.'

'Hush, Joan,' said Lady Agnes. 'You've said enough already to land you in the Tower. He's bringing with him...a husband...for our daughter Virginia.' Her finger moved on, then reversed its direction, Lady Agnes repeating, '...a *husband*...for...*Virginia*.'

'I don't want a husband, thank you, Mother,' Ginny said firmly, 'and I certainly don't want one of the king's choosing. Send a message back. Thank you, but no.'

Lady Agnes pushed the finger farther along while her two ladies, one useful for her wisdom, the other for her energy, leaned in to read the astonishing words in silence. 'One of his gentlemen of the bedchamber, no less. Oh, Ginny! That's a great honour. One of his own personal friends.'

'Oh, good gracious, Mother! One of that crowd. I'd rather...' The words of denial froze on her lips as the picture formed in her mind of yesterday's little scene in the stable yard at Hampton Court Palace when a certain gentleman of the king's bedchamber had appeared at her father's side for no very good reason. At least, that was how it had seemed. What *had* he been doing there? 'Who, Mother? Does Father say who it is? And does he say why the king is involving himself in my future?' Unconsciously, a hand crept up to rest over her heart, pulsing to the heavy thud beneath her stiffly boned bodice.

'Yes. He says the king regards you highly for your comeliness and charm, and for your assistance to Her Grace the queen, and...'

'Oh, I don't mean all that flummery, Mother. I've done no more than anyone else would have.

Who does he propose as a husband and what's the deal? I've learned enough in my short time at court to know he doesn't give something for nothing and certainly not to a woman. Who is it?'

Lady Agnes sat back, clearly taken by surprise, her pale eyes staring about her in bewilderment. 'He's bringing our neighbour, Sir Jon Raemon,' she said. 'He thinks the match would be to both your advantages and Sir Jon has already expressed a willingness for it. Well, what d'ye think of that?'

What did she think? Disbelief. Shock. Rebellion. Elation. Numbness.

'I'll tell you what I think of that, Mother,' Ginny said. 'I think the king has perhaps not been made aware of Sir Jon's rejection of the very same proposal that Father made to him only a few years ago. So to say that Sir Jon is willing must be utter nonsense when he's barely looked my way in four weeks of living under the same roofs. And anyway, *I'm* not willing. Can't stand the man.'

'Because of what happened when you were still a lass?' Lady Agnes said, placing a dish of nuts on one corner of the letter. 'Oh, come now, Ginny. That's all water under the bridge. It was politics. Nothing personal. Your father and he did not fall out about it, so why should you? You know how these things go. A man has to choose carefully who he marries and for what purpose, and the first Lady Raemon brought him far more wealth than you could ever have done, even though Sir Walter's offer was very generous.'

'Which suggests,' said Mistress Joan, 'that the king has made him an even more generous offer that he cannot refuse and that there might also be something in it for Sir Walter. Sir Jon is now a widower and he needs an heir. Sir Walter is ready for a step up in the world and Virginia deserves a reward for her duty to the queen.'

Ginny's tone was bitingly sarcastic. 'Thank you for putting it so simply, Mistress Joan. That seems to be the situation in a nutshell. If ever a woman felt more like a pawn on a chessboard, then I cannot imagine her humiliation. *She's* supposed to be grateful for the reward of a husband she doesn't want, just for doing her duty. The men, however, get their rewards, whatever they are, for falling in with the king's wishes. There must be something here I've missed, but for the life of me I cannot see it, Mother.' With a scrape of her stool through the rushes, Ginny stood up to go. 'I'll go up and change, if you'll excuse me.'

'Ginny, dear, I wish you'd see this differently. It's an honour we cannot afford to refuse. You must know that.'

'It's an honour I can refuse quite easily,' Ginny said. 'There are plenty of marriageable women swarming around the court, waiting for Sir Jon to glance their way, and I'm not one of them.'

'He's so handsome,' said the other lady coyly, thinking it might help.

'Mistress Molly,' said Ginny, scathingly, 'they *all* are. The king surrounds himself with tall, good-looking, virile bucks who dance well, joust and hunt well, gamble more than they can afford, make conversation and music to keep him entertained. That's what he pays them for. Even the new queen thinks them foolish beyond words.'

'Does she *have* any English words yet?' said Mistress Joan.

'Indeed she does. She learns quickly. She's a darling.'

Summoning the servants to clear away the dishes, Lady Agnes rose to her feet and folded the letter into her pouch. 'Such short notice,' she said. 'I wish he'd have given me a week instead of two days. Joan, I want you to go and make a check on the best linen and order the fires to be lit in all the chambers. Molly, your duties will be in the stillroom today. We shall need a mountain of marchpane. Ginny, you come with me.'

Clenching her teeth against a retort that would do nothing to soften her mother's determination, Ginny followed her up the wide oak staircase and along a panelled passageway where carved door frames displayed the very best workmanship and, by association, the money that had been poured into this building by Sir Walter. His efforts had been well worthwhile, for now the king himself felt it was good enough for a stay of two nights, to avail himself of the excellent hawking on the estate. Lady Agnes might have been uncomfortable with the short notice, but nothing could have given her greater satisfaction than to know that King Henry was to visit them twice in the same season and to favour the family with a connection Sir Walter had always been keen on. And it had been worth those years Ginny had spent away from home, not to mention the expense, while she had absorbed the attributes needed for a nobleman's wife and the company of young aristocrats. Things were certainly looking up.

Ginny knew her own feelings on the matter to be irrelevant, however strongly she might try to present her case. Her mother's subservience to her husband's will was absolute. Whatever opinions she had about anything except the day-to-day running of the house, she had been well trained to bend and mould them to her husband's, though even the housekeeping was not secure from his occasional criticism. So however clear-cut Ginny's objections, she knew in her heart that her mother would say nothing to countermand her father's wishes, nor could she expect either sympathy or tolerance from them in a matter that affected them so deeply. For any woman to harbour a preference about her future husband was laughable. Men could choose, women did not, unless they were the flighty kind who fluttered too near the flame of love and burnt their wings in the process, their reputations ruined. And worse.

'Now, Ginny, dear,' said Lady Agnes, imagining her daughter dressed for the great occasion, 'let's just take a look at the rose velvet and see if we can dress it up with my squirrel fur round the sleeves. Is that what the court is wearing nowadays? You of all people should know.'

Ginny went to sit in the large window recess overlooking the squared herb garden where a fine layer of snow etched the scene into tones of grey. Beyond the low hedge stood gnarled apple and pear trees in the orchard, the rose-covered bowers of summer now drooping and dormant, the stream frozen along its banks. In the cosy room behind her, her mother was trying to urge her into the next phase of her life by throwing gowns onto the silk counterpane to make a heap of colour as if there was nothing else more important to discuss. 'Mother…wait,' she said. 'Can we not talk about this? Surely you cannot have forgotten the answer Sir Jon gave to Father when he offered him my hand? How he told Father he would give it his consideration and the next thing we knew he'd married that heiress? Did you not see how hurtful it was to me? Did you not think he could have been truthful from the beginning and said that his future was already decided? How can you agree to it so readily now, after that rebuff?'

Laying down an armful of green brocade, Lady Agnes shook her head at it, then came to sit beside Ginny on the cushioned window seat. Taking the folded letter from her pouch, she passed it to Ginny with the words, 'Perhaps you'd better read it yourself. It won't make any difference in the long run, but you have a right to know, I suppose.'

Ginny unfolded it and read her father's efficient handwriting with sentences as free from sentiment as one might expect. '"The king has noticed our daughter…and feels a need of her company at this troubled time…wants her to be at court…but only within the safety of marriage, not as a maid…to preserve her good name…and to have a trustworthy mate already in the king's employ so that he and she might serve the king as one…"' Raising her head, she tried to read her mother's eyes instead. 'Serve the king as one?' she said. 'What on earth does he mean by that?'

Lady Agnes's reply came rather hurriedly. 'He means you to serve Queen Anna, too, dear, the way you have begun to do with her clothes and…well…whatever else it is that you do. So that you can be at court as a respectable married woman rather than a maid, which might set tongues wagging. And Sir Jon will continue to serve the king as he does now, so you need not be separated as husbands and wives often are when one is at court. A most convenient arrangement.'

'Convenient for the king. Nothing to do with Sir Jon's preferences, then? So he's been commanded, has he? Just like me. To suit the king. To pander to his sudden need for my company at "this difficult time" and for that, I have to be married, do I? As if not being married would set tongues wagging, for some reason?'

'It's not a sudden need, is it, Ginny? You know it isn't. The king saw you here late last year and spent quite some time with you. He made his liking for you quite obvious.'

'Flirting, Mother. As I told you, he flirts with every maid who catches his eye. There's Anne Basset and Kat Howard, the queen's maids, and plenty of others who enjoy his attentions. It's not just me. Really, it isn't. So it's no use you thinking I'm anything more to him than the others.'

'He's particularly asked for you. And he doesn't arrange marriages to his special friends to every maid who catches his eye. This is a great honour.'

'So you keep saying. Marriages are for families, are they not, rather than for individuals? So any woman who thinks it's for her had better think again.'

'Dynasties,' said Lady Agnes, showing no sign of empathy with her daughter. 'Don't think your role is unimportant in all this. Men have to think further ahead than we do. Generations ahead. Sir Jon's wife left him with an infant girl child, but he needs a son, and I know nothing about his reasons for the sudden decision to marry his heiress. Perhaps your father does, but he doesn't discuss such matters with me. It's not my business, except to commiserate when a mother dies in childbed.'

'Well, perhaps he'd already got her pregnant when Father made his offer. Perhaps her parents insisted on a marriage. By the way the women at court flutter their eyelashes at him, it wouldn't surprise me.'

'You should not say such things. If they think him a good catch, that may be as much to do with the wealth he acquired at his marriage.'

'Of which I obviously had so little to offer that I was not even worth looking at.'

Lady Agnes reached out both hands and took Ginny's in her own, layering them for warmth. 'Dear girl, that's not so. If he'd been able, he'd have accepted your father's offer without hesitation. You'd been away up north for over four years at the Nortons' home, remember, and you came back all polished and womanly and well mannered and, best of all, a beauty. Father would have got you a place at court, but you didn't want that, did you? That, and the business of marriage offers, were the few times he let you have your own way. But it cannot last, Ginny, dear.'

Ginny smiled. 'Is it difficult being married to Father?' she said.

'No. As long as I fall in with all his wishes,

it's easy enough. If I ever want to go and let off steam, I go to see your sister Maeve, when she's at home. She brings me back to reality faster than anyone.' A gentle hand came up to rearrange Ginny's long ash-blonde hair that fell like water over her shoulders. 'So lovely,' she whispered. 'I am blessed with lovely daughters and handsome sons and a successful husband. And now I must send for Maeve and George to come over from Reedacre Manor while the king is here. You know how they love a good feast.' Lady Agnes did not mention that her daughter Maeve had also once caught the king's eye with her hair like pale golden honey. But Sir George Betterton had stepped in smartly, too smartly for the king's timetable, made her pregnant and married her before Henry could deepen their friendship. It had not been thought a good idea to tell Ginny of the reasons for the hasty marriage, and the child's earlier-than-expected arrival had caused little comment at home.

'Still,' Ginny said, 'I don't like the idea of being married to a man I despise simply so the king can have the pleasure of my company without it being thought he wishes to marry me. I admire Queen Anna. I want to make her happy and fulfilled, and for her to find out how to make him happy, too. Being on the receiving end of Henry's attentions does not please me the way it does some of the other women. They see it as a way into his bed, but I don't, and I would do nothing to hurt such a dear lady. I don't want his silly notes and jewels. I want her to have them, not me.'

'He sends you notes? And jewels? Show me.'

'I've returned them. It makes no sense.'

'It did to dear Jane Seymour. It got *her* the throne.'

'Yes, stringing him along. She knew exactly what he was about and she was certainly not doing anything to spare Anne Boleyn's feelings, was she? Pious, mousy, unscrupulous Jane, enticing a married man to please her family. Well, I shall not do it, Mother. I'm sorry, but I draw the line at that.'

'You must do it, dear. Would you deny King Henry the pleasure of talking to a well bred and beautiful young woman? Because that is what you are.'

'If he put more effort into his new marriage, he could easily do that with the queen. She is anxious to please him in any way she can, if only he'd see it.'

'Mmm, well, coming here without her isn't going to do much to help, is it? Now come and take a look at these gowns and let's see what's to be done.'

It was not hard to understand where Ginny had acquired her style and elegance. Even though she chose not to be a courtier, Lady Agnes D'Arvall was a keen needlewoman for whom sewing was never a chore as long as she had a team of the best tailors and seamstresses, and a husband to send her bolts of fine fabrics from the London merchants. Her eldest daughter Maeve, now Lady Betterton, spent some of her time in the London house at Westminster near her husband, who was employed in the king's Great Wardrobe. Consequently, the Bettertons and D'Arvalls were amongst the best-dressed families known to the royals, and ostensibly it was this flair that the king had intended to exploit when he'd sent for Ginny to advise his new German wife on the latest English fashions.

Ginny's thoughts, however, were far from the rich heap of velvets, damasks, satins, and silks on the bed and, as soon as her mother had left the room, she returned once more to the window seat, hoping that the stillness of the darkening landscape would help to clear her mind. It did not. Having come home expecting a rest from the empty flattery doled out by the king and his courtiers, she now found herself in a situation where she would have to suffer more of it rather than less.

Even worse was the king's intention to marry her to a man who wanted her only for the rewards he would be granted, a man who'd been told to make himself known to her, for why else would he have appeared beside her father, pretending assistance? She had asked herself this same question all the way home. Now she knew. After four weeks of noticeable indifference and stand-offishness, it had taken the king's command, offer, bribery, call it what you will, to force him to speak, then to make an absurd attempt at flattery by telling her he would not have confused her with another. 'The manners will come,' he'd said patronisingly. As if *he* could teach her anything.

With all the painful sensitivity of a very young woman, Ginny had been baffled and hurt when, after being assured by her parents that finding her a husband would not be difficult, their eligible neighbour had declined Sir Walter's offer in favour of the beautiful heiress Magdalen Osborn. That had been the cruellest part of all, and Ginny was sure he must have known it.

At court, once the shock of seeing him again

had abated, she had done her best to convince both herself and him that he was the very last man she would have chosen as a husband, giving him not the smallest opportunity to revise the decision. Unable to separate sexual attraction from the lingering pain of rejection, it had seemed to Ginny that the natural antidote was to avoid him at all costs and to show that she had always been quite beyond his reach. Even if he had not been the handsomest man at court.

At the royal court for much of the three years since his first marriage, Sir Jon's connection with his neighbours had been brief. When the king had visited D'Arvall Hall last year, Sir Jon had been on a mission for his friend Sir Thomas Cromwell, the King's principal secretary, who occasionally employed him. Not understanding the workings of the royal rota, Ginny had naturally put a different construction on his absence that heaped yet more fuel on her resentments.

'Why?' she whispered angrily. 'Why him, of all men, when he must want this as little as I do? It's so degrading. Bad enough to be pushed into marriage for the convenience of others, but to marry a man who must be *commanded*, after making it clear he doesn't have a mind to it, is shaming. All the court will know of it, for they've seen how things are between us. And now I shall be obliged to face down all the stares and pretend all is well. As for the rest...ugh! It hardly bears thinking about.' Wrapping herself warmly against the icy passageways and open spaces of the courtyard, she crossed over to the stillroom near the kitchen door where Mistress Molly had already begun the task of pounding lumps of sugar in a mortar with a pestle as big as her arm. 'The king loves his marchpane,' she puffed, as Ginny entered.

'Done the almonds yet?' Ginny said, looking round at the benches lined with jars and parchment-lidded pots. 'It might be best to let them blanch while you do that. I'll do them, if you like. For a favour.'

Mistress Molly had been taught the art of sugarwork and simpling by her aunt who, despite being thought a witch, had died peacefully in her bed. There was little that Molly did not know about herbs and their uses, and this was not the first time she had been visited by Mistress Virginia seeking a remedy for some ailment. She smiled at Ginny's bribery. 'I know what it is,' she said. 'I've been thinking about it.'

'*How* do you know?'

The grinding stopped for Molly to shake her aching hand and to dart a look of saucy wisdom at her mistress's daughter. 'Take a glance at your face,' she said gently. 'Anyone would think you'd been given the devil himself to marry. You want me to give you something for it, don't you?'

'For it, or against it. I don't know which. I have to do something, Molly.'

'Depends what. Put him to sleep? Put *you* to sleep? Make him love you? Make you love *him*? Make him impotent? Make you…?'

'No, Molly!'

'I was going to say, make you have twins.'

'How on earth would that help matters?'

Picking up the heavy pestle, Molly resumed the pounding. 'Two for the price of one,' she said. 'He'd leave you alone for a fair while after that.' The pounding continued until she realised there had been no reply. 'Is that what you want?'

But Ginny was staring out of the window, biting at her top lip. Then, rousing herself, she sighed. 'It's getting dark again. Where d'ye keep the almonds?'

Molly lifted down an earthenware pot from the shelf above her and passed it to Ginny. 'Best to put the water on to boil first,' she said with a sly grin.

Not being at all sure what she wanted a po-

tion to achieve, Ginny put the almonds to blanch
and then left Molly to her task. But Molly's
thoughts on the matter were somewhat clearer.
Rather than allow the problem to resolve itself,
which might take some time in Ginny's present
mood, she put aside a basin and began to add
dried herbs picked during the summer months.
Vervain, yarrow, mistletoe and rue, thyme and
bay, chopped and bound together with honey
and oil of roses. These she shaped into tiny
fairy cakes and, that same night under the light
from the rising moon that turned the garden to
silver, she placed them just beyond the bound-
ary where the grass was long and brittle with
frost, whispering a blessing upon each one. The
day of the king's visit, with Ginny's future husband, would be on the fourteenth day of February, Saint Valentine's Day and, although Ginny
had been too preoccupied to notice it, Mistress
Molly had not.

By the time Ginny's sister and her husband
arrived from their home a mere four miles away,
the preparations for the king's arrival that same
day were nearing completion. Outwardly serene
but inwardly anxious about every detail, Lady
Agnes's veneer cracked only for a brief moment
as she threw her arms around her elder daugh-

ter with something like relief. 'Oh, Maeve, my dear, thank heavens you've come at last. And, George, you, too. Such a day! I've had to double the quantities, you know, and now he's bringing women with him.' With more than a hint of drama, she waved her arms aloft.

'Mother,' said Maeve, with a sideways glance at her husband with a warning not to speak, 'stop worrying. There are plenty of places to sleep here. The court is used to it, you know. The palaces are like rabbit warrens. As long as we have enough food and drink, sleeping won't present a problem.'

'They like a bit of indecision about that,' said Sir George.

'George, dear, that's not helpful,' said Maeve, stifling her laughter. 'Where's Ginny got to? You said in your message something about a husband. Is it true?' Unwrapping her fur-lined cloak, she draped it over the end of a bench before her mother picked it up and returned it to her.

'Not there, dear. The steward is rehearsing the pages. Come into the small parlour. And yes, it is true and I expect she's still up in her room, sulking.'

Maeve, whose understanding of her younger sister exceeded her mother's by miles, rose to her defence. 'No, Mother. That cannot be. Ginny doesn't sulk. I dare say she doesn't much like the idea of the king choosing her husband for her, and nor would I, but she won't be sulking. You and she have been quarrelling, haven't you? Is that it?'

Turning her gaze upon Sir George as if to seek comfort, Lady Agnes heaved a noisy sigh, drooping her shoulders. 'Discussions,' she said. 'Heated discussions. You know what she's like. So determined. We'd have had her married years ago if she'd been more cooperative about the business. Oh, I know she'd have married Sir Jon when your father first proposed it, but since that fell through, all the matches he's suggested have been rejected without a single look. It's taken her recent visit to court and the king's command to make it happen, whether she likes it or not.'

'And apparently, she doesn't,' said Sir George. 'So who is he?'

'Same man. Yes, Sir Jon Raemon. You might well look astonished.'

'So what's the problem?' said Sir George, blinking. 'He's widowed now.'

Lady Agnes's eyes rolled with a look of despair. 'She's seen him again at court and now she doesn't like him.'

'Doesn't *like* him?' said Maeve, frowning. 'But she would have accepted him before. So this has to do with her pride, Mother, hasn't it? We have to talk to her, George.'

'We do, dear,' he agreed, 'but can we first get out of these clothes before Henry arrives, or we shall be taken for a travelling merchant and his doxy.' He dodged smartly to one side to avoid the sharp slap aimed loosely at his ears, laughing at his wife's lovely face and the sudden flare of grey eyes. But out of his mother-in-law's hearing, his frivolous tone changed to something more serious. 'You know what this sounds like, don't you?' he said to his wife, closing the door of their chamber. 'Remember how Henry set his sights on you, too?'

'Too well,' Maeve replied. 'If you'd not stepped in when you did, I might have—'

'Shh! Don't say it, love. Trouble is, I doubt if Ginny will understand what Henry has in mind for her. She's such an innocent about what goes on at court, even after a month there, and your mother won't have explained it to her, will she?'

'No, my love. But somebody had better. Shall we warn her?'

'Your father will put pressure on her. Raemon, too, for all I know. They'll make it impossible for her to refuse, with all the lucrative rewards lined up for them. Your father will see it as his big chance to get ahead and your mother will do everything he tells her to, without question. And before we know it, the D'Arvalls will be the new owners of Sandrock Priory and sitting squarely at the top of the tree. Parents of the king's new mistress, otherwise known as Mistress Virginia.'

'I don't want that to happen to her, George. Ginny is destined for better things than that. She's really not cut out for a life at court.'

His sideways smile showed that he knew what she meant. 'Perhaps Raemon himself will explain to her what this is all about,' he said. 'Or perhaps he won't.'

Chapter Two

An hour spent in the frost-bound gardens had done little to clear Ginny's mind of rebellious thoughts, nor had it helped to form any kind of plan to be used against tyrannical parents. Dependent on them for everything she did or was likely to do, the options to please herself did not lie thick on the ground. It had always been so; the nearest she had ever come to being heard on matters relating to husbands had been her refusal to meet any of her father's choices. Until now, that was, when he had turned the tables on her by engineering a meeting first and involving the king. If she found it possible to defy her father, no one knew better than he how impossible it would be for her to defy His Majesty King Henry VIII.

By midafternoon the light had begun to fade again as she trod down the crisp grass, shaking the white crystals off the hem of her skirts and reaching the door in the garden wall just as sounds from the other side made her pause with a hand on the latch. A clatter of hooves in the courtyard, men's voices calling, her mother's sharp words of reply. Could it be the king's party? So soon? Opening the door to look, she saw two men dismounting from horses whose sweat steamed white clouds into the air. Short capes swung from broad shoulders, plumes curled around velvet caps, and long boot-clad legs glinted with spurs.

'Half an hour away, m'lady,' the tallest of the men called. 'His Grace will need wine. A long day's ride and a fast pace. Whew!' As distinctive as the build, the voice was rich and deep, the voice Ginny had last heard in the stable yard at Hampton Court Palace. She could not meet him yet. Not here. Not until she was ready. She was at home now and she, not he, would dictate the pace. And the manners.

Swiftly pulling back her pink velvet skirt, she closed the door, hoping he would not hear the loud clack of the latch, yet fearing that he had when she heard the heavy tread of his footsteps followed by a softer click. The door opened slowly, wedging her behind it to merge with the pink brickwork of the wall, flattened like a naughty child evading capture, her expression already defiant.

Sir Jon's expression was irritatingly amused, though Ginny could tell what else lay behind his lazy scrutiny of her face, her abundant hair splayed over the fur of her cloak, the gentle swell of her bodice beneath one hand. He was experienced. He would know exactly how to assess what lay concealed beneath layers of stiffened fabrics. He closed the garden door and came to stand before her, purposely too close to mask the smell of leather and the sweat of hard riding, handing her the chance to deflate his arrogance with a satisfying shrewishness. His clothes were perfectly tailored and of the finest deep brown velvet with gold edges, his hose clinging to thighs like an athlete's, which she knew him to be. 'You should go and wash, Sir Jon, before supper,' she said. 'Your fast pace leaves its marks, does it not?'

His mouth twitched at the corners and he was close enough, too, for her to see the creases in his tanned skin, like soft leather. 'That's me told,' he said quietly.

'Don't tell me you rode ahead of the king's party to say that he will need wine,' she said tartly. 'When does he *not* need wine these days?'

'Then I won't, Mistress Sharp Tongue. I came early for a private word with you, and you have obliged me. As you will continue to do.'

'I shall exert no great effort in that direction, sir, be assured.'

'Then we shall agree to disagree on that point, for the moment.'

'Oh, do say what you must and let's go in. I have things to do before the king's arrival,' Ginny said with an impatient glance beyond him.

'Then your *things to do* will have to wait, Mistress D'Arvall, until I've spelled out a few ground rules that are more immediate,' he said, suddenly changing tone. 'The first of which is that any infringement of good manners towards me personally will incur a penalty. Is that clear? For a start?'

Ginny's eyes narrowed dangerously, reflecting the deepening sky in their clear greyness. 'I do not usually have a problem in understanding rules of any sort, Sir Jon, but for the life of me I cannot see where or how *you* obtained any authority over me or my good manners. They have always been perfectly adequate, otherwise...'

'Yes, otherwise you'd not have stayed at court for a month, would you? I'm talking about your lack of good manners towards me, and you know that I am. You also know why I've come here and there's nothing you can do to change that. Once His Grace has decided, no woman will undecide him, so you may as well accept it and come off your high horse, lady.'

'Or there will be penalties. I see. Well, that must be the most subtle inducement I've ever received. Guaranteed to succeed with disobedient hounds, hawks and horses, I suppose, but women? I'm not so sure. Me, I'm *quite* sure it would fail dismally. So sorry. Try again.'

Like a firework, their conversation had sparked into the antagonism lying dormant between them for weeks, Ginny's resentment simmering beneath the surface, Sir Jon's usual assuredness on hold, waiting for the right time. Forced into a confrontation by the king's own needs, the right time was still some way off, and Sir Jon's only option was to tackle the problem head-on. Subtlety was going to be of little use here, he'd decided. Bracing himself against the wall with both hands, he effectively caged her with his bulk, making it impossible for her to complete the irritable flounce away to one side. 'No, mistress! That's the first thing you'll learn not to do when I'm talking to you. Stand still and listen.'

'I shall not listen.'

'I think you will. Your manner towards me before others will be polite and respectful at all times. I do not care what you try on in private. I can deal with that in my own way. But do not seek to chasten me by pretending I'm not there, as you have done at court.'

'I can choose who I speak to, sir.'

'Not anymore, you can't. None of us can. We must be civil to everyone these days or make enemies of those who have the means to harm us. You should have learnt that by now. You're about to enter a different world from this—' he tipped his head towards the silver-grey garden '—where a harsher set of rules applies and, if you have the common sense your father tells me of, then you'll allow yourself to be schooled by one who knows them well.'

'Yourself, of course.'

'That's the king's wish and your parents', too.'

'And how much is the king paying you to take on this onerous task, Sir Jon, since nothing my father could offer you three years ago was enough? How many abbeys has he promised you? Which particular titles did he bribe you with?'

There was time enough for her words to fade away on the ice-cold air before he replied, searching her eyes as if to see behind them. 'My, you *are* a bittersweet little termagant, aren't you, mistress? Is that's what's been eating at you for three years?'

'How could it, sir? We have seen nothing of each other until recently.'

'And now we have? Still resentful?'

'I resent being commanded to wed a man who has to be enticed so openly and expensively, sir. What woman could possibly be flattered by that?'

'Wait a minute. That's not the answer, is it? You've only just found out about the king's wish, so why the cold shoulder at court?'

'I really don't know what you mean. I'm not one of the queen's ladies-in-waiting, nor even one of her maids. I have not felt obliged to mingle as they do. We may be neighbours here in Hampshire, Sir Jon, but that doesn't mean we have to like each other. You made your indifference plain from the start. Why should I not do the same?'

'I have never been indifferent, Mistress D'Arvall. I was obliged to bide my time, that's all.'

'Ah, yes, of course. Biding your time. That's done rather differently at court, I notice. A command from the king can make all the difference to one's timing, can it not? There, I see that's hit the nail on the head.'

His head had dropped between his powerful shoulders as she laid bare the facts about timing and, when he lifted it, she could hear how the soft laughter caught at his words, feel the warmth of his breath, and smell the male odour of skin. Standing upright to release her, he replaced the black velvet cap on his head as a sign that their conversation must end. 'Correct,' he said, smiling still. 'A king's command is a powerful thing, but don't forget who else stands to gain from it, mistress. Your family. All of them. Does that mean so little to you? There was a time, I believe, when you would have needed no persuading.'

Freed from his closeness, she pulled her cloak farther around her neck and faced the door, through which shouts could be heard. '*Do* try to understand me, Sir Jon, if you will. I am as set against the king's command, and my father's, as it is possible to be. If I could find a way out of it, I would. Persuasions are superfluous, aren't they, when consent has been removed? It's one thing to be noticed by the king and to have the honour of being his friend, but it's quite another when he tells me who I should marry. It would matter little *who* you were, sir. My resentment would be the same.'

His arm came across her once more, preventing her first step. 'And *you* should try to understand *me*, mistress, when I say that your reasons are far from watertight. But we'll let that go for lack of time. Just remember what I said to you about a more respectful demeanour, for I'll not be made to look foolish by a woman again.' Dropping his arm, he moved away to open the garden door, and there was no time to ask what he meant by that before the king's hounds came bounding forwards to greet them. Sir Jon was relieved by not having to find an answer to his slip of the tongue, as he was by the controversial question of penalties, for if she had asked for examples, he would not have been able to invent a single one.

No one could fail to be impressed by King Henry, for if size alone had been a measure of kingship, he would have won hands down. At forty-nine years old, his girth had expanded to enormous proportions, exaggerated by the winter bulk of padding and furs, making the whippet-like figure of Sir Walter D'Arvall look like a toy beside him. The heavy fur-lined gown was thrown back to expose a chest like a house side, encrusted, embellished, puffed, slashed, and hung with chains and pendants as big as tartlets. Everything about him was large except his prim little mouth and glittering beady eyes that darted over the top of Lady Agnes's head as he raised her to her feet with gentle courtesy. His eyes alighted at last on Ginny, standing with the escort she had not planned to meet until much later, when it suited her. 'Ah, there you are, Mistress D'Arvall. Are you glad to see me again?'

Ginny came forwards to make a low curtsy. 'Indeed, Your Grace. As are we all. Welcome to our modest home,' she said, already practised in deflecting Henry's attention from herself to more general themes. This occasion was going to require all her wits to stay out of deep waters, and Sir Jon's presence would hardly make things any easier. His appearance beside her was immediately remarked on.

'Raemon! Didn't lose much time in finding her, did you? Eh? Made any progress, or is it too soon?'

Sir Jon had expected this kind of tactlessness. It was Henry's privilege. One either had to squirm and accept the humiliation, bluff it out with similar frankness or stand on one's dignity. 'Like you, sire, I made good haste,' he said, smiling. 'As would any man.'

Henry nodded, satisfied. 'Your brothers are here, too,' he said to Ginny. 'We must have them with us at such a time. Can't leave *them* out, can we?'

'Hawking is one of their favourite pastimes, Your Grace. You have chosen a perfect time for it, while the air is clear,' she said.

His smile became paternal as he bent his head towards her. 'Ah, mistress,' he said, so close that she could smell his sour breath, 'that was not my meaning. I invited your brothers along to witness your betrothal to this fine fellow here. Surely your lady mother has told you of our wishes?'

It took every ounce of Ginny's self-control to stifle a cry of defiance at that, having only just learned who her eventual husband was to be, and that there was no way out of it. What was the urgency? Why now? Why the indecent haste for a betrothal, as if she might run away? Forlorn hope. 'So soon?' she whispered.

Taking her response for maidenly reticence, Henry glanced at Ginny's parents, unable to conceal the desire in his piggy eyes. 'Charming,' he said. 'What modesty. She does you credit. Now, Lady Agnes, a glass of your Rhenish would be more than welcome after that long ride. Eh?' Leaning heavily on the arm of a well-dressed young man, he limped away towards the porch where the warmth of the great hall would begin the slow thaw of fingers and toes.

Yet despite Sir Jon's recent warning to her, Ginny's glare of sheer fury could not be held back and, though it was met by the unmistakable caution in his eyes, her snarled question found its mark. 'You knew of this, didn't you? Am I to be the last to know what's going on here?'

'Later,' he whispered. 'We'll talk later.'

'I'll be damned if I'll talk to you,' she muttered, 'or him.'

'Shh! For pity's sake, have a care, woman. He's not deaf.'

Fortunately for Ginny, the hum of voices covered their heated exchange while Sir Jon's hopes of a more compliant attitude from her seemed as far away as before. Obviously it would take more than a hurried warning to make any impression on this fiery creature with a resentment as deep as a well.

For a crowd of courtiers who had ridden hard all day to reach D'Arvall Hall, they still looked remarkably fine and free from the dust that, in summer, would have covered them from head to toe. Around her, the swish and rustle of rich fabrics mingled with excited chatter as skirts were lifted, cloaks trailed, and feathers waved like so many bright birds in an overcrowded aviary. The sheen of silver and gold woven into the silks caught the mellow light from the hall, though Ginny herself would never have ridden a horse wearing such costly garments. She was glad, however, that she'd taken time to dress with care in the pink velvet with the square neckline, the loose outer sleeves edged with her mother's honey-coloured squirrel fur, the under-sleeves of pale cream brocade. To her mother she had pretended not to care that her hair was of the same paleness, but a glance in the mirror had confirmed the radiant confidence that came with looking her best, no matter how dire the situation. 'I shall give you Mistress Molly,' her mother had said in an attempt to thaw the frostiness between them. 'You'll need a maid now and Molly knows your ways better than anyone. She can dress your hair.'

Ginny had thanked her without a smile, suspecting that Mistress Molly would be well rewarded for keeping Lady Agnes informed of all that happened, or did not happen, to the new Lady Virginia Raemon. So the sensational hair had been taken into plaits at each temple, then joined at the back to lie over the top of the rest. Now she felt, as well as saw, the looks directed her way from many of the courtiers she knew and who, until now, had thought her too innocent to include in their worldly conversations.

Her mother's efforts had paid off: gleaming silver and glass on the tables, white napery, liveried servants, musicians up on the gallery, and the delicious aroma of food wafting through the openings of the elaborate wooden screens where tapestries made a splash of colour on adjacent walls. 'Well, little sister?' said a familiar voice behind her. 'You're going to take us all up in the world, are you? Can't say I'm surprised. You could give young Kat Howard a run for her money any day. And the Basset girl, too.' It was Paul, her brother, wearing a doublet of brightest yellow.

Before she could reply to his typically facile remarks, Sir Jon forestalled her with a more apt put-down than she could have devised. 'Your sister is not in competition with Mistress Howard,' he said, 'nor will she ever be. As for going up in the world, that rests with His Majesty alone. Better get that straight, lad, before you get any more fancy ideas.'

Paul D'Arvall's indiscretions had landed him in trouble more than once during his year at Henry's court where he was tolerated for a particular aptitude for mimicry that had been known to take away the pain of Henry's badly damaged leg. Time and again he had been forgiven and excused by Henry for misdemeanours that had had others banished, locked in the Tower, or worse, and others suspected that young D'Arvall felt himself perfectly safe as long as he could keep Henry amused. No reprimand from his father had made him more circumspect, and though his mother could see no fault in him, the rest of the family felt distinctly uncomfortable whenever he was around.

His brother-in-law, Sir George Betterton, was one of the few people to whom Paul would listen, occasionally, and now he happened to be standing with Sir Jon, his neighbour. 'Best keep your opinions under your bonnet, D'Arvall,' he said. 'Such loose talk can get even you seen off with your tail between your legs.' He winked at Ginny. 'Hello, sister-in-law,' he said kindly. 'Maeve's looking for you. Been hiding?'

'Yes,' she said. 'What would *you* do?'

'Oh, I'd certainly hide from this great brute.' He laughed. 'Come and talk to me and your sister. We'll tell you how to handle him.'

But Ginny had seen her other brother, Elion, and her greeting was warmer by far than it had been for Paul, the younger of the two. 'Dear one,' she said. 'Can we talk?'

'Yes, love. But not until after supper, I fear, for here comes Father with that "now you listen to me" look on his face.' He lifted his cap as Sir Walter approached. 'Want me to stay, Ginny?'

His question was answered for him by the quick tip of Sir Walter's head that usually left his subordinates in no doubt about what he intended. Even Sir Jon could only watch as Ginny's arm was taken and she was steered towards a shadowy corner away from the bustle. Foolishly, in retrospect, Ginny hoped she might be allowed to have the first word. 'Father, I know you mean well, but I did not agree to—'

Sir Walter knew immediately what she referred to. 'So your mother tells me, Virginia,' he cut in brusquely. 'But what has that to do with anything? I agreed to it. So did His Majesty the king, and so did Sir Jon. Isn't that enough? Who else is there to ask? God's truth, lass, if we went round the countryside asking for opinions, you'd still be unmarried by Domesday. My duty is to find you a suitable husband and I've been lenient with you till now. But I shall not be here for ever and the king's offer is as good as it's going to get. You must accept it, for all our sakes. It means everything to your mother and me.'

'Whether I like it or not.'

'Yes. Whether you like it or not, young lady. And no more discourtesy towards Sir Jon, if you please. I could hardly believe you and he have not spoken in this last month at court. Have you no thought to the future?'

'Yes', she replied, she had, she did, 'but—'

'But *nothing*!' Sir Walter snapped. 'There are no buts in this business, Virginia. Men make the conditions, not women of your age. Just remember that, will you?'

'Yes, Father,' she responded as he walked away. He did not want answers, reasons, or opinions, only blind obedience, for this was not just about her, but about all he stood to gain by it. In one way or another, a man had to fight for his own advancement by any means open to him, for Henry had grown fickle, unpredictable, and not to be relied on for his favour. Whatever he offered must be snatched up with both hands before someone else benefited; families were at each other's throats, seeking dominance and influence with a king who wanted those around him to agree with every word, to fawn and flatter, to pander to his monstrous ego. Those who were not prepared to do this had no place at court, and no place at court meant no share of the spoils being handed out almost daily, whether positions, titles, or one of the eight hundred or so monastic properties that had been closed down over the past five years. What were the preferences of a young woman worth compared to this?

Nevertheless, it seemed to Ginny that all this fuss simply to have her near the king at court as a married woman was completely ridiculous when he could command her presence at any time, married or not, and to enjoy her company whenever he wished. As he had done since she'd been with Queen Anna, his new wife, walking in the gardens, partnering him at bowls, riding out with hawks, sharing these pastimes with others of her own age until the queen from Cleves could converse in English to his satisfaction. Was this really worth the rewards her mother had told her of? Was there something more she might be expected to do? Was she being used by her family in the same way that plain Jane Seymour had been by hers? Evidently not, for Jane had taken no husband except the king himself, and now he had 'a new wife he didn't care for'…and rumour had it that the dear lady was still a virgin.

The hairs along Ginny's arms prickled. Her

scalp crawled. No…no, not that! Were her parents so insensitive that they could subject her to *that*? With an ageing king? And Sir Jon, too? Had he agreed that, for his rewards, he would allow his wife to be used? Her head reeled with the onrush of questions. She felt nauseous as a wave of cooking smells assaulted her nostrils. Where was Elion? Maeve? They would explain.

From above her, a fanfare of trumpets blasted out across the hall to tell them that supper was about to begin, for however much the king pretended that his informal visits needed no pomp or ceremony, he would not have been impressed if his hosts had taken him at his word. It was too late for Ginny to explore the details of the matter that would affect her for the rest of her life.

Amongst those who had come with the king that day, there were few who were unaware of the coolness between Mistress D'Arvall and Sir Jon Raemon, and now some had even placed bets on how long it would take him to thaw the lady who must have some very serious reasons for her dislike. She must rate herself very highly, they thought, to place herself so far beyond his reach when he was one of the most eligible of the king's gentlemen, wealthy, accomplished, intelligent, and devastatingly good-looking. So it was with some anticipation that the handsome couple was observed together at the table where their demeanour could be judged and the stakes raised accordingly.

But as if in unspoken accord, neither Ginny nor Sir Jon would give them the satisfaction of having anything to gossip about, and to all eyes it looked as if Ginny was prepared to accept the role being thrust upon her, whatever it was, and to be the meek and submissive daughter her father required. The truth was that she would not shame her family, or Sir Jon, in public before the king, although what she did in private would be an entirely different matter. Knowing her as they did, her family was not fooled, and nor was Sir Jon, who did not know her half so well, but had observed her more keenly than she realised. He had seen how her father had spoken to her, how she had paled and how he would not have minced his words. Having gained some idea from their brief talk together how her mind was so set against him, he was thankful, but not optimistic, about her show of obedience.

The lavish supper passed off without incident, King Henry's occasional references to Ginny's talents and Sir Jon's eagerness being taken good-naturedly by them, while she raged inside at all those who sought to manipulate her life for their own selfish ends. There was a point during the banter when, under cover of the noise, Sir Jon murmured to her, 'Well done, mistress. I know what this is costing you in restraint.'

'Do you, Sir Jon? I very much doubt it.'

'Believe me, I do. They're like a dog with a bone. They'll let it go eventually.'

Warming to his role as matchmaker, and assuming that Ginny would be of the same mind as any young woman ripe for marriage, Henry lost no time after supper in bringing the two of them together in a public manner intended to show off his great benevolence, as if his motives were entirely selfless. Upstairs, in the beautiful oak gallery, he took Ginny by the hand while beckoning Sir Jon to stand close by, past the silk-clad legs and crackling skirts, the smiling faces and nudging elbows, causing a silence to descend as he took centre stage. 'Mistress D'Arvall,' he said in his rasping tenor, 'since this sluggard has not seen fit to find you for himself, I present him to you now for your approval. It is our wish, and that of your parents, that you and Sir Jon should plight your troth at some time during our visit. You, sir, are most fortunate. Mistress D'Arvall is a prize worth winning.' He looked down at Ginny with such unconcealed lust that, for once, his next words only squeaked and had to be repeated. 'He will…ahem…he will make you a good and honest husband, mistress. We commend him to you.'

'I thank you, your Majesty, but…'

'Sir Jon, you may take the lady's hand.'

With every eye upon them, Ginny placed her fingers lightly on Sir Jon's rock-solid palm to support her curtsy as the applause and smiles added yet another layer of finality, already too deep for her liking. She felt the net closing around her and pulling her wherever Sir Jon went and nowhere she wanted to be. Certainly not at court and certainly not anywhere near the husband of the woman she had come to admire. She would be moulded to other men's lives, given over to their desires with all her dreams of love fading in one handclasp. He took her hand to his lips, bowing courteously, putting on a good act, Ginny thought, of being pleased by the king's generosity. Her own eyes were downcast, her heart heavy with foreboding, for this handsome creature who had once rejected her would surely have a woman of his own somewhere, maybe one of those watching this charade. Their hearts would probably weigh as heavy as hers. Perhaps they had already planned how to deal with it.

Heavy-hearted or not, Sir Jon concealed it well as he led her through the crowd to meet well-wishers, to acknowledge smiles, slaps on the back for him, and kisses for her from those she would now have to learn to like. Drawn this way and that, parted from Sir Jon, she came face-to-face once more with her brother Paul, his friends already laughing at his witty remarks, the content of which Ginny could easily guess. She would have smiled and moved away in search of her sister, but Paul would not allow the chance to escape him and, leaning heavily against her with his lips close to her ear, he mimicked the king's words of a moment earlier. 'He'll make you a good and honest husband, mistress,' he said in the reedy royal tone. 'And do you see that lust in my eyes, too, sweet wench? I'll have you in my bed tonight, sweet Virginia. Sir Jon won't mind if I have you first, eh?' Laughing at his own adolescent jest, he swung her round by the waist in a parody of a dance until she was caught and held by Maeve, who would not share Paul's sport at her expense.

Nor did George, her husband, whose hand held the back of Paul's embroidered collar as if he were an ill-trained pup. 'Go and sit down,

D'Arvall,' he said in a low angry voice. 'The wine's gone to your head, lad. You'll go too far one day if you're not more careful.' He gave him an ungentle shove into the arms of his companions.

'I said nothing!' Paul protested. 'I was only…'

Sir George turned back to the two sisters and saw by Ginny's white face that her brother's 'nothing' was far from the truth. People moved away sympathetically, leaving them to find a bench at the end of the long gallery beneath a dark portrait of their grandfather. 'What is it, Ginny?' Maeve said. 'What did Paul say?'

'He said…well, he *seemed* to be saying that this is all for the king's convenience and that Sir Jon wouldn't mind. Which is what I'd already begun to suspect. Is it true, Maeve? Is this what the king does when he takes a mistress? I've not been at court long enough to know how these things are done, but not for one moment did I imagine the king would already be in need of a mistress when he's only been married a month or so. Tell me it's not true.'

The brief glance exchanged between Maeve and her husband was loaded with anguish. 'Listen, love,' Maeve said, taking Ginny's hand upon the rich green brocade of her skirt. 'We hoped Mother would have made the position clear to you by now. And Father, too. They know how these things go.'

'The position? You mean, it's *true*? He's expecting me to…?'

'Well, yes. When the king intends to take a mistress, he prefers her to be a married woman so that when she bears a child, there's always a husband to give it a name, so that it won't be a bastard. Bastards can cause a bit of a problem, you see, later on, with claims of royal prerogative, so he tends not to recognise them these days. It's easier for him.' She paused, hoping George might continue.

'It was like that with Mary Boleyn,' he said, 'Anne's sister. She was married off to William Carey before her children were born. They didn't have any choice and Carey didn't care for the arrangement, but he accepted it. It's happened with others, too. He doesn't have affairs with unmarried women anymore. It's too risky.'

'So he's persuaded Sir Jon Raemon to agree to marry me so that I can be on hand? And he knew I'd have to accept the situation because Father would demand it, if he was offered bribes, too? And Mother? How could they *do* that?'

'Henry tried the same thing on with George and me, but I quickly became pregnant and I never got as far as Henry's bed, thank heaven. He took it in good part, but now he's seen you, Ginny, and he's got Father to assert his authority because he knows how much Father wants Sandrock Priory and this is the carrot he's using. I don't know what he's offered Sir Jon, but if I were you, I'd not assume he had to be bribed heavily.'

'Of *course* he must. He didn't want me three years ago,' Ginny said heatedly. 'He's been persuaded to change his mind.'

George would have said more, but Ginny was in no mood to accept that Sir Jon's change of heart might have had much to do with the beauty she had become. Even in a roomful of Henry's select courtiers, Ginny and her sister stood out like perfect blooms in a winter landscape. And he had seen a look on Sir Jon's face that he'd never seen before, not even for the late Lady Magdalen Raemon. She had been a beauty, but Ginny had a rare loveliness that took men's breath away and made wives nudge their husbands peevishly when their eyes lingered too long in her direction. At eleven years her sister's senior, Maeve had a more mature loveliness and a serene nature that Henry had once found more to his liking than Queen Anne Boleyn's fault finding. But by that time, she and

George were deeply in love and George had
never been one to let the grass grow under his
feet. He had not even waited for Sir Walter's
permission to marry his daughter, and it had
taken the birth of his first grandchild to soften
his heart towards them.

'Ginny, listen,' he said. 'We'll help. It doesn't
have to go all the way. Sir Jon will find a way
round it, as we did.'

'By getting pregnant as fast as possible…
yes…well, thank you for that, George. I'm sure
you meant it for the best but, as it happens, I
don't want to go to bed with either of them.'

'Is there someone else, Ginny?' Maeve said,
watching the approach of Sir Jon and wondering guiltily why any woman would *not* want to
go to bed with him. What a virile creature he
was, for sure.

Ginny stood at Sir Jon's approach. 'It would
make no difference now if there was, would
it?' she said, looking directly at him, intending
him to understand the question as well as the
reply. 'It's a risk we both must take, husbands
and wives.'

'Congratulations, Raemon,' said Sir George,
standing to meet his neighbour. 'It's been an
eventful day. Would it help for you and Mis-

tress D'Arvall to find a quiet corner where you can talk in private? I can show you...'

Forgetting Sir Jon's views on her manners, Ginny was already moving purposefully through the parting crowd, leaving some stares in her wake at her determined expression. With the intention of shaking him off by weaving in and out of groups, darting through doorways, round corners, and into a series of linking rooms, she glanced over her shoulder to see if she had lost him and bumped, with a din that echoed off the panelled walls, into a servant bearing a tray of drinking glasses. The crystal splinters seemed to wet the floor with glittering fragments, bringing forwards a rush of servants to clear it and stranding Ginny in an island of clear flagstones. 'I'm sorry,' she whispered. 'That was my fault.'

'No, mistress. Mine entirely. Oh...sir?' the poor man said, indicating Ginny's plight, 'could you...er...assist? Ah, thank you, Sir Jon.'

Before the request could register with her, she was being swung off her feet by strong unyielding arms that held her hard against a velvet doublet with, just above her forehead, a white linen collar edged with blackwork, a neatly bearded jaw, and the scent she recognised as dangerously male, indefinable, and unique.

'Now, my flighty bird,' he muttered, swinging her round, 'is this where you were leading me? Over here, was it?'

Above her, the plasterwork ceiling tilted and revolved. 'I was not leading you anywhere,' she scolded, clutching at her skirt as they passed through yet another doorway. 'Put me *down*, sir. I can walk!'

'Following Henry's instructions to take you in hand, mistress,' he said, striding ahead as if he knew exactly where they were going.

'He didn't say that!'

'He did to me. He knows of your reputation. Perhaps your father warned him.'

'I don't need to be taken in *your* hand or anyone else's,' she said, gasping at the pace. 'Put me *down*!'

With the squeak of an iron door latch and a noticeable fading of light from the wall sconces, she was carried into the small private anteroom overlooking the chapel and tipped without ceremony onto the cushioned bench. There was no room for her to manoeuvre a way out. The heavy door clicked shut and, before she could protest about being alone with him in the semi-darkness, Sir Jon was beside her with one arm along the back of the bench and his knees intimately wedging her in. Down below them in the body of the chapel, distant candles in tall wooden stands shed a glow over the altar and panelled reredos, the step, and very little else. In the dimness, Ginny strained her senses to pick up the messages of his body and the face too close to hers. She had never before been lifted and carried by a man, or held helpless in a small space, not even in the dance where she could move away easily. Now her instinct told her that talk was her best defence. She drew breath, too audible in the closeted space.

She could not see what was about to happen in time to prevent it. With characteristic speed, he pulled her towards him, tipping her head against his shoulder and covering her scolding mouth with his lips in a kiss that, if she'd been less of an innocent, she might have anticipated. A man did not usually sit so close to a woman with his arm across her back for no very good reason. Meant, she was sure, to silence her, his kiss sent a shock through her body of a kind she had never known before, tasting of mastery and a world of experience that had little to do with her own relatively uneventful years. She would have struggled to free herself but, for that moment, nothing existed but the sensation of his mouth moving over hers, the soft brush of his beard on her chin and the hard pressure of his arms across her back. Making it clear that her participation was not required, he moved one hand to take a fistful of her hair, sending another shock deep into her body as it instinctively recognised the male force of his desire and her helplessness against it. Her lips parted under his fierce grasp and a quiet yelp of fear escaped them. His mouth lifted at once, his arms slackened and she was held upright, her hair released.

Dazed and shaken, Ginny moved away as far as she could, resisting the temptation to adjust her hair or wipe her tingling lips. She would not show him how she was affected. 'So,' she whispered, 'that's taking me in hand, is it?'

'It's a start,' he said huskily. 'You let that tongue of yours run away with you in public again and I'll stop you. That's as good a way as any.'

'Indeed, that's as great a threat as ever I heard, Sir Jon.' She stood up. 'Now let me pass.'

'Sit down. We haven't finished.'

'In which case, sir, perhaps you can explain to me how much you know about the king's intention to make me his mistress. Am I really the last to know of this?'

'Let's get this straight, shall we?' he said, taking her chin in his hand and turning it towards him. 'We are both pawns in this game, mistress. The king offers me a wife and I accept. He offers your father a good marriage for his daughter and he accepts. Neither of us has much of a choice, with or without the rewards you're so concerned about. We do as we're told. There's nothing new in that.'

'Oh, wait a moment. What I'm so concerned about is not so much the rewards you're being offered as *my* role in this particular charade. You see, I *do* like to have some say in who fathers my child, when I have one. I would say that was reasonable, wouldn't you? Otherwise I'd not be much different from a breeding mare that has no choice in which stallion covers her. Would I?'

'So you don't see it as an honour to be the king's mistress? Many women would.'

For a few seconds, Ginny struggled to find words to counter the crassness of his question. Henry was forty-nine years old, monstrously overweight, and suffering from a painfully ulcerated leg, bad temper, and bouts of depression. He was probably the most unattractive bedfellow any woman could possibly be saddled with, yet she knew that there were women who would climb into bed with him if they thought the rewards were great enough. The possibility was a favourite topic of conversation at court, although Ginny's closeness to Queen Anna, the lady from Cleves, had afforded her little understanding of the process, except the initial flirting. She had believed this to be relatively harmless coming from a newly married king, and certainly she had never taken her own involvement seriously. She had not been the only maid to be sent letters and jewels. Fifteen-year-old Anne Basset, daughter of Lord Lisle, had been given a horse and an embroidered saddlecloth, much to her lady mother's delight. 'His Majesty has a new wife,' Ginny said, 'of whom I am fond, sir. I would be shamed, not honoured. You, apparently, see things differently. You stand to gain. I stand to gain the title of king's whore. That leaves you unmoved, does it?'

His reply was not quite what she'd expected. 'Believe it or not, mistress, I am not as eager as you seem to think to propel you with all haste into the king's bed.'

'Yet you accept his offer—me—without demur. He must have made the position clear to you.'

'I accepted the king's offer because it suits my purpose. I need a mistress for my home at

Lea Magna, a stepmother for my daughter, and an heir of my own.'

'Thank you. How very honest. Three years ago, it *didn't* suit your purpose.'

'Correct. Things change.'

'Obviously.'

'Try to forget your resentment, mistress. It was not personal.'

'So my mother insists. Of course, it *was* personal because I am a person and I had been led to believe that no man was likely to refuse my hand in marriage. I was well past my sixteenth birthday and the truth of the matter hurt my pride. It serves me right for having some. What's more, this sordid business has done nothing whatever to salve it, being now a bartering tool in a game for men. That's *very* personal, Sir Jon.'

'Then listen to me, if you will. While I cannot refuse to obey the king's command, as your husband I shall do all I can to delay what you fear for as long as possible. Indeed, it may not happen at all if Queen Anna finds a way to please him. Try to place some trust in me, Mistress D'Arvall, even though you find it difficult. I am no more eager than any other man to be cuckolded, even by the king, nor do I particularly want my wife to be his whore. I can manage without his rewards, but unfortunately your father thinks differently about that side of things. And before you remind me again that I accepted, just consider a few of those leering faces who looked on you at supper, and ask yourself which of them you'd have preferred. I was not the only one the king had in mind, you know.'

'I might ask you the same question if I thought you'd give me a straight answer. Which of those women out there would *you* have preferred? We may not have spoken at court, Sir Jon, but I have eyes in my head. You have never been short of female company.'

'It's a requirement that goes with the job,' he said wearily. 'It means nothing, and you will have to close your eyes to what goes on, or make yourself miserable with jealousy.'

'To be a jealous wife, sir, I would have to *care* where my husband bestows his affections—somehow I cannot see that happening. Thank you so much for making our respective positions clear. I may still be unhappy with the situation, but at least I now know where I stand on your list of priorities. Let us both hope that the king's eye will alight on another maid before our betrothal. Who knows? If he can change wives with such speed, perhaps he'll do the same with mistresses.'

'And if you think that will make a difference to my agreement to make you my wife, then think again. It won't,' he said, pulling back his shoulders. His head was silhouetted against the white plastered wall, his profile almost classical in its beauty of line and proportion, and Ginny knew, as she had known before, that her boast about not caring was likely to fall far short of the mark. His friendships with so many admiring women would be difficult for her to accept, for men who strayed were unfamiliar to her and undeserving of respect. Her father would never have looked at another woman.

'Is that all you have to say?' she retorted. 'Shall you escort me back to the others to pretend all is well after being taken in hand by the experienced Sir Jon Raemon? Tell me, what are the signs they'll be looking for? Weeping? Or quaking, perhaps?'

'As a means of silencing you, mistress, the kiss didn't work too well, did it?'

She had nothing to say to that. Would he try again?

'So *you* tell *me*,' he said, 'about what you were saying just now to your sister. Is there someone else? I need to know.' That young assistant of Father Spenney's?

Here was the perfect opportunity, Ginny thought, to invent some mysterious and handsome lover to whom she had given her heart, to show Sir Jon she could play the dalliance game as well as he. But for the life of her, she could not do it and the chance slipped away before she could make the slightest dent in his arrogance. 'No,' she whispered, looking at the little gold aglets on his sleeves. 'There's no one.'

Again, he lifted her chin to make her eyes meet his, for him to search deeply through the clear grey pools rimmed with lashes so long and dense that they appeared darker than they were. But the shadows were deep and there was little for him to recognise except the blaze of hostility, of which he already knew. What Ginny saw in his was the distant reflection of a flame from the altar candle, but nothing that would give her a clue as to his true thoughts, only those she cynically imposed upon him from her limited experience.

The splendid oak gallery came alive with the colours of richly clad guests, vibrating with the strains of half-heard melodies and laughter. Sir Walter's minstrels were not as good as the king's, but they were enthusiastic. The gallery was one of D'Arvall Hall's largest chambers built for entertaining on a grand scale, projecting over lawns and knot gardens with views of gently rolling fields, now in darkness. Hundreds of candles shed light on the white plasterwork ceilings and on the oak panelling of stylised linen folds, falling in a blaze of colour upon King Henry himself. He saw them at once and beckoned. 'Mistress Virginia, ah! I see you have been persuaded. That's good. Did this whelp allow you to get a word in edgeways? He usually presents a good case.'

'No, Your Grace,' said Ginny artlessly. 'He did not. I doubt he heard one word I said.'

Gently, Henry punched a great ham fist into Sir Jon's chest. 'Shame on you. Come, mistress. You'll find a better listener in me, I promise.'

Ignoring whatever message was in Sir Jon's eyes, Ginny was led by the hand to a cushioned window seat where Henry sat like a colossus beside her and proceeded to break his promise as if it had never been made. His questions required only one-word answers. Did she know he wrote music? And poetry, too? And played several instruments? Which he would show her when they returned to court. Was she afraid of the marriage bed? Well, Sir Jon would make sure she had nothing to fear and she must regard him, Henry, as her advisor, sharing her problems with him at all times. He had her interests at heart, he told her, stroking the skin of her folded hands with a caress much more than parental. He praised her voice, her looks, her stormy grey eyes, his unctuous flattery betraying a lover-like esteem totally inappropriate to the time and place, or to an advisor. With nerves already as taut as bowstrings, Ginny wondered how she was expected to respond to a married monarch who, in theory, could do no wrong, yet whose eyes roamed freely over her without pause. So when Sir Jon approached and slipped like a shadow onto the seat beside her, she caught her smile of welcome just before it showed.

Henry was not annoyed. 'Puppy!' he chided. 'Come to claim her, have you?'

'Yes, sire,' said Sir Jon. 'My turn again.'

'See?' said Henry to Ginny. 'This is the esteem in which I hold him. There are few of my courtiers I would allow to interrupt a tête-à-tête with you, mistress. We were having a merry chat, were we not?'

'We were indeed, Your Majesty.'

'Eating out of my hand already. That's the way to do it, lad. But see, we're making the

maid blush, between us. There, mistress,' he
said, patting her hand. 'We'll resume our talk
later, shall we? *Later*, eh?' His eyes crinkled
and glittered.

'Your Grace does me much kindness.'

'Humph!' He nodded, clearly agreeing with
her platitude as he watched the pair drift away
into the crowd. Immediately, courtiers engulfed
him like an incoming tide.

It grew late, but there were those to whom
Ginny wished to speak, and others, like her
parents and Paul, she did not. It went without
saying that the king's visit had set a seal on
everything they'd hoped for, not only for their
daughter's future but for the acquisitions that
were sure to come their way. In view of her dis-
taste for the methods used, they did not feel it
necessary to thank her for any of this, but nor
could they quite wipe the satisfaction from their
faces as the evening progressed. Her words to
them were understandably brief, dutiful if resentful, and laced heavily with a bitterness they
chose to disregard. She would come round, they
assured each other.

Elion, Ginny's twenty-eight-year-old brother,
was far more sympathetic, though there was
nothing he could do about it except to antici-

pate, with some feelings of guilt, the knight-hood that would certainly come his way. There would be no question of him refusing it. With his sister Maeve and her husband, George, he did his best to lighten Ginny's heart by suggest-ing that, with her help, Queen Anna would learn to appreciate music and dancing, gaming and glamorous clothes and thereby win the king's affection and admiration, making Ginny's role redundant. This would not, of course, eliminate the forthcoming marriage to Sir Jon, but per-haps she would learn to tolerate this, as others did theirs.

For some reason, it seemed important for Ginny to know what the first Lady Raemon looked like. Was she as beautiful as they said? Popular at court? Gracious? Kind? Had she merely been a dutiful wife or had there been love between them? Their replies, on the whole, were less than satisfactory. They couldn't really say. They hadn't had much to do with her. Pop-ular, yes, but not a personal friend and hardly ever at Lea Magna, so very little contact as neighbours. To their relief, Ginny dropped the subject.

Paul, the younger of the two brothers, was as usual intent on ingratiating himself with some of the king's gentlemen of the bedchamber, of whom he was not one, but had a friend who was, Thomas Culpeper. Their nonsense kept the weary king awake and, as no one could leave the festivities before he did, it was well after midnight when Culpeper whispered to Sir Jon that, tonight, his services would not be required. The other five would put Henry to bed so that, if Sir Jon wished, he could try for a lingering goodnight with his new woman.

Thanking him, but rather wary of such un-usual cooperation from one he spared no love for, Sir Jon entertained not the slightest hope of any kind of goodnight from Mistress Virginia D'Arvall, lingering or otherwise, so took his leave of his hosts and went to find his bed. Vir-ginia, they told him, had already gone to hers. They would all have to be up in good time for the hawking.

Safe at last from the court's social demands, Ginny lay spreadeagled on her wide bed, still fully dressed, her dangling feet being mas-saged by Mistress Molly, who did not need to ask about her new mistress's state of mind. Too tired to begin undressing, she stared up at the carved wooden tester while snatches of conver-sation flitted darkly through her mind like bats, too fast to be caught. In a vast warren of interlinked buildings added on at various stages of ownership, her room was cosy and warm with a crackling fire in the iron grate and walls lined with seasoned pine and gold-framed portraits of ancient ancestors. Outside in the passage-way, the patter and thud of feet, the slam of doors and distant squeals of laughter added to the usual bedlam of guests finding their quarters, though a discreet tap on her own door was not what she'd expected, unless it was Maeve come for a last chat.

Molly answered the door, exchanged a few inaudible words with the young man, then closed it and came to stand beside Ginny with an expression of deep offence written clearly on her sensible features. 'At *this* time of night?' she said, looking back at the door as if it were personally responsible. 'I can scarce credit it! Really!'

Ginny sat bolt upright. 'What? Who was it?'

'A royal page. The king's lad. He's sent for you.'

'The king? Sent for *me*? You cannot be serious, Molly.'

'I am serious, mistress. I would not jest about something like this. He says the king would like the pleasure of your company and to take a glass of wine with him, if you please. In his room.'

'In my *father's house*? Molly, what on earth is he thinking of?'

'Well, what does His Grace usually think of at this time of night? No marks for guessing what he wants *you* for. You can't go. Not alone.'

'Of course I can't go, but how do I disobey? There would have to be a good reason, Molly. I can't just say, no, thank you, Your Majesty.'

They stared at each other, dredging up reasons good enough to sound genuine. 'I'm ill,' Ginny suggested. 'I have the plague. He's terrified of that.'

'He knows you're not.'

'I'm asleep.'

'That's unlikely, too, with this racket going on.'

'I'm betrothed, and...'

'And with Sir Jon! Yes!' Molly caught the drift. 'That's it!'

'But I'm not, Molly. Am I?'

'You could be. What's to stop you? It'll happen sooner or later.'

'No, that's ridiculous. We've only just met. I need time...'

'Mistress Ginny, you don't *have* time. The king is waiting for you. The only convincing excuse not to obey is that you and Sir Jon are already in bed together as a newly betrothed couple. Henry's not going to argue with that.'

'But he would have to *be* there, at the betrothal, wouldn't he?'

'Not necessarily. You were in a hurry. There were witnesses. Father Spenney came to conduct it. It's perfectly legal. I'm going to get your sister and brother. They'll agree it's the only thing to do.'

'No…no, wait, Molly! What's Sir Jon going to say to all this?'

'We'll soon find out, won't we?' said Molly, turning to go. Relenting, she came back to Ginny's side, her face softening at the stricken expression. 'Listen, he's not going to tell you to go to the king, is he? Given the choice, what do you think he'd rather do? He's not an ogre, mistress. The king is, but not Sir Jon. Leave it to me.'

Covering her face with her hands, Ginny recreated that same dimness of the chapel anteroom where she and Sir Jon had bickered and fought a verbal battle while sitting close together, his warmth flooding her side, the scent of him and, yes…the taste of him, too, the shameful pressure of his arms and body. No, she could not do it. Not with a man who didn't want her. She would need weeks to prepare herself for it, for the courage to satisfy her parents whose future security depended, apparently, on her obedience. This was all going too fast for her. 'Not my parents too, Molly,' she whispered into her fingers. 'They would not agree to it. They would take me to the king themselves, if necessary. And Paul, too. Don't bring him back with you.'

Climbing off the bed, she went to stand before the fire, shivering in spite of its warmth, waiting for the help she both needed and feared.

Chapter Three

Help was not long in coming. A quick succession of taps on the door admitted first Maeve with Molly, both of them comfortingly adamant that this was the only safeguard, convenient or not. Next came Sir George with Sir Jon and Elion. George had found them talking together before bed, agreeing with him that to invite Sir Walter, Lady Agnes, and Paul would be counterproductive when they could not be trusted to consent to such a drastic method of escape. Ginny's doubts about Sir Jon's reaction were instantly dispelled, however, when he took her wrist in his hand, gently but firmly asserting a kind of instant possession that said more than words about his reading of the situation. If it was somewhat arrogant in its boldness, Ginny felt relieved that he had shown no sign of reluctance, so she left it there, putting up no resistance to its message. Last of all came Father Spenney, Sir Walter's chaplain, quietly spoken, sensible, and scholarly, a man in his fifties who had no qualms about conducting a hurried betrothal if it meant saving Mistress Virginia from the king's bed. Nor did he need Sir Walter's permission, he said. They could, if they'd wished, have done it without him, too.

His unassuming and authoritative manner brought sighs of relief from several of them, but it was Ginny's brother Elion who needed more confirmation. 'What's His Grace going to say?' he whispered in the crowded little room. 'Wouldn't he expect to be present? Is this all perfectly legal, Father?'

Father Spenney placed a lean hand on Elion's arm. 'It is perfectly in order for two people to plight their troth,' he said, 'at any time in any place, no matter who is or isn't there, Master Elion. His Grace will either be furious or he'll think it all highly amusing. We shall not know until tomorrow. All that is certain is that he wishes Sir Jon and Mistress Virginia to pledge themselves to each other while he's here and that is what they're about to do. So for this night, and probably tomorrow also, His Grace will have no claim on the lady's company, which is what we all agree must be prevented.'

'And His Grace,' said Sir George, 'will have his own ideas about where the marriage should take place. But Sir Walter has not hesitated to browbeat Ginny over this business, so I can understand why she would not want her parents as witnesses.'

'Well, George,' said Sir Jon, glancing down at Ginny, 'that's a nice way of putting it, but correct all the same. Even so, I think the lady ought to be allowed to say, before it's too late, whether she is willing to go ahead with it. I would rather not be accused of browbeating, though it has to be said that we are only hastening the business, that's all.'

'I do not know exactly what His Grace has in mind for me this night,' Ginny said, noting their sympathetic faces, 'but whatever it is, I would rather *this* than *that*.' She felt Sir Jon's hand slide carefully from her wrist to her fingers and hold them, silently approving the choice that must have been far from easy. Neither choice had been what she wanted.

'Shall we begin, then?' said Father Spenney.

There was so much that was wrong about this, thought Ginny. The haste, for one thing. The pressure, for another. Her reluctance. The uncertainty, not least about the king's reaction on the morrow. His temper was notoriously unreliable. An almost imperceptible squeeze on her fingers brought her back to reality, reminding her that she must not waver, that this, as Sir Jon had reminded them, would have to happen one way or another and there was little she could do about it when men had agreed.

It was all over in a matter of moments, whispered promises with clasped hands and a short prayer thrown in for good measure by the kindly priest. Then smiles, hugs and kisses, and words like *safe now*, and tightly grasped arms and hands, and it was all done. Elion and Sir George were the ones to offer to go to the king's rooms to convey apologies from Sir Jon and Mistress Virginia. They were in bed together, they would say, and did not think the king would wish to disturb them. Consummation would make the betrothal not only more valid, but marriage inevitable.

Looking back on that particular night, as Ginny did so often in the following months, she realised that she'd been in a daze, rather like a dream that she knew made no sense yet could not be halted. 'I shall have to stay, mistress,' Sir Jon said to Molly as the door closed on the last of their guests, 'if I go out there, I may be seen and that would not help our cause.'

'Then, if my mistress doesn't need me?' she said, looking at Ginny.

'Er…no, you go, Molly. I'll manage,' Ginny whispered. 'Goodnight and thank you. Sleep well.'

Molly would have wished her the same, but had the wit not to. Once they were alone, the antagonism that had worked so well in the garden only hours before seemed inappropriate after a ceremony in which they had promised to marry 'at some time in the future', which, if the king had his way, would be sooner rather than later. Spreading her hands in a helpless gesture, Ginny shook her head, looked for a chair, and sat down heavily as though her legs had softened. 'This is quite ridiculous,' she whispered. 'I'm sorry you've been pushed into this, Sir Jon. You could not have expected it to happen this way any more than I did. I don't know how a man must feel when he's been manoeuvred into—'

'Shh!' he said. 'I haven't been manoeuvred, mistress. If I had not wanted to take you for my wife, then believe me, I would have refused. He wouldn't have killed me for declining his invitation.'

'He would not have offered you rewards either, would he?'

Sir Jon came to squat on his haunches before her where his head was on a level with hers. The candlelight caught at the high cheekbones, and the dark line of his chin covered with soft hair that she had felt upon her skin. Pouches of laugh lines gathered beneath his eyes and she knew he was amused, which she thought odd, in the circumstances. 'Shall we not go into all that again?' he said quietly. 'You are tired. You've had an eventful day that hasn't been easy for you. Perhaps we should delay talking about the future until another time. It's too late to go into all that again.'

As before, talking was her best defence against something she did not want to happen, so when she began again, his response was to take one of her hands to stop the flow of protests, whatever they were. 'I know what the problem is, mistress. So this is what we'll do. We have to make it look as if we've been to bed together. In theory, that is what's required of us.'

'In theory?' she said, revealing at once by the squeak in her voice that he had cleverly identified the cause of her concern. 'How...in theory?'

'We shall be asked if we have actually lain

together and we shall have to say yes, because that's what this is all about, isn't it? You not being available to the king.'

'Yes.'

'So all we have to do is to share the same bed and lay side by side. That's all. I have never taken a woman unwillingly, mistress, and I shall not start with you. You are more than safe, from me and from His Grace. I'm sure that's what you'd prefer, isn't it?'

Whatever she had been expecting to happen, this was something she had not thought of, and now it came as a shock to her to hear Sir Jon finding a way out of a delicate situation that any man would have taken advantage of without a second thought. It was true that she had no wish to go to bed with him on this night or any other. He did not want her and she did not want him, but he might have given her the option of refusing him in a maidenly fashion, instead of conspiring how to deceive the interested parties who would ask questions tomorrow. Not that she'd had much time to imagine how it would be to suffer his lovemaking, but she *had* thought of how she might offer various excuses that would be sure to disappoint him. After all, how many women would have refused him since his wife departed? she wondered. Probably none. Yet how else was she supposed to make her disapproval of him clear except by being so reluctant in bed that he would derive absolutely no pleasure from it? And now he had removed that chance from her with his damned chivalry. Was his suggestion what she would prefer? Or would she have preferred him to make just a small attempt to win her? Something like the kiss in the chapel?

'Yes,' she whispered. 'That is what I would prefer, too. I believe that would suit both of us, Sir Jon. I'm sure you cannot be any more eager for the intimate part of the business than I am. But heaven only knows how I'm to shed these clothes when I cannot reach the back. I may have to ask for your help, lacking Molly's assistance.' It was, she thought, an inspired idea that would show him what he had just forfeited.

Recognising a certain confusion in the young lady's mind in which her curiosity conflicted with her reluctance to satisfy it, he continued with the chivalric conduct he believed was probably the safest while her nerves were so on edge, her body tired, her thoughts too packed with happenings beyond her control. 'Of course, mistress. If you will turn, I'll do my best,' he said. 'Are the sleeves to be untied first? Or the laces?'

Ginny suspected he knew the answer to that when he began deftly to untie her sleeves, then peeled each layer off and laid it aside as efficiently as Molly would have done. Steering her round with firm hands on her waist, he began to unlace her bodice, removing each of the pieces one by one with none of the chatter that Molly would have offered. By the sureness of the process, Ginny was sure he'd done this before, more than once.

She had tried to be matter of fact about it, telling herself that, having been forced into this commitment against her will, she would now have to make the best of it and accept those aspects about which she could do nothing while making her objections plain in every other way open to her. Including intimacy. She now began to see that this was not going to be quite as straightforward as she had planned. His fingers, warm and firm, touched her skin here and there and, whether he knew it or not, sent tiny shivers of delicious shock flowing through her before she could control them. Even though he was doing no more than Molly would have done, the male presence of him, his bulk, his scent, his breathing, the concentrated attention so close to her, all contributed to an overwhelming desire for more than the accidental touch of his hands,

more like the sudden swoop of his mouth, as
it had been in the chapel. She had expected to
arouse him. Now it was she who was being
aroused, if that was indeed what this vague and
disturbing longing was, deep within her body.

'Thank you,' she said, more sharply than she
meant. 'That will do well enough. I can manage the rest on my own.' She moved away from
him, stepping out of the pile of rose-pink velvet and slubbing off the petticoat like a second skin, heaving the discarded fabrics onto
the chair while clinging to the fine linen kirtle
she wore underneath. That, she decided, would
have to stay on.

But now Sir Jon was undressing. Though her
intention was not to watch, the room was small
and, short of closing her eyes, it was impossible not to be aware of his performance when
he took up so much of the space. He was graceful and strong in every movement and apparently oblivious to his audience of one, sitting
on the edge of the bed, too curious to climb
between the sheets. She had expected that he
might spare her modesty by keeping his shirt
on but, before she could avert her eyes, he had
whipped the shirt over his head and thrown
it aside, revealing to her the full length of his
body, the powerful shoulders, the rippling mus-

cles of his back, the small rounded buttocks, the slender waist and long, shapely, sinewy legs. Some parts of him were a slightly different shade from the rest, hidden from the sun or exposed to it, darker at each extremity. She had last seen her brothers like this when they'd swum as children, when they were all skin and bone, scrawny and white. This creature was fleshed out, beautifully proportioned and superbly fit, without a trace of self-consciousness in the presence of a woman. And though she had taunted herself repeatedly, without any hard evidence to go on, with the knowledge that he was experienced with women, what she saw now only helped to confirm that, with such a body and so much self-assurance in her company, his casual mention of never having taken an unwilling woman was not a boast but sure to be fact. For what woman, seeing him like this, would not wonder how it would feel to lie with him? Growing more and more aware of the train of her thoughts, Ginny covered her face in her hands so as not to see him turn in her direction, for that would either quickly dispel her growing desire or fuel it, she did not know which.

Sir Jon was not so insensitive that he would have knowingly shocked her, just for effect. Instead, he took advantage of the hidden eyes to turn down the sheets, then to scoop her up into his arms, deposit her carefully between them and cover her over. Without another word, he entered his own side of the bed, leaving a very decent gap between them, and blew out the candle. She neither moved nor spoke and in only a few moments, by the sound of her regular breathing, he knew that she had fallen asleep as soon as her head touched the pillow. This, he told himself, might just as easily have happened even if they'd been friends, for she was desperately tired and fraught with anxiety, and that was not how he would have wanted their first night to be. It remained to be seen what King Henry would say when he discovered they were already ahead of him and his plans. His last thought before sleep was that it was very uncharacteristic of Henry to summon a young unmarried lady to keep him company last thing at night while staying in her own father's house. What had got into the man? How difficult would he find it in the future to keep Henry's hands off this ravishing woman by his side?

His thoughts turned, as they still did in the dark hours, to that other woman, the beautiful Magdalen, and of how the king had ogled her, too, quite openly, during his third wife's pregnancy. Of how she had first lain by his side, naked and desirable, but consumed by her own needs, not his. Then, too, he had been tempted to overcome her, physically, except that force was not his way and he had preferred to wait, as he would do with Ginny, until she could see her way to replace duty with desire. Not for a king's ransom would he accept a woman's pity, or anything less than joyful surrender with at least the stirrings of love. Unrealistic it might be, but his pride had already suffered a setback, and he'd be damned if he'd allow it to happen again. This, he knew, was a second chance to obtain his heart's desire and if it was yet only a masquerade, he would need time and patience to make it real.

Ginny woke several times during the night with the level of her downy mattress slightly altered, the sheets not where they should be, the sound of breathing so close. Her hand crept towards the warmth of his body, but stopped before it reached it, in case he should wake and think she had relented. The dying fire cast a pink glow over the room and once again the enormity of what she had done, or rather *allowed* to be done, came around her like a cage from which there would be no escape. Never.

Bleakly, she saw the future where a complete stranger had been handed control of her life, where she would breed to supply him with heirs and, if she could not evade the function of being mistress to the king, keep *his* bed warm, too. Between queens. Tears of anguish rolled down her cheeks to be soaked up by the pillow, her sobs stifled as best she could by the linen sheet stuffed against her mouth.

Trained to be vigilant, even in sleep, Sir Jon felt the sobs and heard the muffled gasps for air and knew what ailed her. Waiting a little, debating what best to do, he shifted himself into her space and pulled her backwards into his arms like a father with a distressed child, smoothing her damp hair with one hand and bending her into the curve of his body, closing the space that had been between them. The sobs died away, except for the occasional disturbance of her lungs that remembered the cause of her weeping, and sleep returned without her registering that it had ever left.

The vague remembrance of some kind of physical contact lay at the back of her memory as they rose next morning before the light had begun to show, but Ginny could not be sure about it. Like some other things that might or might not have happened yesterday, it was filed away for later inspection and, since Sir Jon had duties with the king on rising, he left after the briefest exchange. Not, she supposed, how genuine lovers might have behaved. Sir Jon had seemed preoccupied.

He had hardly gone more than a few paces along the passageway, however, when he was stopped by Ginny's brother-in-law, who looked relieved to see him. 'A word, Raemon,' said Sir George, 'if you don't mind. Best you should know this before the king discovers the deceit. He still doesn't know you and Ginny are betrothed, so you're going to have to tell him yourself when you go in to him.'

Sir Jon frowned, not quite understanding. He had expected Sir George and Elion D'Arvall to take that message to His Grace last night. That had been the arrangement.

'We went,' Sir George told him, 'but the king was fast asleep. He had sent no message to Ginny.'

'*What?* You mean…?'

'Yes, it was a hoax. And no prizes for guessing who was behind it. Apparently, Culpeper and Ginny's brother Paul decided between them that it would be interesting to have Ginny arrive at the royal bedchamber and see the king snoring his head off. They didn't stop to wonder if she would see the funny side of it, but whatever they had in mind, neither of them thought that she or any of her family would react as seriously as we did. Elion and I told them what had happened as a result of their disgraceful behaviour, and they're now pissing themselves in case you or I tell His Grace, for he'll not take it lightly, will he? If he thinks Ginny has been embarrassed by this, there'll be all hell let loose.'

'There certainly will, George. Paul cannot continue to behave like this. The little toad is getting to be a liability. As for Culpeper, well, you know my thoughts on him. He's a dirty piece of work, though the king will believe no ill of him, even when it's true. We'd be wasting our breath complaining of him. Best to keep quiet about it.'

'Yes, and best not to let Ginny hear of it, either. She will not be pleased.' He knew, as Sir Jon did also, that this was an understatement. Ginny would be mortified and humiliated to think that her own brother would not hesitate to put her in such a position and was taking Henry's interest in her so lightly as to make a jest of it. 'I've told Maeve already that Ginny shouldn't know, but now I'm going along to my father-in-law's room to tell him. Don't worry,' he said, seeing the concern on Sir Jon's hand-some face. 'I know him better than you and I can explain why he and Lady Agnes were not invited. I've dealt with his anger before. He doesn't really have a leg to stand on, does he? It was he who wanted it so badly. Well, now it's happened and he'll have to pretend he's de-lighted.'

Sir Jon did not feel inclined to say anything about how things were between himself and Ginny, but he thought George might possibly guess. Now he would have to face Henry. He did not look forward to it with any degree of optimism.

As it turned out, the king had had a peace-ful and pain-free night, so when a roar of royal laughter bellowed through each of the small chambers in turn, Sir Jon's relief confirmed that it would take more than what the king was pleased to call 'his damned impatience' to upset the favour he'd enjoyed so far. Sir Jon, said the king, had done no more than he himself would have done in the same circumstances, so if he was in so much of a hurry, he must prepare him-self and his lady to take the next step of mar-riage. Yes, right there in Sir Walter's chapel, that very day. They would go hawking first,

while the day was still new, and give Lady
Agnes time to prepare for a wedding feast. The
idea of consulting Mistress Virginia or anyone
else did not occur to him. Convenience was the
king's privilege.

Unrepentant, and still secure in the king's
regard, Thomas Culpeper grinned at Sir Jon as
he left. 'No harm done, then?' he said. 'Perhaps
I've done you a favour.'

Sir Jon swung round, his eyes revealing nothing of the dislike he felt for this irresponsible
young man. 'No harm done at all, Tom. I'll do
you a similar favour one day, perhaps, and hope
for the king's understanding. Eh?' There was
no doubt of the young woman they both had in
mind, a certain Katherine Howard, one of the
queen's maids and a relative of the powerful
Duke of Norfolk. With connections like that,
one would have to be very careful how one trod
around *her* sense of humour.

The news that Ginny was to be married that
very day, at home in the private chapel where
she and Sir Jon had wrangled about their future, was not taken lightly, as those nearest her
had anticipated. Sir Jon had broken the news
to her about the king's wishes as gently as he
could, but had not stayed long enough to hear

the complete version of Ginny's views. Particularly those on the king's hurry to meddle with her happiness. Didn't a woman have the right to choose her dates?

The morning was like a bright jewel sparkling in a sapphire-blue sky, the air sharp and as clear as a bell, cloudless, stinging the nostrils, crisp underfoot and perfect for sport. Ginny loved hawking as much as the rest of her family, but this day she had to suffer the king's laughing references, mostly to his courtiers, that Sir Jon had taught her, at last, to come to his hand. Nevertheless, Henry was never coarse or vulgar, and though Ginny was obliged to stay beside him for much of the time, there was a moment when her brother Paul managed to speak to her without being overheard. 'Sorry, Ginny,' he said in a low voice. 'We meant no harm by it. Thought you'd see the jest. Better be more careful in future, hadn't we?'

It was his use of *we* that puzzled Ginny. 'Are you talking about your indelicate remarks yesterday, Paul? If so, they're best forgotten. By both of us.'

'I'm talking about the message we sent you last night, sister. We neither of us thought you'd react like that, to go and get betrothed, I mean. That was a bit extreme, wasn't it? Now Henry's insisting on going the whole hog with your marriage. I never meant that to happen, when you and Sir Jon have hardly spoken to each other till now. Still, I expect you're a mite better acquainted after last night. No?'

Ginny was well able to piece together what he was saying, having been the butt of Paul's so-called pranks all through her childhood. 'So what did you mean to happen, then? For me to march into the royal bedchamber and announce myself? Was that it? To throw myself at him, unasked? Like the whore Father and Mother wish me to become? For pity's sake, Paul, do you still not know me better than that?'

'Shh! Keep your voice down, Ginny, or they'll all know.'

'I think they *should* all know what kind of a brother I have.'

'We meant no harm, sister. We thought you'd be amused to see him snoring loud enough to wake the dead. I've never heard anything like it.'

'Paul, I know you hanker after a post as gentleman of the bedchamber, but you'll never pass the test if you cannot be more discreet about His Majesty's functions. I suppose I need not ask who let you into the royal presence so late at night. If the king learns of this, you know what'll happen, don't you? To you *and* Culpeper?'

'He won't,' said Paul, dismissively, turning his horse's head away. 'I'm sorry you take it so ill, Ginny. It would have to happen soon anyway, wouldn't it?'

'My wedding? Yes, Paul. But I'd have rather it had not been *you* to say when.' Digging her heels into the mare's flanks, Ginny swung round in time for her bridle to be caught by Sir Jon's gloved hand. She saw his eyes flash in the sunlight, cold as ice, his voice rasping with controlled anger, directed at her brother.

'If you were worth the effort, D'Arvall,' said Sir Jon, 'I'd have you down off that horse for the thrashing you deserve. If your own sister doesn't merit your good manners, then who does, I wonder? It's time you grew up, lad. Come, Ginny. We have more interesting things to do today.' He led her clear of her brother's presence and then let the bridle go. It was the first time he'd called her Ginny and the first time she had looked at him with something approaching a smile.

'Thank you,' she said. 'I was running out of words.'

'Well, now,' he said grimly. 'That would not be one of my methods.'

She could have pursued the subject on several levels, but thought that now was neither the time nor the place for such a discussion, or for a release of the fury she felt at being manipulated yet again by men, least of all by her own brother. What was more, the acceleration of their nuptials was not Sir Jon's fault in any respect, so to berate him for what her brother had done would be quite unfair. He had, after all, fully cooperated in protecting her from the king's attentions, even though they had turned out to be false, and had tried to keep from her the humiliation of discovering her brother's disrespectful behaviour. She also realised, as they moved to join the lunch party spread out in the copse, that by calling her Ginny, he had shown her brother that the ice had been broken already. That vague memory of an intimate warmth returned to tease her, but hunger overtook it before it could be examined.

Her sister Maeve and her brother Elion joined them for the outdoor meal, keeping the conversation general and well away from weddings as long as the king was nearby. Afterwards, Maeve and Ginny were able to talk more specifically about what she might be expected to do, to wear, to say or not to say, particularly to their father and mother, who had stayed at home to prepare. They had, naturally, been shocked to have been excluded from the betrothal ceremony and had been prepared to scold her soundly for this piece of thoughtlessness. But it was too late to make a fuss about the manner of it when they'd insisted on her obedience, and when Sir Jon reminded them of the advantages to be had, their objections had become less strident, though Ginny could not help but be cynical about the importance of her own happiness compared to her father's acquisition of Sandrock Priory. When she said so, Sir Jon refused to discuss it. 'Let's not go down that road again,' he said. 'It can do no good. It's too late now and we have no choice but to move on at the king's pace. We'll get the wedding part over, then I'll take you to Lea Magna tomorrow. We'll go early. I don't want to be cross-examined by this crowd about...'

'About what?' Ginny said, knowing what he referred to, but wanting him to say it.

'About anything.'

'So we shall not return to London with the king?'

'I'm off duty for a few days. Special dispensation. We'll take a day or two to look round your new home and see Etta, my daughter. Then we'll go on to Whitehall and you can rejoin the queen there. Will that suit you, mistress?'

'Thank you, yes, as much as anything suits me these days. Believe it or not, it's the first time I've been asked since I came home.'

'Then maybe it will not be the last, once you bear the title of Lady Raemon.'

His tone, while not exactly frosty, bore the slightly defensive edge it had held at their first talk in the garden when he'd told her what he expected of her, reminding her that he was probably no more pleased about the speed of events than she was. She watched to see if he favoured any particular lady in the party, either by look or speech, but found no sign she could identify. He was as courteous to them as he was to her, no more and no less. What she knew, however, now that she'd seen beneath that fine velvet doublet and linen shirt, was that he was even more worth looking at than she had supposed, and that, whenever she rode next to him that afternoon, she could not keep from her memory the graceful movements as he'd pulled off his shirt, the undulations of his skin lit by the fire's glow, and the way he had lifted her in his arms and placed her on the sheets, lingering over the task as if he would have done more before he covered her. She recalled also how his fingers had touched her skin and set it alight, making her gasp and tremble. She must be on her guard, for something similar would happen again tonight unless she disallowed it.

The wedding in the small private chapel, on this occasion more crowded than usual by the king and his courtiers, passed in a haze of unreality like a dream over which she had no control, unable to wake, or believe, or protest, or seek help to escape from. At no time did she believe that this was her day or that she was the most important element in it, only that she was doing this because she must, rather than because she wished it. Her parents smiled, the king smiled even more, and everyone told her and Sir Jon how fortunate they were not to have to call the banns, with the king being head of the church now and able to give permission for it and to have a private chapel here at home, with its own chaplain, Father Spenney. His assistant, twenty-year-old Ben, was in love with her, she knew, and contrived to emulate her mechanical demeanour throughout the ceremony and the mass that followed, earning him a frown of reproof from the priest when his hands shook so much that he almost dropped the prayer book. Ginny could give him no comfort.

Later, wearing a gold ring provided by her mother from her best jewel box, Ginny accepted the light kiss from her new husband before the smiling congregation, a kiss so fleeting that she hardly noticed it compared to that of King Henry, who took full advantage and almost suffocated her with the smell of onions and the mint leaves with which he'd tried to mask it. The food that followed, lavishly heaped upon Sir Walter's best plate, tasted of nothing, even those delicate bits placed before her by Sir Jon, who knew what the problem was. 'Just drink,' he advised her under the cover of the laughter. 'We'll make our excuses and go. He won't mind and I don't really care if he does. The rest of them could be here till the early hours.'

'I don't want them to follow us,' she said, taking the beautiful Venetian glass by its twisted stem and emptying it. 'Will the king insist on it?'

'No, he won't. He's surprisingly prudish about that kind of thing. And anyway, he knows we've already been bedded, doesn't he?' The way he said it made her blush, partly for the pretence, and partly for the evocative word itself. The preparation for the bedding ceremony could have been riotous, but it was not. Not this time. In fact, so few saw them slip away after the feast ended that they were spared all the superfluous advice usually thrown after newly-weds to embarrass them, then they were alone in Ginny's small firelit chamber like a couple of runaways without even Mistress Molly to attend them. The sound of music and laughter floated through the passageways and under the doors.

Deliberately, Sir Jon locked the door and, as if to keep in the warmth that the wine had provided, threw another log on the fire and watched as the sparks flew and crackled and flames licked at the dry bark. 'There,' he said. 'I think this day has lasted long enough, don't you?'

'We have denied Father Spenney the pleasure of giving us his blessing, Sir Jon. Was that your intention?' Ginny said, yawning.

'Do you want me to send for him? I have no objection. It was an oversight.'

She shook her head. 'It doesn't really matter, does it? He'll understand, I think.'

'But who is Ben, exactly?'

Ginny was glad of a reason to talk, to delay whatever was to come. She sat at one side of the fire on a heavy floor cushion, clasping her knees over her brocade skirt. 'Father Spenney's nephew. I don't know any details and my father won't talk about it. Ben's uncle longs to return to Sandrock, so if the king allows my father to have it, he'll have to spend some money putting it to rights again. Mother sees herself as Lady Agnes of Sandrock Priory because that tells everyone they're favoured by the king, doesn't it? All the best people have a priory or an abbey these days, don't they?'

'And you? Is that what you want, too?'

'Me, Sir Jon? No. My aspirations are less grand than that, as you know.'

'Like being the mistress of Lea Magna, perhaps? The idea appealed to you once, didn't it? Three years ago?'

'That was only because I liked the idea of being close to home, in case we didn't get on, sir. Nothing else was in my mind, I assure you, but convenience.'

He smiled at that. 'So you're still of that mind, are you?'

'No, not anymore.'

'Why not? Are you thinking we might, er… get on well together after all?'

'I'm thinking, Sir Jon, that after what's happened, my mother is the last person I would want to run home to. Or my father. I had not understood their ruthless ambition until now, or that their daughter's happiness meant so little to them. I hope they get their priory, for then they'll be farther away and Elion will be here at D'Arvall Hall. Perhaps that'll encourage him to marry someone he can be happy with. As for me, if I need advice I shall turn to Queen Anna. She'll understand.'

Ginny's bitter words seemed hardly the best topic of conversation at such a time, yet Sir Jon knew they had to be said, to clear the air between them so that things could move on. There was, he knew, much more to come, but not tonight. So he let the matter rest and, for a long interval while they watched the fire blaze, she seemed half-expectant, yet content in his company. Or was it resignation?

She looked up as he stood and went to sit behind her on the floor, close enough to begin untying her sleeves without disturbing her. 'Perhaps I ought to send for Mistress Molly,' she said over her shoulder. 'To prepare me.'

'For what?'

'Well, I don't know. For whatever it is you're supposed to do to me,' she said, rather hoping he'd not ask her what she was expecting.

He went on untying. 'And that is?'

She was silent then, but heard a soft chuckle as he pulled the sleeve down her arm. 'Listen to your husband,' he said. 'Lovemaking is not something a man *does* to a woman, it's something they do together. The only experience I have of virgins is when I was fifteen and, as I told you last night, I don't relish having an unwilling partner. So until you tell me that you are ready to accept me in bed, as a husband, our nights will be as chaste as they were last night. I take it you are still not willing? Or has anything changed?'

His honesty was one thing, but she thought he might have sounded more eager to woo her, just a little. Was he telling her he was not interested? Could she blame him? 'No, nothing has changed,' she said, holding out her other arm as he nudged it. 'But I thought it was a requirement. Part of the essentials, so to speak. What about the bloodstained sheet and all that? Won't they want to see it?'

'Nonsense,' he said, pulling her other sleeve off. 'That's an old wives' tale. There's no reason at all for there to be a bloodstained sheet, as if you're being torn to shreds. You ride, don't you? Well, that would have done the trick long ago, very likely. And anyway, no one but your Molly is going to see our bedding, is she? Does she talk?'

'She was my mother's lady until a few days

ago. Then she was given to me as my maid, and I would not be surprised if Mother expects her to find out all that happens, or doesn't happen. Still, I don't think she'd talk. She's not like that. But what did you say just now about virgins? Did you know the first Lady Raemon when you were fifteen? Is that—hic—what you meant?'

'No, that's not what I meant. She was not a virgin when we married.'

'Oh, I see. She was s'perienced. Well, many women at court are, aren't they? I s'pose it's almost s'pected these days. Some of the young women around the queen are, even if she thinks otherwise. I must be one of the few ex-pec-shuns.'

'Which makes you a richer prize, in men's eyes. You'll have to stand up, Lady Raemon. I cannot reach these last few laces. Your hair's getting tangled.'

Yawning again, she clambered to her feet, but stumbled against him, felt his hands on her bare arms, steadying her, pulling her back to his body while her feet untangled from the hem of her dress. The wine, her father's best, was working its magic and was preventing her eyes from focusing as quickly as usual, making her feel heavy and clumsy, her face flushed. Sir Jon's warm hands moved over the soft skin of her arms, then went to finish undoing her laces and, before she could stop him, to remove the bodice that had held her rigid all day. She watched, bewildered, as the boned contraption flew past her to hit the chair and then slither to the floor as if it had a life of its own, and by the time she had turned to move away, the flimsy linen kirtle had dropped over her shoulders as the drawstring slid open, revealing far more to Sir Jon's interested gaze than yesterday, when she'd been angrily sober. Pausing in its flight downwards, it was caught first on the swell of her breasts, then on her hips, sliding to the floor like a white pool around her feet. Instead of catching it up again in horror, Ginny looked down the length of her figure as if to reacquaint herself with what had been hidden for at least two days, giving her new husband the chance to do the same. She was not so tipsy that she could not recognise the raging desire in his eyes, already dark but now almost black, soft, and perceptive of every detail, roaming over her like a man starved of comfort, and so unlike that barefaced assessment she had suffered at Sandrock years ago. She allowed him to look, then picked up her kirtle, knowing that, in doing so, she was testing him to his limit as her lovely body bent, swayed and read-

justed to gravity. Something inside her gloated
with satisfaction, reaping some kind of reward
for what she'd suffered at men's hands: the use
Henry hoped to make of her, the compliance of
her husband, the bargaining of her father, the
unkind prank of her younger brother. She held
the trump card, even if they did not know it,
for she could withhold her body for as long as
it pleased her.

The facts did not quite accord with this, however. When he lifted her and carried her to the
bed, as he had last night, it would have been all
too easy for her to relent and to meld herself
into his maleness with abandon, to give in willingly to whatever he asked of her, trusting in
his carefulness. And there were moments when
she wondered whether she was holding on to
her virginity to no purpose, or whether she was
punishing him as she thought. Wine was not a
good friend at such times. And though she slept
at first, being tired after a long day, the night
was punctured by sleepless hours when she
longed for his touch again, or a stolen kiss she
could protest about, or even his arm on her side
of the bed, the hand of which she might hold
without him knowing. How long, she wondered,
would she be able to hold out against him? And
what would she lose or gain by doing so?

* * *

Aching for her touch, Jon lay as silently and patiently as he had with Magdalen during those nightmarish years when she had never even pretended to want him. Then desire had eventually dwindled to periods of undiluted male lust that were more difficult to control, lying there in torment, knowing in his heart that duty had been allowed to triumph over conscience, just as Ginny had said it could. He had been so sure of himself then, all those wasted years ago.

Chapter Four

The new day brought with it all Ginny's previous aversions to the schemes that threatened to blight her life and the independence that had never, sadly, been tested. Whatever slight wavering of her resolve she had experienced last night under the influence of too much wine, she must now make the best of whatever lay ahead and show that she had control enough to make her objections clear. It would not be easy when plans were being made without her consent, but she would find a way.

She was able, before she and Sir Jon set off for Lea Magna, to thank her parents so frostily for their hospitality that they could hardly have missed her meaning, that it would be some time before she would find the charity to forgive them, or to visit. King Henry was too intent on his own business to note the strained family at-

mosphere, parting with plenty of advice on how
to be an obedient and loving wife, by which
Ginny supposed he meant her to be available
whenever he summoned her. His instructions
for them both to hurry back to court seemed to
confirm this, though Maeve told her she was
reading too much into it. Ginny hugged her and
Sir George, and Elion, too, who assured her that
they would be there for her wherever the king
was, which put a smile on her face as they and
their small party moved off through the bright
morning as Sir Jon and Lady Virginia Raemon
of Lea Magna in Hampshire.

They were there in less than an hour, riding along rutted tracks hardened with frost and
white spikes of plants waiting for spring rain,
past low timber-framed cottages interspersed
with a few taller, sturdier ones, the ale house,
blacksmith and priest's house by the stone
church, the village cross, with the great walls
of the house in the distance that took the name
of the village, Lea Magna. Through the tiled
gatehouse, an array of buildings sprawled inside
a very large courtyard where household staff
went about their business of carrying, cleaning,
supplying and ordering, then running to welcome Sir Jon's party, to hold the bridles and to

take a first look at the new mistress with grins
of approval. Even before she entered the house,
Ginny knew that she would like to live here as
its mistress. She had made a mental list of concerns, but this was on it no longer.

Their first stay here was to be too short for
Ginny to do more than absorb the flavour of the
place, to find out how it worked and to meet its
inmates before removing to Whitehall where
the queen awaited her services. There was no
question of delay, for her attempts to make the
queen more attractive to her husband in so
many ways would also help to decide Ginny's
own involvement with the king. One could not
predict Henry's mind these days; even the greatest men in his employ dared not do that, except
by being certain of his unpredictability, so what
chance did a new queen have? she wondered.

But one little person of whom Ginny was
most eager to make the acquaintance was Sir
Jon's small daughter, who lived here with only
a staff of nurses to deputise as parents. Not
that the child would know any different, Ginny
supposed, but how sad that her father had had
so little time for her in those most formative
years. At the noble household in the north of
England where Ginny had lived and been 'polished', along with other daughters of wealthy

and ambitious parents, there had been several
very young members of the family whom she
had been expected to supervise occasionally
with games and exercise, with learning to eat
correctly and grown-up manners, reading and
writing, too. It was all good practice for her
when she would have a family of her own, they
said. Fortunately, she had enjoyed this part of
things, so the thought of being stepmother to
the infant held no fears for her, only concerns
that any bond they were able to forge would be
continually broken by her absences. One remedy would be to bear a child of her own, but
the thought was fleeting and not particularly
attractive after what she'd just learned about
the uncertainties of who might father it. Sir Jon
had tried to assure her of his protection. She believed he meant it, but how far did that stretch?
Paul's unkind prank had frightened her. It was
all so very possible.

'Will you take me to see her now?' she asked
Sir Jon. 'I long to see where she lives. I've heard
no child noises. She must be a very quiet child.'

'I'll take you, if you wish,' he said, holding
open a very wide carved door under which a
draught blew icily. 'She lives in the far wing, so
I never hear her. I expect she'll have grown by
now.' He sounded far from enthusiastic.

Ginny noted the unemotional tone of voice, the distance between them, the lack of sight or sound. It was inevitable and not something she could change easily without changing him, too. The little girl registered no recognition or cries of welcome for her papa. As they entered, she was energetically propelling herself across the wooden floor inside a walking frame, like a small cot strapped to her waist, with wheels at each corner, requiring all her concentration to avoid the furniture. Her staggering walk showed that her legs were strong and that there was little wrong with her determination, either. 'May I pick her up?' Ginny said to one of the two nurses, a youngish woman wearing a white apron over a dark gown. The lack of colour in the room was noticeable, bare of comfort, containing only a few stools, tables and a large wooden cot for the child, a chest and a dresser, with a roaring fire in the chimney piece, the dark-curtained windows wet with condensation.

The child, Etta, was sturdy and as pretty as any two-year-old Ginny had ever seen, with a shock of red-gold hair the colour of new copper, tightly curled under a padded band tied round the crown of her head, known as a 'pudding' to prevent injury when she fell. Ginny went to pick her up, but removing her from the walking frame did not meet with Etta's approval, her howls of protest being enough to convince Ginny that practising this skill was far more important than relationships. Clearly, the little lass had a mind of her own, and a temper to go with it. 'Psh! Psh,' she yelled, telling Ginny what was on her mind. Mobilisation.

Placing herself in front of Etta, squatting on her heels, Ginny held out her arms. 'Come on, then,' she cooed. 'Come on, push! Push it to me!'

The child's face lit up, clearly delighted that someone understood the seriousness of the game. 'Psh!' she yelped, steering herself towards Ginny with an energy so unexpected that the crash, when it came, resulted in a tumble of bodies that ejected Etta into Ginny's arms, squealing and laughing with excitement.

The nurses rushed to help, but Ginny waved them away while Etta struggled to her feet and wriggled back into the frame. 'Gen! Gen!' she cried, eager for a repeat. Much to the disapproval of the audience, Ginny allowed a repeat of the crash that gave her the chance to hold her new stepdaughter without the awkwardness of introductions, to carry her to the window and open it wide, to smell the sharp air and to see the courtyard below where men went about their work. The child was entranced and responsive to the quiet invitations to look and to tell Ginny what she saw. Clearly, Ginny thought, she was an intelligent little thing, but lacking as much in stimulus as in cuddles. For although she was well kept, the nurses revealed that she had not been out of that room for weeks because of the frost and snow, and no one told her stories, sung to her, or played the rough games she obviously enjoyed. Taking her role as stepmother seriously from the start, Ginny asked them questions about how Etta's days were organised, but was not entirely happy at her findings.

Undoing the clinging arms of the adorable little child from her neck, Ginny found herself almost in tears at having to leave her in that dull room. 'It's more like a prison in there,' she whispered to Sir Jon on the way down the passageway. 'You see how she needs companionship and fresh air. Can she not come out with us?'

'No,' he said. 'She's too young for adult company yet.'

'But you saw how she responded to me when I talked to her. She *longs* for adult company. She'll never learn to talk properly if she doesn't hear it.'

'The two women are doing their best,' he said.

'I'm sure they are, Sir Jon, but I could do better.'

'Really? It's difficult to see how, unless something changes,' he said.

Ginny blushed at the criticism, for she had not so far been a dutiful wife. Withholding herself had seemed to be her only weapon against him and his part in her controversial relationship with the king, yet something deep within her body had stirred like a yearning, an ache for something she was denying herself just to gain some kind of control. Or was it revenge? She had felt it up there when she'd held the child in her arms, felt the soft weight, the clinging arms, the warm, moist little mouth and lisping words, those amazing brown eyes like hazelnuts, and the scent of baby skin. Sir Jon was right; she would not do better than that, nor would she even equal it unless she had a change of mind about a husband's rights. She was not able to answer him or to broach the subject again as he showed her round the many rooms, the outside buildings, introducing her to the senior staff who ran the place in his absence.

But there was a distraction in his manner that grew as the day progressed, which Ginny believed might have much to do with seeing his daughter again and the home where he and his late wife had once been happy, where now he was bringing a new wife in the most unusual circumstances. A wife who did not want him any more than he wanted her, or so she had tried to convince him. She was not sure she'd convinced herself after two nights of trying to sleep alongside his naked body, which, until only recently, she had done her best not to look at. She knew it would have taken only the touch of her hand to reverse all her resolutions, for she also knew that, however loving his memories were of his late wife, he could have taken her at any time. Men, she had heard, were like that. So she was not too surprised when he left her to her own devices later that day. He had his house steward to consult, his bailiff and his accountant, while she and Molly needed to see her housekeeper about the stores and where to put her few belongings, the dairy and laundry, the stillroom and larder, and, of course, the gardens. Without him, she would also return to see Etta.

Standing beside the cot in the semi-darkness, she felt again all those strange yearnings and the beginnings of a bond that would inevitably weaken with distance. Time and time again.

Would they ever be more than strangers to each other? she wondered. Would Sir Jon ever know his daughter as well as a father ought? The older nurse came to stand by her, watching fondly.

'We shall take her out tomorrow, mistress,' Ginny said. 'After breakfast, wrap her up well and we'll show her what the frost and snow and sun really feel like.'

'My lady, I doubt very much whether Sir Jon will allow it,' the nurse said. 'He's very protective.'

'Sir Jon will agree,' Ginny said firmly. 'I'll change his mind somehow.'

For Jon, the old house was filled with memories both pleasant and desperately sad, for it was the family home as well as the place to which he'd brought his first wife, hoping to make the marriage work. As he walked along the dark passageways, he heard the echoes of his parents' voices, the merry singing of his mother before his father's departure for France. The singing had stopped when they'd heard of his capture and the appallingly high ransom demanded for his release; his mother's despair, her gradual decline, her death, the desperate efforts to keep the estate going while fulfilling his duties to two demanding masters, the king and his private secretary, Sir Thomas Cromwell. Life had presented him with the mother of all dilemmas, although in reality there had been only one solution.

His chamber held no comfort for him now. Conflict of duties had seen to that. Succumbing to a moment of bleak sadness, he sat on the oaken chest while his mind played out a scene where Ginny would come to him, submissive and sweet, to offer him the unconditional love he craved. The clack of the latch brought him back to reality.

At the sound of Ginny's entry, the head lifted and the hands slid down the handsome face, but stopped over his mouth, as if to stop himself speaking. Cupping his chin, he held a look she could only identify as despair, raw and harrowing, and far from the arrogant, assured, insouciant expression he was used to wearing at court. 'Sir Jon,' she whispered, shocked by the change in him. 'What is it?' Quietly, so as not to disturb the silence, she closed the door and placed her lantern on a nearby table, but hesitated to approach what must surely be a profound grief. What else, she wondered, could cause such pain in his eyes?

As it had only an hour ago in the child's room, a small part of her melted deep inside, calling for another soul to comfort her body's craving in some small way, even if she could not identify the reason. At the same time, she felt that he needed her, too, though nothing had been said to make her sure of it. What was she to do? Should she ask him? Ought she to offer herself, to comfort them both for what they'd lost? Even though she could not approve of what he was doing? It would not be the sacrifice she had at first pretended, for now she knew how her body had responded to his touch and how she had thought of little else since then. Would she hate herself for it? Would she not be what he required after all? Would she care if he took her as a substitute for his late wife rather than for what her own body could offer him?

There was no need for her to make a decision, for she had only to move into the arms he stretched out towards her and place herself between his knees as silently as a ghost, with no explanations. His embrace closed around her hips while his head, smooth and velvety, pressed hard against her bodice. His eyes were closed and now it was in her power to speak the words and to know that he would act upon them, to bridge the gulf, to make a beginning on her promise to him as a wife, which to her shame she had not yet kept. 'Husband,' she whispered to the top of his head, 'let me comfort you.' She smoothed one hand over the short cap of his hair and down one cheek like a mother with a small child at her apron. Perhaps, she thought, there were times when a man might need a mother as much as a wife. Was this going to be one of those times?

From his throat a hoarse sound emerged, half pain, half excitement, the kind of triumphant cry a man made when he'd won a bout with his sword master. But however Ginny had imagined her first time with a man would be, she thought—she was sure—that this would not be it. In the semi-darkness, he would imagine her to be his beloved late wife, the one for whom he longed, here in the home they had loved. She could not expect him to treat her like the virgin she was. That would be too much to expect. Whatever happened, she would have to accept it and give him back without complaint what she owed in terms of lost nights, his patience with her caprice, his attempts to understand her, his protection, and his cooperation in shielding her from what they'd thought was the king's demand. So when his kiss was more searching by far than the one in the chapel, Ginny was convinced that her expectation of a certain pretence was accurate. He would surely not have kissed a virgin as if she were an experienced woman. Would he?

These concerns vanished, however, when she realised he was treating her as an equal, not like the young unmannerly girl of D'Arvall Hall, but as a married woman capable of pleasuring him in the height of his passion. Their undressing, already practised, was conducted with trembling fingers in the semi-dark and chill of the room, helping each other over every lace and hook punctuated by soft caresses in places where usually only hooks and laces went. This time, his hands lingered over her skin, purposely setting her alight in secret places that had always been covered and chaste, and hardly looked at. Her beautiful firm breasts were fondled, lifted and weighed in his palms, turning her knees to water. It was the sweetest and most startling undressing Ginny could have imagined, with mouths and lips being used for other things than talk, for talking might spoil his illusion. Or was it hers? Or were they sharing it?

Then, with her skirts falling away from her feet, she was scooped up and carried over to the bed, already melting in the strength of his arms and the assertive power of every movement. Pretending not to, she had seen how he moved at court, masking her desire from others as well as herself. Here in the dimness of the candlelit room, there was no more need of the mask, for she had already revealed, even in that short time, that her willingness had only been waiting to be kindled. Lifting her arms to enclose him, she drew him to her like a blanket. This would be no time for reticence. Whatever she had intended in her earlier moments of resentment no longer had any merit, for now she could not have held back for even a moment when he was teasing her body along its length with hands and lips. There was no part of her to be spared from his quest, hands exploring every surface, every luscious curve, every detail usually hidden from view and imagined, played upon with fingertips and lips, tormented into life, making every part of her long for more. Hazily, through a surge of ecstasy, she wondered if he had made love to his first wife like this, or whether after all this was for her alone, as a virgin. Would she have known the difference?

Although she had no means of knowing exactly what to expect as a preliminary to coupling, or indeed that there was much to expect at all, she discovered that lovemaking took longer than she'd supposed when he sought out every small and delicate area of her skin for his attentions. As if he knew how all her sensitivities were combined in those places, he touched, teased and drew from her lips the moans of delight and gasps of pleasure that neither of them had expected to hear with such abandon or so soon. Now she could begin to understand the stricken expression on his face as she'd entered the room, for, if this was how it had been with the beautiful first wife, he must indeed have missed her more than he had divulged to anyone. Still, there were no words between them and none needed when she used all her innate knowledge as a woman to pleasure him, as if she had always known what was required of a wife by her husband. It appeared to succeed when she explored and stroked his taut muscular body and smoothed the rippling back with its valleys and silky contours, like hillsides under her hands and when she whispered, 'Show me what to do,' she fully expected him to take her to the next level of fulfilment, for she could feel the hardness of him against her body.

'No,' he whispered, 'not this time, my amazing wife.' Smoothing her hair away from her face, he kissed her forehead and, drawing her into his arms, lay on his back with a deep sigh.

Puzzled, Ginny tried to understand what was happening. 'Why?' she said, passing a hand tenderly over his chest. 'Why not this time?'

'I cannot accept your offer,' he replied. 'I told you when we made our vows that I would not take advantage of you until I was sure you came to me for all the right reasons. You saw my pain and, even without understanding the reasons for it, you gave me the comfort I craved. And for that I must be satisfied. And I am. You are everything a man could desire.'

'But I do understand your reasons, Jon. You lost a beautiful wife. I know I cannot replace her, but at least I can give you some release. And anyway, you have shown me what I've been missing and I'd like to know the rest.'

'Your curiosity delights me, Ginny. But...'

'No...no, I don't *mean* curiosity. Oh, dear, I don't know the word for it.'

'Then until we can be more sure of each other, I think it's best to take things one step at a time. Be satisfied that you have done your wifely duty in comforting your husband when he needs it. I shall not demand more than you feel able to give.'

Wifely duty? Is that what he believes I've been doing while his hands tormented me? 'I did not see it as a duty, Jon,' she whispered, chastened by this unexpected turn of events. It served her right, of course, and there was no use now in regretting it, for she had made it clear from the start that she intended to withhold herself, and now she must accept the same from him, for whatever reason he gave. She had not thought he would be able to stop once they had reached that point, but he was disciplined and well in control of the hardness she had felt pressing against her and, after all her strident protests of the past few days, she now realised that it was he who would decide, not her. The unsettling ache within her body kept her awake for hours while the arms that held her gradually slackened and slipped away, and the slow rise and fall of his great chest indicated that sleep had come to him easily.

After days of brilliant sun and frost, the next day was noticeably warm enough to have begun melting the white crystals that covered every surface, dripping them with diamonds. Ginny rose late and missed Sir Jon's silent exit from their room and his absence from their breakfast, such as it was, though Molly made no comment on her mistress's thoughtful expression. Their visit to Etta's nursery was conspiratorial, however, for Ginny was aware that the child's father had not so far approved of any venture into the winter landscape. It was, she was sure, simply a sign of his ignorance where infants were concerned, and although she'd had more experience of them than he, she had no wish to make her own views too much at odds with his. Wherever he was, he was not likely to see them out there until it was too late. Then he would relent, of course.

Dressed in warm clothes and swathed in blankets, the bright-eyed child was accompanied by her nurse, by Mistress Molly and by Ginny, who took it in turns to hold her tiny hands along the pathways and through the gardens, stopping frequently to look at lace-like trees and hedges, at the pattern of thawing puddles, inquisitive blackbirds and perky robins. Staggering along the gravel pathways with hands in theirs, everything she saw seemed to entrance her, for it was clear this was the adventure of her short life so far. The distant figure of her father talking to his horse master was not as visible to her as a new snowdrop pushing through the soil, so when he walked towards them, the only greeting was from Ginny herself.

Sir Jon looked anything but pleased. Frowning his displeasure at the nurse, he said, 'I thought I'd made my wishes clear about this kind of thing, mistress? Did you not convey them to Lady Raemon? The child could take cold out here.'

The nurse, happy to be outside, too, had a quick reply that she supposed would make him smile indulgently, as new husbands often did. 'Oh, yes, Sir Jon. Last evening. But Lady Raemon assured me she could find a way to make you change your mind. It's such a beautiful...'

'Did she, indeed?' he replied in a dangerously low voice. 'Well, then, I'd better try to look as if I've had my mind changed, hadn't I? Clever of you, my lady. Why didn't that occur to me, I wonder?' His meaning was clear to Ginny, but not to the others, and before she could find anything to remedy his misconception about her apparent change of heart, he had turned on his heel and walked away back to his horse master, his boots crunching heavily on the gravel. A hard lump rose in Ginny's throat, preventing her from calling after him, to come back, to allow her to explain and not to think what he was so obviously thinking. It had not been like that at all. She had wanted to comfort him, not to wrangle for favours.

What lay between them was so delicate and difficult to explain that neither of them dared take the metaphorical bull by the horns and wrestle it to the ground for fear of wreaking more damage. With so many potential misunderstandings and impediments to clear away and no means of doing this as long as Ginny's fears remained, what chance was there of ever finding harmony and trust and the love they both desperately longed for? That one night of passion had been for both of them a step in the right direction, but that alone was not enough to clear the way for a better understanding. Not while she was still so uncertain and angry about her future and about her husband's complicity in it. It was true that there had been more to her capitulation last night than compassion for his grief, if that was what it was. Her own body's rampant desires had had a lot to do with it, too, and her curiosity and her need for a child of her own. But if she had been uncertain whether he would understand her reasons, she had not expected him to get them so terribly wrong, either. Now they were back where they'd begun, suspecting every word and look, and wondering how, if ever, they would break the deadlock of antagonism. Their night spent in each other's arms seemed now like a stupid mistake they had wandered into like a couple of dreamy adolescents, to be put behind them, not referred to, not thought about. Except that they *did* think. How could they not?

That night, their last at Lea Magna, Sir Jon did not come to her bed, though they had eaten a subdued supper together in the hall, the local musicians filling the void where conversation might have been. Ginny slept with Molly to keep them both warm, and it was the maid who comforted her without asking any questions. Perhaps, she thought, even magic needed nurturing sometimes.

They and their party were away at dawn next day, Ginny on a new mare introduced to her by Sir Jon's horse master instead of him, an event she interpreted as a continuation of his extreme displeasure. Which she thought was a great pity, for the horse was a very beautiful creature with a creamy mane and a coat the colour of combed flax, a tall, elegant mount with a new saddle of golden tan over a rich saddlecloth of quilted velvet. When Ginny tried to thank her husband, his reply was sour. 'Think nothing of it,' he said. 'I shall expect something in return, of course. That's what we seem to be doing these days, isn't it? Rewarding each other.'

'How can you think that?' she said.

'Because, my lady, I don't yet know you well enough to think otherwise.'

'And at this rate, you never will, sir,' she said, allowing him to lift her into the saddle.

'Nor will you know your child unless you spend more time with her.'

'An occupational hazard. She doesn't appear to be harmed by it.'

Ginny's heart was too full to make a sensible reply, having only half an hour before said a tearful farewell to the little mite who had clung to her like a limpet and wanted to know, in her broken lisping words, when Ginny would came back. Would it be that day? she wanted to know, having no conception of longer periods.

'Soon,' Ginny had lied. 'Soon, little one.' Already the bond was there between them, though she knew Sir Jon had not said goodbye to his daughter. The distress stayed with her for the rest of the journey, which Sir Jon took for the same resentment because he had no way of knowing about the pangs of emptiness vibrating within Ginny's heart. The days—weeks—ahead would be stark indeed while they were at Whitehall, he with the king and his friends and she with the queen, both of them pretending that all was well.

This time, leaving his little daughter had touched Jon more than usual and more than he cared to admit. The instant bond between her and her new stepmother had surprised him and tweaked at his conscience after his long and frequent absences; the child's loneliness was something he'd thought little about, so occupied had he been with his own bitterness. Now, for the first time, he saw how she was the innocent by-product of his own past and that she could no longer be ignored as a person. That was regrettable, but how much more so was it to visit his own problems upon Etta, whose life was only just forming. How might it have been, he wondered, if Etta had been Ginny's, and how easy would he find it to allow that bond to grow naturally and flourish? He thought of that night when she had gone to him, and of the family she was prepared to make with him. Had he gotten it wrong? Were his own conflicts clouding his perception of her motives?

Keeping up a relentless pace throughout the day, they managed to arrive at the palace of Whitehall just as darkness fell on that chill February afternoon, the torches already lit round every corner of the vast complex of buildings, more like a village than the other royal palaces. It often took weeks for newcomers to find their way round the warren of corridors and courtyards, the galleries, anterooms, offices and staterooms, those for the queen, those for the king, those for receiving guests and eating.

Mistress Molly had not been there before either, but had the good sense to look as if she had and to attend to her mistress's needs promptly. Discreetly, she moved aside as Sir Jon came to lift Ginny down from her saddle.

'I may not have time to see you again today,' he told her. 'I shall be on duty with Henry until late, then I'll probably have to sleep in his chamber. Will you be all right? The queen will be glad to see you again?'

'Yes.' She nodded. 'I suppose so.' She had not expected anything more.

He began to turn away, but evidently thought better of it, and, instead of leaving her to accompany Molly across the courtyard, he pulled her roughly into his arms for a kiss as fierce as some they'd shared in their bed. Off balance and taken completely by surprise, she trembled with fatigue in his arms, wondering what it meant to him, but also taking what she could from the moment, knowing that it would not be repeated until he felt the need, perhaps to remind himself again of his first wife. His skin tasted of the cold ride along the Thames, of a hidden warmth beneath and of thwarted desire, despite himself. And when he released her, he had to hold her arms until she could find her balance again. 'Just to remind you, lady,' he said gruffly.

'Of course,' she said, fighting the pain in her throat. 'Or I might easily have forgot.' His gaze stayed upon her upturned face long enough to show her that her remark had hit home. But she was unable to hide the wealth of unspoken desires that flooded her eyes, and he found it equally difficult to believe what he saw, having gazed at similar messages in other women's eyes, particularly one.

A sudden wave of regret softened his scarred heart as he drunk deeply of her beauty. 'Forgive me,' he said. 'I didn't mean it like that. What's done is done. Go in now, out of the cold. Give my regards to Queen Anna. I dare say Henry will visit tomorrow and I shall come with him whenever I can.'

Wordlessly, she nodded and left him without a backward glance, thinking how much pleasanter it would have been if he'd escorted her to her new quarters to see that she had all she needed. Of course, he had his duties to perform, too, but although she was now Lady Raemon, she had no intention of chasing after him or even making herself more available than she had before. The queen would keep her equally busy, she was sure, and there was nothing like work for taking one's mind off unpleasant matters.

'I thought you'd left the queen at Hampton

Court,' Molly said as they tripped up the stone staircase to the hall. She saw men's heads turn to look at her mistress in open admiration, even some of the older ones.

'Yes, I did. But she must be where the king is most of the time, and he does most of his business here nowadays. Now he'll have diplomats to see and councils to attend. Where he goes, she will go, too, except for the odd occasion.'

'He still goes to her bed, then? Even though he doesn't care for her?'

'Shh! Not so loud, Molly. Of course. It's expected.'

'Poor woman,' Molly muttered. 'Is she as plain as they say?'

'You'll see,' said Ginny, following the page along yet another corridor. 'I don't think she's at all plain. I think you'll like her as much as I do. This way.'

Molly hoped she would not be asked to find her way out of here alone, as they passed through room after room hung with brightly coloured tapestries and painted woodwork, past solid furniture and carved doors, under plasterwork ceilings flickering in the torchlight, and beneath gilded arches where renovations were still only partly complete. Like worker bees, liveried pages and gold-badged guards marched past them on errands, groups of whispering ladies and dark-gowned men with rolls of parchment under their arms, their servants carrying boxes of writing equipment. Finally, Ginny slowed down as they came to a door outside of which a guard stood holding a long halberd at an angle. 'Mistress D'Arvall!' he said in surprise.

'Lady Raemon now, if you please,' said Molly importantly.

Ginny smiled at him. 'Is Her Grace within?' she said. 'May we…?'

'Of course, m'lady,' he said, and opened the door into a brightly lit room where the soft strains of music and chatter washed over them like a welcome cloak after the dark and cold of the evening. The music stopped and cries of delight drew Ginny forwards into smiling embraces, and it was all she could do to hold back the prickling tears behind her eyes as she was engulfed in the genuine affection of friends.

One voice in particular called out to her. 'Mistress D'Arvall! Is back with us, yes? Come!' The accent was unmistakably Germanic and Molly had no need to ask if this was the Queen Anna she'd heard so much about, for there was something in her manner quite different from anything she'd heard or seen of the

king's previous three wives. Molly could tell at
once why Ginny enjoyed this queen's company,
even if she was less than enthusiastic about life
at court. She saw a tall, elegant woman of some
twenty-four years, not exactly petite, but well
shaped, narrow waisted and graceful. Her becoming French hood framed a sweet face that
tapered to a neatly pointed chin, and smooth
cheeks that bunched into a charming smile for
Molly and her mistress. The fair brows, recently
reshaped into a fine line, arched over rather
drooping lids that half-concealed intelligent
brown eyes, which might otherwise have been
unremarkable except for the steady regard and
honesty of her gaze.

The queen had known nothing about Ginny's
recent marriage, for Henry had not discussed
these matters with her before he left for Hampshire, and she was as astonished as the queen's
ladies and giggling young maids to hear that it
had happened with such speed. They begged
her to tell them the reason for this remarkable
development in the light of Ginny's well-known
antipathy towards one of the king's most eligible gentlemen. Why the hurry? Had Sir Jon
developed a secret passion for her? Was it her
father's doing? Why had the king himself inter-

fered? Had it been, after all, what Ginny herself wanted?

Both Ginny and Molly were hungry. While they waited for dishes to arrive, there was time to offer the explanation she'd formulated on the way here. To Ginny's relief, the queen accepted this, for she, too, had been a victim of the king's impatience, though it had not turned out quite so happily for her, being unused to his ways. Whether she suspected the king's interest in Ginny as his mistress there was no way of telling, though Ginny thought it unlikely when Anna was as innocent in such matters as she herself had been, until this. If her Henry found pleasure in the company of the young ladies around her, she was either far too intelligent and diplomatic to complain, or she cared little one way or the other. Anna could not have been unaware of the fate of one of her predecessors who had complained too stridently and too long about Henry's amours.

The possibility of hurting Anna by diverting her new husband's affections was one of the worst parts of Ginny's involvement in a marriage she had never wanted. Anna, too, had not been given any choice in the matter of her marriage to Henry, but now she saw it as her duty to do everything possible to please him. She would not have expected that the one to help her in this would also be the one to wreck her chances.

The welcome food had arrived, yet to Ginny it tasted of nothing more than old parchment. She made her excuses to retire to her rooms with Molly before returning to dress Anna for the king's evening visit. Then the game of evasion and capture would begin again.

Chapter Five

Whitehall was now the centre of the king's government offices, as close to the bustle of the city as it was possible to be, yet surrounded by courtyards, gardens, and orchards and within walking distance of the great abbey of Westminster, the towers of which were visible from Ginny's windows. Dressing quickly with Molly's help, Ginny left her to unpack and went along to the queen's sumptuous apartments to help her in her choice of gown and accessories, determined more than ever to present Anna at her most attractive. Laying a gown of silk grosgrain over the oak chest, she smoothed it lovingly. 'This one, Your Grace?' she said. 'The aquamarine is perfect for your colouring. The gold damask oversleeves and forepart are the colour of your hair.'

Mistress Katherine Howard, one of the

queen's youngest maids of honour, had scarcely noticed that her foreign royal mistress understood more of the language than she could speak, so felt it necessary to say what many of them were thinking. 'You think the king will visit, now you're here?' she said pertly to Ginny. 'He hasn't been near Her Grace since his return from Hampshire. Except at bedtime, of course. When he has to.'

Mistress Anne Basset, a well connected and pretty seventeen-year-old, did not care for the Howard girl's impudence. 'He's been busy with state affairs, Kat. You know he has, or he'd have been here before. Mistress…oh, no, I mean *Lady Raemon* is correct. The golden forepart is exactly Her Grace's colouring. Would you put the aquamarine headdress with it, too, my lady?'

'And the ruby biliment?' said the queen, removing the headpiece from Kat Howard's pudgy hands, leaving the girl open-mouthed at her perfect pronunciation.

'I think Mistress Basset is right not to introduce another colour, Your Grace,' Ginny said. 'The aquamarines and pearls are perhaps the soft pale effect we should strive for.'

''Tis well,' said the queen. 'Whatever you think.' Turning her head this way and that be-

fore the mirror, she saw with pleasure how
the sun caught the gold highlights after recent
washings with infusions of parsley and rose-
mary, nettle and watercress. Ginny had dressed
it for her in the most becoming styles, ready for
when Henry should wish to reveal it, and she
had eventually agreed, laughing with embar-
rassment, that it was one of her loveliest features. So far, Henry had not commented on it,
but had left it to others to do so. Anna caught
sight of Mistress Howard's disappointed face
and knew the reason. Handing back the ruby
biliment, she smiled at the girl. 'Lend?' she
said. 'For tonight?'

'Borrow, Your Grace,' Ginny corrected her,
glancing at the girl's confusion.

'Ah, *borrow*. Yes. To match *your* hair, no?'

Katherine Howard's hair was auburn and
she did not need anyone to tell her what her
best features were. 'Thank you, Your Grace.
Oh, thank you!' she said, pulling off her tiny
hood and fixing the jewelled biliment around
the curve. Her eyes sparkled with excitement
as she replaced the hood well back to show off
her smooth, glossy hair. It was at times like this,
Ginny thought, that one wondered whether the
good-natured queen understood just how intense was the rivalry for Henry's affections,

whether she knew and did not care as much as she ought, or whether she had some scheme of her own in mind that none of them had given her credit for.

In the mirror, Ginny's eyes met Anna's on their return from watching the silly young thing whirl away with a shriek of excitement. 'She means no harm,' Anna said quietly. 'She knows how to get what she wants.' Ginny waited, knowing there was more to come. 'I would like to have been there,' Anna continued, 'at your wedding. I did not know Henry was going until it was too late. Nor has he been to tell me about it. Can it really be that his matters of state are so great that he cannot spare me a moment of his time? Was he like that with...with the others?'

'Sometimes, Your Grace. Sometimes the king's matters are pressing and then he has time for little else. But I didn't know of the wedding either until it was...'

'Was what? Too late? And do you like Sir Jon any better now, Ginny?'

I don't like having to make up excuses for the king. I don't like what I'm caught up in. 'We have not had time to get used to each other yet' was what she said.

'But you sleep together? There will be babies? I, too, shall have babies soon, God willing.' She pressed a hand over the skirt Ginny was tying around her waist.

'Heirs, Your Grace? Is that so? The king is... considerate?' Ginny had tried to avoid hearing gossip, but she knew there were those of the queen's ladies who were quietly concerned that all was not as it should be in the royal bedchamber. Perhaps they, too, had looked in vain for bloodstains, but she had not questioned them. It was not her business, yet the queen appeared to be saying something different.

'Yes, indeed. We sleep in the same bed each night and he is always courteous. He bids me goodnight, sweetheart and good morning, darling. So gentlemanly. I cannot complain of that.'

'And is that all, Your Grace? Simply goodnight and good morning? Just that?' Had they moved on no further, after more than a month? Could the rumours be true, then, after all?

Anna turned to study her friend with steadfast eyes and the hint of a query. 'Well, yes? And a kiss, just there,' she said, placing the tip of her finger on the corner of her mouth. 'His Grace smells of onions,' she whispered impishly. 'But what do you mean by is that all? Is there something more he should do?'

So it *was* true. The royal marriage had not been consummated, and if Ginny didn't explain it to her, how it felt to lie naked with a man, then one of the other women would, and not so carefully, either. Years ago, she had discovered from her friends in the north what husbands and wives did to make a child, but ought she to take it upon herself to describe an act that sounded so ridiculous and unlikely it would scarcely be believed by a woman of twenty-four? Anna was sensible to a degree, but would she submit to such intimacies with a man like Henry? Some would, for power. Anna might do it for the sake of duty. 'Your Grace,' she whispered, glancing at the young maids huddled over the queen's clothes chest, 'there *is* more. A man cannot get a woman with child with only kisses, or even by just sharing her bed.'

The sheltered life Anna had lived in Cleves had done her no favours. She looked at Ginny with dismay. 'More? Oh. I see. Then perhaps someone—you—should tell me or I shall not get the heir the king wants, shall I? Don't look so, Ginny. It cannot be as bad as that. Can it?'

She had misread Ginny's face. Memories of that single night when Ginny had expected so much more came like a wave of sweet longing to catch her breath on a shuddering sigh, closing her eyes against the intruding light and squeezing a single tear onto her lashes to shimmer there like a pearl. Unthinking, she covered her face with both hands as the ache shook her. As she had never thought it could. Wanting him, whatever it cost her in pride. She felt Anna's arms come round her in a womanly embrace. 'Oh, my dear. It was bad? So sorry. Poor... poor...'

Whatever Ginny said now would probably fail to convince the queen that the experience was anything but repulsive, for Anna was a sensitive woman, despite her quiet undemonstrative manner. Would her sense of duty be enough? Was it already too late? Had the king stopped trying? Had he ever...? 'No,' she said, 'it isn't bad at all, Your Grace, but I think the one to tell you ought to be Mother Lowe, your Flemish lady, who can explain it to you in your own language. It's not my place, you see.'

Concerned for Ginny more than herself, Anna agreed. 'You're right. I should not distress you. I shall ask Mother Lowe. I shall tell her she must show me.'

Ginny's concerns went further than that, however, for the queen's revelation was disastrous. If Henry had shown so little interest in her after so many opportunities, then his need of a mistress would be greater than ever.

* * *

Ginny's prediction that the king would visit
that evening after supper was correct. Although
he brought with him a crowd of courtiers to
the queen's rooms, the time he spent with his
wife was noticeably less than that spent with the
other young women, including herself. Sir Jon's
appearance could not be ignored this time as it
had been before, but between them there was a
restraint that only they knew the reason for, and
only they could amend, if some privacy could
be granted. It was never going to be likely. Their
exchanges were politely formal and, as he left
her to speak to another woman, the pain became
more intense when Thomas Culpeper came to
her side with a smile she would have preferred
to see on her husband's face. He was a pre-
sentable young man of noble parentage whose
knowledge of court etiquette was unimpeach-
able. He had everything Henry liked in his companions: good looks and a way with women, a
reputation for recklessness, and a natural arrogance that won him frowns from the older
courtiers and simpering smiles from their older
wives, who lapped up his condescending flattery like cats with cream. The maids of honour
could not get enough of him, yet Ginny thought
him superficial, potentially dangerous, and too

smooth-tongued to be genuine. She found it difficult to respond with anything like politeness to him now, after hearing from her brother how they had both wanted her humiliation at the expense of a good laugh. She did her best, for appearances' sake, when he swept off his hat with a flourish that made the jewelled brim sparkle.

Culpeper's attention returned to Ginny with a sigh. 'A pity,' he said softly.

'Pity, sir? Whatever for?' said Ginny.

'Pity she doesn't make her husband laugh like that as he does with you. Perhaps you should tell her how it's done. But that would be difficult, I think. It's a special gift you have, my lady. Which is why, I suppose, he much prefers your company to the queen's. You must have noticed. Your father certainly has, hasn't he?'

'Master Culpeper, this is dangerous talk. If His Majesty were more in the queen's company, he would discover her many attributes. She is eager to please him, as I said. All she lacks is the chance. And you have the means to encourage him in that, too, instead of bringing other women to his attention.'

'By which you mean yourself,' he said, turning the full beam of his smile upon her. 'But, my lady, I understood *that* to be the reason for your marriage to Sir Jon. So that Henry could have—'

'That's enough, Master Culpeper! Whatever you understand to be the reason for my marriage to Sir Jon is of no account. At His Majesty's request, I am at court to give his new wife the benefit of my assistance, however small, and to be with my husband. That's all. I have no intention of becoming your cat's paw in whatever game you have up your sleeve.' As she spoke, a high giggle of girlish laughter cut across the room like a knife, turning heads to confirm what most of the assembly already assumed, that young Katherine Howard had said something to amuse both herself and the king. Again. A sparkle of rubies caught the candlelight as she whirled in front of him, wantonly, like a plump little elf, while in a shadowy corner the Duke of Norfolk watched his niece's capers with satisfaction.

Culpeper's wide smile faded as he caught Ginny's eyes upon him, reading his mind, seeing the flash of desire and jealousy that flitted across his face before he could wipe it away. He knew she had seen it. 'Where did the rubies come from?' he said, as carefree as he could manage. 'From Henry, was it?'

'Who else?' Ginny said. *There, Master Culpeper, now our scores are even.*

But now Thomas Culpeper had given Ginny more food for thought than she was comfortable with, making it quite certain that he would prefer her to take Henry's fancy rather than Kat Howard. Ginny had no doubts that Culpeper was in love with the Howard girl and, like any normal man, was not happy about the idea of sharing her with the king. It was a tricky situation Ginny would rather not have been a part of. Not for the first time, her feeling of insecurity was almost like a pain, for she would have liked it better if Sir Jon had shown the same kind of concern for her that Culpeper did for Kat Howard.

Making her way across to the queen, her arm was caught in a strong grasp, and before she could protest at the urgency, she was propelled towards a door cut in the poorly lit tapestried wall usually used by servants unobtrusively. By the feel of him, and the faint scent that haunted her dreams, she knew even without looking that it was Sir Jon. There had been a time only recently when she would have made a fuss, made it difficult for him to manoeuvre her into darkness and through to the deserted passageway beyond, but not now when her senses were alive and responsive and needy, after two days of wondering how to make him want her again as he'd wanted her before, once. She did not protest at his roughness either when he turned her round to face him and slammed her without ceremony against the panelling with a soft thud, at the same time holding her fiercely, more in anger than desire, she thought.

'I was watching,' he said, his face close enough for her to feel his warm breath on her lips. 'He upset you. What did he say? And don't say it was nothing.'

'I wasn't going to,' she said breathlessly, wincing under the pressure of his hands. 'He's concerned about Kat Howard being so close to the king. He would rather I was in her place. He's jealous. Nothing I didn't already know. Or you.'

'And I expect he offered you his friendship, too, did he?'

'He would have done, if I'd given him half a chance. Why? Do you think I would have accepted it? Do I need friends like him?'

'I don't know what you need, lady. Perhaps one day you'll be able to tell me.'

'Do I have to tell you, then?' she whispered. 'With all your experience, do you not know? I thought perhaps we'd found something out about each other, but perhaps I'm wrong. Perhaps I dreamed it. Or was that for someone else? Was it?' Her free hand had begun a slow ascent along his shoulder and up to his face, and now, finding his bearded cheek, held it in a soft caress with her fingertips reaching into his velvet hair. She would like to have gone on to tell him the reason behind her softness on the night of their loving, and how he had got it so wrong, but she was given no chance before his mouth, already close to hers, took what they had both wanted and could wait for no longer.

With a fierceness that matched his, Ginny's needs were poured into her kisses as they had been that night, after which they'd had unfinished business to attend to, and that, this time, there would be no pretence about who or what it was for. She sensed that his hunger was as great as her own when he bent her in his arms and cradled her head against his shoulder to reach the silken curve of her throat, and she felt his warm lips tasting her, possessive, assertive, as if to refute her taunt of unsureness.

If he had taken the chance then to explain to her the complications that beset him and his deeply felt reasons for doubting her, even after he'd affirmed his authority at the very beginning, she might have been more able to place

her own problems in context. But they had
started off on the wrong foot with her anger
over the previous offer, over the king's interference, her father's domination, and the humiliation of being rushed into a marriage against all
her wishes. On his side, there was his previous
marriage to haunt him, as well as Henry's determination to use both him and Ginny for his
own ends, as if they were both there only for
his convenience. And now, with no time to get
to know each other at all, they were in a place
where explanations were well-nigh impossible,
in an undignified scuffle where families wres-
tled each other for power, using their women to
play rings round the king's unstable emotions.
And Ginny in the middle of it all like the innocent she was and not fully aware of the dangers
that lay like snares around her feet, the false offers of friendship, the nasty jests that even her
brother could play on her. He himself could
have gone to Henry's chamber that night to see
if the message was indeed genuine, but the suggestion of a betrothal had come from Ginny and
her relatives, and why would he question that,
with such an early prize to be had? The delay in
consummation he had understood and accepted
at the time, thinking it might be a long wait,
but within days, nights, she had offered herself

to him, and afterwards, still unsure of her, he had taken it the wrong way, thinking that, because of what had happened to him years ago, that was what women did when they wanted something. After seeing his child, she had no doubt worked it out for herself that a pregnancy would keep her safe from the king, at least for a while. It was all her earlier angry protests and unwillingness that had made him wonder how she could suddenly want him for any other reason but that. That, and a kind of reward.

If, of course, he had known more about the heart's waywardness in matters of love, he would have accepted it without all the painful heart-searching. But being clever at jousting and ciphering—which he did for Sir Thomas Cromwell—did not automatically make him wise in other ways, and sometimes even love charms buried in frost-covered gardens were not entirely controlled by the ones who planted them.

In the stuffy darkness of the passageway, they snatched at a physical need that neither of them dared to question. Still feeling the unfulfilment of their previous loving, they remembered both its sweetness and bitterness and now, for whatever reason, logical or not, their hunger overpowered them for the short time available.

'I shall come to you tonight, in your room,' he said, taking a deep breath to steady himself. 'Wait up for me, wife. Henry will have to wait on my pleasure.'

'You want me, then?' she said, hoping for a softly spoken word.

'If I don't, I'll try to put up a good enough pretence of it,' he said, adjusting the tiny French hood over her hair. 'Come, we must go before we're missed.'

It was not the answer she would have liked, but philosophically she had to accept that it was all she could expect until they could trust each other.

He took her back to the queen's rooms, stealing through the concealed door like lovers while one of Henry's musicians sang to his own lute accompaniment. Only moments later, Sir Jon was asked to sing, which he did in a rich, clear baritone that Ginny had heard before. This time, as a married man, he was able to sing to his wife the words of love that, so far, he had never spoken. It was a good act that brought applause from those who were convinced by it and a lump to Ginny's throat for the feigned sentiments of the haunting 'My Heart Awaits the Spring' that were still frozen in her mind by doubts.

Thankfully, her elder brother came to her side as the song finished, walking her away from the others into a recess from where they could see the colourful swirl of fabrics and the soft glitter of jewels, the sheen of gold threads and the animated faces of courtiers whose task was to entertain and be entertained. 'I saw you and Culpeper talking,' said Elion. 'You should beware of him, you know. Is that what Raemon has advised?'

'After what happened at home, you mean? Yes, I am wary, I assure you.'

'Not only that. He's…well, perhaps I should not say.' Looking down at his hands and then away from her, Elion conveyed his unease as clearly as if he'd written it. Like Ginny, he tended to wear his heart on his sleeve, his comely young face being a mirror of his soul, reflecting every nuance of feeling, good or bad, unable to pretend for long what he did not believe.

'Perhaps you should,' said Ginny. 'No one else will, unless it's to his credit.'

'That's the problem,' he said softly. 'He has the king's favour, even when it comes to crime. I say this only to protect you, Ginny.'

'From Culpeper? Elion, you have no need. I

don't like the man. But what's this crime you speak of that the king overlooks?'

'Rape,' he whispered. 'Last year, he and his friends took the wife of a park keeper by force, in the forest, for a laugh, while his cronies held her down. And when the bailiff came along to try to arrest them, they killed him. That's the kind of man he is. I believe Paul might have been one of those involved, but I have no proof.' Hearing Ginny gasp, he placed a hand over hers, squeezed it, then took it away. 'And since I cannot find proof, I cannot say anything to Father. He'd banish him. You know how Father feels about misconduct of that kind.'

'Elion! This is…is *dreadful*! And you say the king knows about it? How?'

'It was reported to him. He told Culpeper off, but decided to forgive him for what he was pleased to call *high spirits*. Can you imagine? That's the kind of relationship he and Henry have. The lad can do no wrong, it seems. Not even that.'

'And does Kat Howard know of this?' Ginny said, trying hard not to reveal on her face the horror of what she'd heard.

'I doubt it, love. And if she did, it would not make the slightest difference to her feelings for Culpeper. The thing is, Ginny, I fear that one day he'll go too far and she won't be able to stop him, and then there'll be trouble. From Henry, I mean.'

'Maybe she won't want to stop him. She's besotted. And very indiscreet. But I never thought Paul would do something like that, Elion. That has shocked me.'

'As I said, I have no proof, but I know that to be in Culpeper's crowd means a lot to Paul. He'd do anything to stay there.'

'Even that?'

'My advice, for what it's worth, is to keep well away from them. All of them. I believe they'll go too far one day and then the king may not be so tolerant of their high spirits. If Culpeper takes what Henry wants, he certainly won't be amused.'

'All I hope is that Henry wants Kat Howard more than he wants me,' Ginny said in a low voice. 'I know that sounds selfish, but I cannot help it. Do what you can to push her under his nose, Elion.'

His large grey eyes blinked at her like an owl. 'That's not like you, lass,' he said. 'Is Raemon not doing what he can? Are things not going well with you and him? Have you still not made up your differences? I'm sure he means to protect you.'

She preferred not to answer his questions directly. 'Did you ever meet his wife, Elion? Maeve and George couldn't tell me much.'

'Nor can I,' Elion said, looking away. 'She was very lovely, but I was not in her sphere. I know very little about her, actually, except that she had wealth that Raemon found very useful.'

Since any husband would have found his bride's wealth very useful, Ginny attached no great significance to that, but Elion either knew little about the first Lady Raemon or would not to go into detail. She wondered if that was part of his protection, too, or if there was truly no more to tell.

As she had feared, the evening could not end without Henry claiming her attention for a good hour and talking about his need of a beautiful companion, by which she knew he meant 'mistress'. Were she and Sir Jon getting on well together? Was she enjoying being a married woman? She tried to be positive, telling him of the young child left behind at Lea Magna. She asked about the young Princess Elizabeth and the Prince Edward, always a safe topic of conversation, for he was as proud of them as any father, though not as involved as he would like to be. To Ginny's great relief, he did not suggest a meeting that night, but asked her to be in the queen's gardens in the morning to walk with him, and she wondered if he'd asked the queen's maids to be there, too. She saw her husband watching Henry from a distance, though he did not, this time, interrupt them as he had done before.

The candle had burnt down to its last inch before Sir Jon came to her room with the muffled bells of Westminster pealing quietly through the blackness. Ginny was on the edge of sleep. She stirred, then sat up to lean on one elbow. He had begun undressing even before the door was closed behind him, throwing his clothes upon the floor like a trail left for the hounds. Expecting him, she had not anticipated the urgency that impelled him towards her. Nor could she possibly have known of the overpowering need that had occupied his mind throughout that evening when he'd been obliged to manufacture small talk to those he had nothing in common with. Pressed back into the pillows by his arms and body, she gave herself, in half sleep, to whatever it was he desired, wondering if this might be the kind of passion that comes with love, or whether it was the kind of thing men could do at will, whether they loved or not. She had no way of knowing and it was too late to ask, for her arms instinctively wrapped themselves around him and her legs entwined his lithe body to experience along every surface what she had missed over two whole days of longing.

Bleary with delayed sleep and tiredness after the long ride to London, Ginny let her remaining thoughts fade into oblivion, giving herself up to the comfort of his attentions, for he seemed to understand that consolation and relief would come together in the tenderness of his arms. Soothing her with his hands and lips over the satin smoothness of her skin, he stroked back the lethargy he had interrupted, demanding nothing more than her willingness and sleepy appreciation, her languid caresses, and the cooperation of her lovely body. His gentle preparation came as a relief to Ginny, for although her need of him was great, she was still new to the rigours of passionate lovemaking. And in spite of, or perhaps because of, his blissfully unhurried loving, she felt the growing desire ignite within her thighs and spread into her belly like a slow flame, wakening her to deeper responses that could wait no longer for fulfilment. 'Take me now,' she whispered, moving her hips against him teasingly. 'Will you take me to the end this time, Jon?'

'I *will* take you,' he said. 'I could have taken you at any moment this evening. I should have taken you nights ago. And if he'd sent for you tonight…'

'Don't!' she said. 'Don't spoil it. He hasn't. He didn't. I don't suppose he will. Now, let's forget that…please?'

I cannot forget it. I cannot. For it's that which haunts me. 'Yes, you're right,' he said. 'I cannot allow it to get in the way, or I stand no chance, do I?'

The exact meaning of his words was lost on her, not only because she did not understand what he meant by them, but also because his tenderly thrilling invasion closed her mind to everything else. There was no force, no pain, only a certain resistance on her part and an insistence on his, and a strange perception of accommodating part of him in a new and untried place. Instantly, she felt both safe and deliciously vulnerable under the gentle weight of him where no one but he could reach her. Stormed by a torrent of contentment, she gave herself up to him, for in this if in nothing else, she was learning to trust in his care.

Yet even in his careful loving, there was an

anger in the magnificent body lying just below the surface where she could sense it through her fingertips, trembling like a bad dream on the point of waking. His silence puzzled her, for it was as if he was afraid of saying something he might regret and of hearing something he might not want to know. Only days ago, he had talked of ways to keep her silent, yet she could not believe he meant it to apply to times when pleasure might be expressed in words. These were early days, however, and so as not to disturb this special experience, she went along with the inarticulate lovemaking that had a language of its own after all, thankful that he found her pleasing enough to have wanted her all evening, rather than some other woman. For years she had tried to persuade herself that he was not the man she wanted, that he meant as little to her as she apparently did to him. Now she could no longer deny her feelings for him, even if the method used to bring them together had humiliated her beyond anything, when he'd had to be bribed and rewarded to bring it about. So had he really meant it when he'd shown concern at Henry's interest this evening? Had that been show, for her sake? Was that what men did when they possessed something new? Refuse to share it?

Well, since talk of love so soon would be sure to embarrass him, she would not talk of it. She would take what he offered and be glad that he desired her, for whatever reason. But as for telling him so, she would not take that risk. She would have to cultivate acceptance and serenity, like clever Queen Anna with her marital problems. She would confide in her. Ask her how it was done. Having reached this point, she was not going to spoil what she had by telling him what he obviously did not want to know. That her feelings for him were not what she'd led him to believe.

She knew, somehow, that she had satisfied him as she would like to have done before, though the warm contentment she felt after his withdrawal was obviously not of the same intensity. When he had braced himself above her, she had been aware of a change of pace, deeper and faster, as if a new urgency spurred him on to something just beyond his reach. She would like to have known what and where it was, and why he groaned into her hair as if he would never let her go.

Chapter Six

Dreamy with memories of the previous night and her body still alive with sensations, Ginny gowned Queen Anna in her finest furs and most becoming greens to walk in the gardens at Whitehall, determined that if the king wanted to walk with her, he would have to walk with Anna, too. Crystals frosted the garden like a confection, glistening on the long colour-striped posts that decorated the corners of each pathway where, in the raised beds, crocuses, snowdrops, and hellebores were hardly noticed by the groups of courtiers strolling with their faces towards the weak sun. Topping each pole, mythological beasts bearing shields shone with gold leaf, adding rich colour to the silver-white frost, Anna's soft velvet gown being the only sign of green on that occasion. Ginny saw the king looking hard at her but, after the shortest of enquiries about her health, left his queen in the company of Sir Jon Raemon and took Ginny by the arm to walk with her apart, too conspicuously for her comfort. Others fell back to give them some privacy, though she could feel Sir Jon's eyes upon them.

Henry tucked her hand into the soft bend of his elbow and patted it in a fatherly manner. 'I'm glad you've returned to us, my lady,' he said. 'I knew you were the one to set the queen's wardrobe to rights. You have style, you see. More than any woman at court.' He sighed. 'I thought I, too, would have a wife with a liking for our culture, for music and singing, for poetry and fine things. Mistress Howard has an eye for pretty things, does she not? Now, if *you* were my wife, my lady, we would have so much more to talk about, I know. But my new wife will never understand me, I fear, the way you do. Charming, of course, in her own way, but, ah…I cannot see how I shall ever come to, well…be with her as a husband should. It's so hard for me to find a way forwards on this matter. I have no heart for it anymore.'

'The queen has many fine qualities, Your Grace. Once you get to know her better, I'm sure you will find you have much in common. And she's so eager to learn our language and our customs. She has the most wonderful sense of humour, too.'

But Henry was feeling sorry for himself, sure he'd made a mistake that could not be rectified by any effort on his part, with not a thought about how his foreign wife must be feeling far away from home amongst strangers. He had done little to rectify the situation, or make things easier for her, nor had he offered her more than courtesies in place of the love she would have preferred, and Ginny was left with the impression that things would not improve when he had now begun to leave Anna to her own devices, especially at night.

She need not have been concerned that Henry, on that occasion, would try to suggest seeing her in private for, disregarding royal protocol, Katherine Howard danced past to chase after a ball that bounced ahead of them, her skirts swishing, her hair fraying across her face as she turned, laughing. Her cheeks were flushed with mischief as she tossed the ball to the king without a word of warning, obliging him to catch it, and Ginny knew then that their conversation, such as it was, was at an end.

Joining Sir Jon and the queen, she thought sadly how blind the king was to his wife's qualities, for even now she was chatting animatedly to her escort in her limited English about the differences between a pavane and a galliard, making Sir Jon laugh at their linguistic problems. 'Come here, my lady,' he said to Ginny, holding out a hand, 'and show Her Grace the steps. See... Watch this...'

At once, Ginny entered into the spirit of the lesson and there, on the frosted lawn, they joined gloved hands and executed the steps, slowly and gracefully, for the queen to watch. Then, as Sir Jon took the queen for his partner and others joined in with Ginny, they hummed the tune and clapped hands for the rhythm as if they were in a candlelit hall, their fur bonnets and booted toes making them look like solemn, woolly, well-dressed dancing bears.

If Katherine Howard had hoped to monopolise the king's attention, she must have been gratified to see how the courtiers gathered round the dance on the silvery grass where the queen laughingly counted her steps out loud, with Sir Jon talking her through the moves, stopping, starting again, correcting the details. And by the time the dance was mastered, the king and his young friend were nowhere to be seen. It did not matter to Ginny or to Sir Jon, for they had at last enjoyed something together in public instead of each pretending that the other did not exist. Ginny felt almost heady with pleasure. Perhaps, she thought, they were beginning to make some progress.

However, it was only a short time later when she saw her husband, as she had seen him many times before their marriage, enjoying the company of a very pretty woman with black hair and a deeply cut bodice who was openly flirting with him as if he was still single. They obviously knew each other well. Feeling it beneath her dignity to comment on it, she called to mind what he'd said to her only a few days ago in the chapel at home, that she must learn to look the other way. At the time, she had not believed she would care enough for that. Now she did.

Thomas Culpeper turned out to be a convenient accomplice as they stood in a group behind the queen where Sir Jon could not fail to see them. Ginny had not noticed that Culpeper was standing closer to her than she would have liked, but nor did she prevent him when he bent his head to hers to compliment her on her beauty. She'd heard it all before. It meant nothing, although, in retrospect, it was foolish of her to stay when there were so many others she could have talked with, rather than a man she despised for his unprincipled behaviour. Afterwards, she wished she'd had the sense to walk

away, but the pert and self-satisfied expression
on the face of Sir Jon's companion made her
reckless with jealousy and that moment of hesitation gave Culpeper all the encouragement he
needed to make what trouble he could. 'To continue our conversation,' he said, being careful
not to be overheard, 'I wanted to ask you how
you liked your new home at Lea Magna. Did
you get to meet your new stepdaughter there?
Is she growing to be as lovely as her mother?'

Ginny sensed the not entirely innocent nature of his questions, but here was a chance to
discover something about the first Lady Raemon that her siblings had been so reluctant to
remember. 'You probably know that the child
is adorable,' she said, speaking to him over her
shoulder. That, at least, would be giving nothing
away. 'As for her being as lovely as her mother,
I have no way of knowing that, have I, Master
Culpeper? The child has all the makings of a
beauty, certainly, but that is hardly surprising
with such a handsome father. Perhaps you can
tell me who she favours.'

'Oh, Magdalen was his match in every way,'
Culpeper said, smiling at her curiosity thinly
veiled under the careful words, 'but if you'd
seen her portrait, you'd have been in no doubt
about the child's—' Whatever he'd been going

to say was cut off sharply by a scuffling sound that made Ginny turn to look. Thomas Culpeper's shirt front and doublet were caught fast in the grasp of a man's fist being used to propel him backwards with a thud into the stone wall of the passageway. His face, contorted with outrage, showed that he had been taken as much by surprise as Ginny had. 'What the *devil*…?' he croaked, knocking the restraining hand away and pulling down his ruffled doublet. 'Have a care, Raemon. You know the penalty for violence in the king's ward, surely? Not to mention the regulations about the courtesy due to His Majesty's gentlemen? Do I have to remind you?'

Sir Jon needed no reminding that the penalty for any kind of violence within a certain distance of the king was to lose a hand, no less. Yet the sight of his wife receiving Culpeper's insidious gossip was worth the risk and only force would have stopped him in time, though it had already whetted Ginny's appetite for the rest of the revelation, whatever it was. 'A little harmless fun, Tom,' he said smoothly, dusting a hand over Culpeper's well-made doublet. 'Sense of humour deserted you, has it? Forgive me for interrupting, but I need my wife rather urgently. Come, my lady.' Taking hold of Ginny's elbow through her fur cloak, he escorted her at speed down the passageway, telling her more clearly than any words that whatever Culpeper had been about to say was not something he wanted her to hear.

Wrenching herself free from his hand, Ginny swung herself away from him in anger, putting space between them in the now-deserted passage, snarling at his high-handedness. 'That was not harmless fun,' she said, checking to see that no one was within earshot. 'Was it? If *you* can talk to who *you* like, why should I not do the same? It was perfectly innocent.' She knew it was not.

The expression on Sir Jon's face chilled her heart, so far was it from the laughter he'd been sharing with the black-haired woman. 'I cannot prevent him speaking to you, my lady, nor can I prevent you from speaking to him. But don't for one moment imagine that anything he tells you will be *innocent*. What did he tell you this time to warp your mind against me?'

'*This time?* What on earth can you mean? Does it warp my mind to know that your first wife was beautiful? Do you think I'd not heard that before? Do you think,' she panted, 'that I'm not reminded of it when we are in bed together, when we make love, do I not become *her,* the one you still grieve for? Do you think I cannot tell, Sir Jon?'

'Is that what you think?' he said. He jerked his head back as if she had struck him. 'Is that what it's all about? You think…?'

'What am I supposed to think?' she cried. 'All I know is that we're going in different directions in this marriage of convenience and that the only times we come near to behaving like husband and wife is in the dark, and in silence. Is that good enough for you? Is that what you're used to? Personally, I had no expectations at all, knowing as little about you as you do about me, which is why I have to rely on what I can glean from others, even some who're not my friends. It's better than nothing.' As she spoke, she knew the words to be less than the truth and unkind, meant to hurt him. But the days of wanting him and the few nights of loving, although rapturous, had left her more unsure of his motives than ever, or even whether he would come to her at all. Added to that was the ever-present threat of the king's pleasure when, any evening, he might send for her. She would not be able to refuse any more than Jane Seymour had, or Mary Boleyn, or Queen Anna, for that matter.

After her talk with the king that morning, she

had begun to see the chances of Anna's marital harmony slip away as he became more and more dissatisfied and determined, it seemed, to escape from his dilemma. Ginny herself was doing her best to promote Anna's rare qualities, and today she'd even had the help of Sir Jon, too. Yet her fear was that, if Henry was to find a way out of his marriage, it might also bring about her own separation from Sir Jon. She would return to Lea Magna and he would stay with the king, and their life would then resemble that of her parents, who preferred it that way. The choice, if there was one, would be unbearable, with the all-consuming mothering urge growing daily inside her like a craving after having held his beautiful child in her arms. She would never remain at court as long as Etta needed a mother so badly, and Sir Jon would never relinquish his position there.

The alternative was even more uncomfortable for, if Henry and Anna were to stay unhappily together, she would be in greater danger than ever from the king's attentions. Unless, of course, they changed direction. Then, Katherine Howard's compliance and Thomas Culpeper's comeuppance would be her dubious rewards.

'No,' he said, 'hearing what gossipmongers say *isn't* better than nothing. I know there is

still much you've not been told, but the king
has put me in a *damnable* position, Ginny, and
I like it no more than you do. You will have to
trust me to keep you out of his way for as long
as I can, but listening to what Culpeper has to
say about it isn't going to help matters. He has
the opposite in mind. You must have seen that.'

'So if you prefer me not to listen to him, Sir
Jon, shall you be listening less to that black-
haired strumpet with the bare front from now
on? Or is that different?'

That had been enough to light the tinder of
her tightly held emotions, and now her temper flared, fuelled by the brazen black-haired
woman. Jon saw the fire flash in her eyes and
recognised something he could respond to with
his own brand of anger. 'Jealous, are we?' he
said. 'In spite of me telling you to look the other
way. Do I see green in your eyes? Eh?'

'See what you damned well like!' Ginny
snarled. 'Talk to who you like. See if I care!'
Aiming a push at his chest, she was not prepared for the hand that closed around her wrist,
pulling her into a deserted angle of the passageway where a window had once been. Before she
could protest, Jon had swung her round onto
the wide windowsill where, losing her balance,
she was held back against the wall, unable to

right herself. This time, she knew she had tried his patience too far, their combined duties disallowing anything more than fleeting contact and no time for the gentler aspects of an early partnership.

'Then I *will* see what I like, since we're talking of bare fronts, lady,' Jon said. 'Maybe this will convince you of something, if words do not.' As he spoke, his hand expertly pulled apart the laces of her bodice, snapping them as easily as cotton threads and exposing the fine lawn chemise beneath. Stopping her protesting hands with one of his, he pulled them together behind her back as her chemise gave way before his force, revealing her breasts to the subdued light as they had not been before.

Far from being dismayed by her husband's ungentle disrobing of her, Ginny felt the excitement flare into her nostrils as she breathed in the closeness of his body and the heat of his arousal at the sight of the perfect expanse of nakedness. Though she could have struggled against him, her body told her to watch instead, without shame or fear. Partly supported by the open bodice, her breasts seemed to rise to his touch like soft silken orbs, palest pink tipped with deep pink nubs that hardened as his palms brushed past provocatively, asserting ownership. Hearing her gasp, Jon watched her eyes half close with sudden desire and he knew then that she *would* be capable of reaching a climax, if he were to think of her more like a passionate woman than a tender virgin.

Accordingly, he pursued her desire, skilfully diverting her outrage and jealousy into safer waters, caressing her more boldly than he had done so far, bending his head first to one breast, then the other, leaving her in no doubt where his lips, teeth and tongue had been. 'There,' he whispered. 'Convinced now?'

'Of what?'

'Of my wanting you. And of something you might have found out for yourself before flying off the handle—that the strumpet is my cousin. We almost grew up together. She was laughing about the suitors my uncle has lined up for her. And I've no wish to see her breasts. Never have done.'

Her amazing eyes widened as he spoke and now he saw that the fire had been replaced by dark desire, genuine and unashamed. Her glance moved towards his mouth and he knew she awaited his kiss. Releasing her hands, he held her beautiful breasts as he kissed her, long and passionately, thinking that of all the ways he'd tried to have the last word, this had been by far the most successful. In silence, he pulled the edges of her clothes together, covering her with the cloak to conceal all signs of his intrusion before escorting her along the passageway, smiling to himself at her meekness.

As for her accusation of making love in silence, that was partly because his hunger for Ginny had been so great that to be talking when they could be making love had seemed to him a sad waste of time, of which they had so little when their combined duties rarely coincided. What was the need for talking when lovemaking could say it better? More telling than that, though, was her belief that she was not the one in his thoughts when they made love, but his first wife, and that *that* must be why he'd spoken to her so little. It was as far from the truth as it was possible to be. There was much to be said that he'd kept to himself for a variety of reasons, one of which concerned his own pride, wounded at a time when the world had seemed to be his. She would have to be told eventually, but not until the time was right. And certainly not in bed. Emotionally, she had enough to concern her for the present. Or so he thought.

He did not, nevertheless, stop to ask himself whether he was the best judge of that or whether, by keeping Ginny in the dark about things she ought to have known, he was destroying the trust he'd asked her to find. Or even whether, by trying to protect her from perceived harm, he was actually doing the opposite.

Having changed the bodice of her gown, Ginny set off once more for the queen's apartments, where the furniture was draped like a market stall with lengths of fabrics, braids and laces, patterns and parts of garments, many of them unidentifiable except to the queen's tailors who had their own intricate ways of piecing, seaming, attaching and lining, facing and binding. Anna stood with arms out like a scarecrow while the tailor knelt at her feet with a row of pins held between his lips that reduced his instructions to a series of squeaks. A group of her maids and ladies sat over by the window with their embroidery before the light faded, their tiny black stitches on white linen making scroll patterns on shirt wristbands and collars. Others sewed narrow white seams on nightgowns and kirtles so fine that one could see through the linen. For the queen's wardrobe, Ginny was choosing a soft honey-coloured cloth of cashmere and wool, and a rich fabric that rustled with the silver weft and silken warp, a two-coloured miracle of plum and blue. But Anna looked pensive instead of excited and Ginny believed she knew the reason. She had been talking to Mother Lowe, her Flemish lady, about the getting of children, which her own mother ought to have explained to her many years ago and certainly before her marriage to a king.

An hour later, with the fabrics still heaped upon the table in a darkening room, Ginny and Anna sat by the fire, warming their hands on beakers of mulled wine and watching the steam rise in convoluted swirls. Anna shook her head slowly from side to side, her lovely almond eyes darting away to one corner, where two maids sat with a young musician and his lute, before coming to rest on Ginny's sympathetic face. 'As if that was not enough,' Anna whispered, 'why was I not told at the time? Now it seems I'm supposed to make myself more—what is the word—allure?'

'Alluring, yes. Is that the word the Earl of Rutland used? Did he say how?'

'Nothing I could understand, Ginny. I think the poor man was as…'

'Embarrassed?'

'Yes. But to have a man, my own chamberlain, talk so to me… Oh! I cannot tell you how I felt. Of course, it was that man Cromwell who said he must.' Her hand covered her mouth, then as quickly resumed its place on her lap. 'I think you might have said it better. At least I'd have been able to understand you.'

'So Mother Lowe had already told you what a woman's part is?'

Anna nodded, her eyes darting again, searching for some point of reference. 'She did, but I cannot believe it, Ginny. Is that what *you* do? You and Sir Jon?'

For different reasons, Ginny joined in the queen's sigh. 'Yes,' she said. 'It sounds dreadful when it's spoken of, but really it's not, Your Grace. It's very comforting and, well…exciting. There is no language difficulty then, you see. One hardly needs words. If you love the man…' She was stopped by the bleak look of despair on Anna's face and by the words that echoed inside her own head, finding some resonance there. *If you love the man, one hardly needs words.*

'That's the difference, then, isn't it? I could never do that with the king. Could you? Answer me, Ginny. *Could* you?'

By some convenient quirk of fate, Ginny was saved from having to answer by the entrance of a burly figure she recognised at once as the artist who had been sent to Cleves to paint Anna's portrait for the king. It was on this por-

trait that Henry had based his decision to make
her his queen and, since then, Master Holbein
had had to make himself scarce for a while until
the king's anger abated. Turning sharply to see
who had entered unannounced, Anna's gasp
was audible to Ginny, though not to the others,
and as Master Holbein came forwards into the
glow of the fire, she witnessed the serene ra-
diance on the queen's face that Hans had cap-
tured. The half smile of burgeoning desire, the
demure yet steady gaze of interest in a man, the
anticipation in the curve of her lips, the contained excitement generated by his presence,
centred on her alone. Anna could never have
done 'that' with the king, but Ginny knew that,
with Hans Holbein, she could. The question
went unanswered as the king's painter doffed
his cap and greeted them both, then sat down
and began to speak to Anna in their own language, neither of them noticing when the stool
opposite became vacant.

Preoccupied with her own troubles, Ginny
had intended to talk to the queen in the hope
of discovering the secret of her serenity, her
acceptance of things beyond her control, and
her thoughts on duty as opposed to preferences.
Now she realised that Anna was perhaps less
accepting than she had thought, that it was dis-

cipline that held her desires in check and not so much the natural composure of an obedient daughter. And since Ginny's situation was in some ways paralleled by Anna's and in other ways diverging, it occurred to her in the long walk back to her own rooms that she had the best of it with a husband she desired and who, for whatever reason, desired her enough to take her to bed. He was also concerned for her safety, for he must have known about Culpeper's crime, too. She had overreacted. It had not been her intention to stir up trouble. But the desire Jon had incited in the passageway was still vividly in her memory. The boldness of it, the spontaneity, the sheer lust between them generated by anger had made her wonder what he might have done next had they been more private.

She found Sir Jon reclining on their bed reading a paper that he quickly folded and packed into his pouch as she entered. Taken aback by his presence at this time of night when he would normally have been with the king, she put aside their last acrimonious bickering. Had he come to continue where they'd left off?

'I've been with the queen,' she said, unfastening her fur cloak and holding its warmth in her arms. A single candle burned by the bedside, casting long dancing shadows across the bed curtains.

'And I've been with Sir Thomas Cromwell,' he said, swinging his long legs to the floor. 'He's not a happy man. Things are not going well for him.'

'As the one who proposed the king's marriage in the first place, I can see why. Anna was not happy either, when Cromwell suggested to her own chamberlain that he should give her some advice about…' She pursed her mouth, deliberating how to say it.

Sir Jon's laugh was husky, sending shivers down her arms. 'I know what it was about. You can see how desperate he's getting, then, to send a man to give the queen that kind of instruction. Not that it will do any good, I don't suppose.'

Ginny felt sorry for her friend and said so. 'Well, none of us knows exactly what either of them gets up to in the bedroom, do we? The king can say what he likes, and probably has done, but there's only his word for it. Poor Anna doesn't get to put her side of the story. I cannot imagine how *anyone* could even pretend to…ugh!'

'And will she pretend to?' he said, smiling at the wry face.

Ginny shrugged. 'Is there any way she can avoid it, if that's what he wants?'

'It looks, Lady Raemon, as if we were not the only ones to delay our consummation, only theirs appears to be mutual, whereas ours was not, was it?'

'Yes, it was. You agreed to it.'

'For your sake. Not because I was unwilling. Come here.' He stood up and, reaching out, took the cloak from her arms, tossed it onto the bed, and pulled her closer to him. 'And you needed no advice, did you? Even the first time.'

'I was not offered any, sir. We don't speak. Remember?'

He wore only his shirt, breeches, and hose, and she could feel the warmth of him taking the place of the cloak, his male scent filling her nostrils. Perversely, she wanted to delay him, not to make it too easy, though she knew where this would lead. 'What will Sir Thomas do?' she said, tilting her head to look up at him. 'Henry has not banished Master Holbein for his painting of her. Would he banish Cromwell?'

'That's anyone's guess,' he said, his fingers pulling at the strings of her headdress. Tossing the contraption aside, he searched for the pins that held her hair up. 'But he's been told to find an escape clause in the marriage contract, so even with the chamberlain's advice to the queen, Henry is quite determined…'

'No!' Ginny protested. 'Not that! He cannot do that. It was all so thoroughly investigated. What will her family say? Will he put her aside on some trumped-up clause just because he doesn't desire her?'

'He wants heirs, remember? As I do. He's not going to get any heirs with Anna.' His fingers raked through her hair, fanning it out like a silver cloak over her shoulders, piling handfuls of it on top of her head and letting it fall over her face, playing like a boy with water. Like a man with his lover.

Ginny felt her words drying up, but she persevered, just to delay him. 'So what clause can he possibly invent?' she said through her hair.

'He doesn't have to invent one. Nonconsummation is one, and the other might be that there was a precontract to a previous suitor in Cleves.'

'That's nonsense. He knows it is. Henry accepted her brother's assurance that there was no legal contract. She was a child at the time. He can't use that.'

'He's the head of the church in England, my sweet. He can do as he likes.' He might have said *and so can I* when he kissed her through an opening in the veil of her hair, tangling their eyelashes in the fine silvery strands and taking some into their mouths.

Ginny pulled away at last, blowing wisps aside. 'He'll send her home? In disgrace? Surely he'd not be so cruel, knowing how she'd be shamed before her family? After all her efforts? She's tried so hard to please him. This one unlaces from the side, not the back.' She felt his hands relocate, beginning their journey down her bodice, taking time to investigate beneath the openings, making her lose the thread of her enquiries.

'Henry needs the goodwill of her brother, the Duke of Cleves,' he said, kissing her neck. 'He'll not do anything to shame the duke's sister. Will she contest it, d'ye think? Make a fuss like his first wife did? Henry hates it when his wives argue.'

'It's not the same, is it? He and Catherine of Aragon had been married a long time. This marriage is only weeks old. Between you and me, I think Anna would find life perfectly bearable without Henry in her bed every night with his, ah…fumbling…hands…ah!' She gasped and writhed as his hands found an expanse of bare skin and pushed her gown down to the floor, then, before she could tell what he was going to do, she was lifted up to him with hands beneath her buttocks to sit astride him, clinging to his shoulders, her face tucked into his neck. It had taken only this to make her ready and for him to bare himself to her.

'Not like this, then?' he whispered. 'Put your legs round me. Rest your feet on the bed. Yes, like that. Hold on, sweetheart. This is what I wanted to do earlier, jealous little cat.'

He was immensely strong and easily able to hold her securely, and though this was not to be the tenderest of acts, being so spontaneous, it had all the excitement of which she had tried to convince Anna, and more. And since Anna's dilemma was so recent in her mind, it occurred to Ginny also that this method would probably have sounded more off-putting than the one she'd heard from Mother Lowe. She thought Anna would now never experience the passion that was pouring through them in that most intimate of embraces and that she would be the poorer for not knowing. She felt his animal urges meld into her, giving her pleasure she had so much desired where she did nothing except cling and caress with her lips, and savour each delicious thrust as his body met hers. Grasping his head, she showered him with her kisses as he groaned and finished, finally falling back onto the bed, spent, laughing, and speechless. This time, it seemed not to matter that there had been no words, for neither sight nor sound were needed to describe the sweet lethargy that followed.

'Well, my lady?' he said, breathing the words into her hair. 'Are you tamed now? Have I found a way to silence you?'

The best way to reply would be with silence, and Ginny was learning, on each occasion, that she would have to be patient with this enigmatic man who would not be pressured into telling her anything more about himself than was convenient. That he had some kind of secret, she understood, for she had felt it again in his energetic loving that had been for him a release of emotion only partly connected to desire. She had heard it in his breathing. A certain desperation. Was it a need to control? Revenge, perhaps? Or possession? Or some deep wound he was trying to comfort? He wanted her not to ask questions, particularly not from Culpeper's set. He preferred not to discuss the welfare of his fatherless and motherless child. He preferred not to go into the specific dangers that lurked around her, of how to avoid Henry, or of how exactly he meant to protect her. She was to be silent on these matters, though they could discuss the queen's problems in some detail. Ap-

parently, he now assumed that this was what
it took to make her pliant. And silent. It was
something she would soon have to resolve in
her own way, which would probably not be his.

Nudging his soft earlobe with her nose, she
wondered whether he would know that, for her,
his wonderful loving had fallen short of bringing her to that same place he'd reached when
he'd groaned, and convulsed, and strained into
her deepest parts. Would he ever take her there,
she wondered? And if so, how soon? Or was it
her own doubts that held her back?

To please him, she nestled closer before saying drowsily, 'Take off your breeches, Sir Jon.
They're scratching me. I'll embroider you a new
codpiece tomorrow, if I find time.'

'Bigger than Henry's?' he whispered.

'No, he wouldn't like that. Just more colourful.'

Ginny's resolve to take matters into her own
hands was given a boost early in March after a
lecture from her father about the need to fulfil
those obligations for which, in his book at least,
she had come to court. Why had she not managed, he wanted to know, to get as far as Henry's bed? What was the meaning of the delay?

Did she not know how to go about it by now?
Had Sir Jon taught her nothing?

'Father!' she said. 'Please, not *here*.'

They had met by chance in one of the galleries that linked the older parts of the palace
to the park where, although servants were not
allowed to linger, privacy was rarely possible.
Sir Walter took Ginny's elbow, drawing her towards a recess, indicating that he was not about
to let the matter rest. 'Well?' he said, present-
ing his back to the traffic. 'What's the problem?
Has the king not asked for you?'

'Not yet, Father. I think he's more interested
in Mistress Howard at the moment, but he's not
found a husband for her, so *she's* not going to
become his mistress any time soon, is she?'

Sir Walter's sigh came out like a dying note
on an organ. 'Virginia, she's related to the *Howards*, remember? The Duke of Norfolk is her
uncle, lass. Norfolk is pushing her like a de-
mented miller towards the *throne*, as he did
with the Boleyn woman. He's not going to allow
silly Kat Howard to climb into Henry's bed before she's *married* to him. Don't you see that?
What Norfolk wants is the *power*, Virginia, that
comes with having one of his family bear the
king a son. A *legitimate* son. What I want is
Sandrock Priory. What your brothers want is

knighthoods. What Henry needs right now is a mistress, and he takes mistresses from families like ours, not aristocrats like the Howards. See? God's truth, lass, do I have to spell it out for you *again*?' His breath ran out as his complexion reached the same brick-red as the walls.

'So if the king is not so interested in making Kat Howard his mistress, Father, I wonder why he goes across the river each night to visit her at Lambeth at the Norfolk residence before he returns to the queen?' Ginny could see by his face that this was news to him. 'You are not informed of *that* little detail?' she said. 'Well, if you remember, I told you and Mother that, from what I'd seen with my *innocent* eyes, the king's fancy is both unpredictable and unreliable. So perhaps you should not have built up your hopes too high.'

'I was relying on you, Virginia.'

'And I find your morals too confusing for me, Father. For a man who professes to be disgusted by other men's infidelities, like Jane Seymour's father, for instance, you now want to know why I haven't already been unfaithful to my husband. You must try to explain that to me one day. Preferably when Sir Jon is present. But you'll be pleased to know that my manners toward him have improved, of late.' She curtsied and skipped round him. 'Do excuse me. The queen waits.'

After that, she felt as if a load had shifted from her shoulders, even if her father had been wrong about one thing. The king *had* taken a member of the Norfolk clan as his mistress in the form of Mary Boleyn, sister of Anne, who was Norfolk's sister's girl and therefore as much his niece as Kat Howard, his late brother's orphan. Howard was the family name. It was a wonder, Ginny thought, how any outsider could fathom out who was related and who was not, with so much intermarriage and assorted stepparents. But Ginny was now aware, as she had not been before, that in his ambition for power, compared to her father, the steely Duke of Norfolk was like a warhorse to a Shetland pony. With the king's ear and as a member of the Privy Council, Norfolk had only to keep his niece dancing in front of Henry in a way that Sir Walter could not do with her. He had hoped Sir Jon would do that, but Sir Jon had not so far obliged, and her father had noticed how, as long as she stayed in the queen's company, the king would see less of her than he'd hoped.

Only moments later, it looked as if her brother Paul might have been drafted in to tackle the problem in his usual ham-fisted way.

'Where's my knighthood, then, Ginny?' he said, catching up with her farther along the gallery. 'The old man's getting a bit hot under the collar. Thinks he's going to miss out on Sandrock. So has Henry gone off the boil?'

'I'm sure he'll have *you* on his list of rewards, Paul,' Ginny said. 'Remind me again, what was the knighthood to be for? Services to…?'

'Oh, come on, Ginny. Don't be like that. You know what it's about.' He was like a child, as sure of a favour as he'd always been with their mother. Wearing the latest fashion in jewelled and plumed caps, he depended on his boyish humour as much as on his appearance, yet Ginny knew from Elion how deep he was in debt to his tailor and goldsmith, saddler and wine merchant, and how the allowance from his father was lost at cards each month. Now, however, she had learned a far more unsavoury report about him from Elion, which, although without proof, could not be discounted when he was in many other ways so irresponsible. She would rather not have believed it of him, but could not quite disbelieve it either.

'Is that what you said to the park keeper's young wife?' she said.

'What?' he said. 'What do you know about it?' A deep pink stole up his neck and reached his cheeks while his knuckle pushed at his nose, this way and that. Momentarily stuck for an explanation, he watched his sister walk away without another word, hardly noticing that he was being jostled by passing shoulders.

Judging by the wave of shrieks and yelps that greeted her, Ginny could tell at once that the queen was not in her room. Kat Howard and two other maids, however, were taking every advantage of the absence by wading almost knee-deep in a pile of royal finery that Ginny had ordered to be made and which, if the concerned face of the tailor was anything to go by, had not yet been approved. 'Mistress!' he was bleating. 'No, not that one, that's delicate… please!' Mistress Howard laughed at him, demanding that the laces be pulled tighter round her plump figure, careless of the stitched holes, the straining fabric and the hem that was being trodden on. He cast a pained glance at Ginny as she entered. 'My lady?' he said, waving a hand over the crumpled gowns. 'Could you…?'

After what she'd just heard, Ginny would have to use some diplomacy, for she might just be about to give a dressing-down to the future queen of England. 'Not quite your style, Mistress Howard, and by far too long,' she said,

removing the laces from the hands of the maid
who pulled. 'And the queen is on her way, so
the sooner you get out of this the better. Come
on, wriggle out! And you two, pick up these
dresses and fold them. Hurry up or you'll all
lose your jobs.'

Mistress Howard complied, but was unrepentant. 'They look better on me,' she pouted. 'I'm
more petite. His Grace calls me his—'

'Never mind what His Grace calls you,'
Ginny said briskly. 'As far as Queen Anna is
concerned, you're still her maid. Take my advice, mistress, and don't make too many assumptions.' *Cleverer women than you have
done that, to their cost,* she would like to have
said, thinking of Katherine's cousin.

'I do believe you're jealous, Lady Raemon,'
Mistress Howard said, making a grab for her
own gown. 'His Grace has not yet invited you
to his bed, has he? Isn't that what you're here
for, really?'

'And who can blame him, mistress?' Ginny
said, smiling at the pert face with a good nature
she did not feel. 'With you here, why would he
wish to see more of me? It's the queen I feel
concern for, not myself. She's the sweetest of
women.'

Picking up a gown from the floor, she had

not seen the astonishment on the maid's face, nor had she heard the door open, or the queen's quiet entry. Anna pretended not to have heard the last remark, but her smile at Ginny showed that she had and that she knew what had been happening only moments before by the relief on the face of the tailor and the hanging laces on the Howard girl's bodice.

If Ginny had been making her own assumptions about the king's interest in her, both she and Katherine Howard were proved wrong that same evening when he sought Ginny's company straight after supper, while the queen was deeply involved with a group of courtiers intent on teaching her the game of cent. Casting a scolding glance over the merriment where Anna had already been discovered cheating, Henry took Ginny to one side as if she were no more than a diversion. But Ginny found the king's polite interest in her background something of a comfort, for it filled a gap left by her husband, who had never shown any curiosity about her capabilities, her love of nature and skills in languages. Taking care not to tell Henry about the new library bought from Sandrock Priory, she was at least able to talk with him in Latin and French, which she suspected would not be

the case with Mistress Katherine Howard, for
all her winsome ways. He appeared to enjoy
it, although Ginny dreaded the conclusion that
might be a request that she should go and take
a glass of wine with him in his room at bedtime
to continue their discussion. The glass of wine
being, of course, a euphemism for something
else. She would not be able to avoid it and Sir
Jon would know of it, and the night with him
to which she had been looking forward would
not now happen. The thought of the king in his
place was almost unbearable.

She was saved again when the king noticed
the appearance of Mistress Howard with Culpeper, his two favourites, and Ginny's conversation with him came to an abrupt and timely
end as the king called them over. There was no
invitation that night. But though she waited for
Sir Jon until the early hours, he did not come,
and Ginny could only assume that he was en-
gaged in the king's duty until late. Either that,
or he had found some more enticing company
of his own.

Next morning, unable to hide her discontent,
she went to seek her sister Maeve, whose house
was conveniently near to the Royal Wardrobe
at Westminster where Sir George worked. For

Ginny, the longing to escape from the royal court had never been so strong as it was at that moment when she saw the domestic warmth of Maeve's house with its homely furnishings and the happy sound of children, the lingering baking smells and smiling servants. Bowls of primroses reflected yellow patches onto the polished tabletops and a tattered hobby horse leaned drunkenly into one corner, like the one she'd had as a child. When she told Maeve of her longing to be with Etta, Sir Jon's child, Maeve's reply was predictably sensible.

'You're not bound to the queen as the maids are,' she said. 'Take a few days off and go to Lea Magna. Sir Jon will not prevent you, surely?'

'He need not know,' Ginny said. 'He's going with Henry down to Greenwich for a few days to see some new ships. I could be there and back before they return.'

'Sir George will give you an escort. I'd come with you, but there's too much going on here at the moment. George is frantically busy.'

'No coronation robes to be dug out of the Wardrobe, then?'

'There won't be one for Anna, Ginny. She's not going to get that far.'

'You know that for certain?'

'They'd have started by now, if he intended to crown her. Come to think of it, poor little Jane Seymour didn't get that far either, did she?'

Chapter Seven

It was poor little Jane Seymour's sister-in-law with whom Ginny stayed overnight on the journey to Lea Magna, as she had done on previous occasions when the dark came too early to continue in safety. Elvetham Hall in Hampshire was a vast and impressive place owned by Sir Edward Seymour, Jane's elder brother, a statesman and one of the king's right-hand men, as ambitious as the rest of them. Having had a sister who reached the throne and produced a son before her untimely death, Sir Edward was in a position of influence that he took good care to exploit. Being uncle to a future king was no mean feat these days when the king was having trouble producing the required 'spare' heir.

His wife was not one whit less aware of her status than her husband. If anything, she was more so and strident about it. Not a popular woman with courtiers, she was far too outspoken and keen on her precedence above other more senior ladies, so she was glad to offer hospitality to a young neighbour on whom she could impress her superiority without fear of argument. Ginny knew better than to argue with one such as Anne Stanhope, Lady Seymour, aunt by marriage to Prince Edward. She was Sir Edward's second wife and he had been trained from the start to do as he was told. It was as well, for while she exceeded expectations in managerial affairs, his first lady had not lived up to expectations in other respects, and Lady Seymour was determined that no breath of scandal should taint the family while she was in charge.

The hospitable Lady Seymour, however, had been tainted by association with the earlier story affecting her husband and his family, even though it had had nothing to do with her personally, and it suited her to talk in wary and mistrustful terms about men in general rather than to appreciate the benefits, dropping hints about their perfidy as if she had been the one to be affected. It was not what Ginny needed to hear, when she herself was wavering between trust and doubt in her own new marriage. 'Men need careful watching, my dear,' she said to

Ginny as they sat together after a plain but generous supper. 'Sir Edward is meticulous in his affairs, but I have to remind him sometimes what is due to his family as the king's brother-in-law. One must keep up one's standards these days, when it is so easy for men to go astray. Even your dear father, for instance, had to be reminded of his duties once, I believe. But then, that was a long time ago, and now Lady Agnes has your sister and the boys, and yourself, of course, to keep an eye on him while she is at home. Such a good thing to—'

'I beg your pardon, my lady?' Ginny said, wondering if she had heard correctly. Lady Seymour reminded her of a slim black starling with the sheen of iridescent feathers and a sharp-eyed stare too direct for comfort. She was always to the point in any conversation, but this point had passed Ginny completely. Sir Walter had always been the first to condemn any kind of marital misbehaviour, including that of Sir Edward's late father, who had got two sons on his own daughter-in-law. The affair had been going on for years without anyone knowing, and the two young lads had been disowned by Sir Edward, his wife banished to a nunnery. It had been the scandal of the year at the time, though now the king had decided to let the matter rest, and to take the Seymours back into favour. He had chosen his third wife, Jane, from their family, which the second Lady Seymour had never let anyone forget. Now she pretended surprise at Ginny's ignorance. 'Surely you knew, dear? Oh, then perhaps I should say no more. 'Tis not my place after all. A long time ago, I believe. More punch before you go up? It's going to be another cold night.'

'Er…no, thank you. But tell me, if you please, what were the duties my father needed reminding of? He's usually the most dutiful of men.' She understood that Lady Seymour was eager to tell her something she did not need to know, some scandal that would show her own impossibly high standards in a better light. It was what she did so well.

'Oh, it was just a fling, I suppose, taken when your mother was carrying. It's what men do, my lady. It's what the king does as a matter of course.'

'A fling? You mean…a mistress? My *father*?'

'My dear, I would never have spoken if I'd thought for one *moment* that your dear mother had not confided in you. Now, the best thing to do is to ask her, isn't it? I was never one for speaking out of turn. It can do too much damage.'

Since damage seemed to be what Lady Anne Seymour thrived on, her refusal to go into details only added to Ginny's confusion, even after the more recent shocks of finding that her parents cared less about her moral behaviour than about their personal acquisitions. As for her father's infidelity, Ginny felt sick with shock, not only because he'd been unfaithful, but because he'd always made such a fuss about other men's lapses, except the king's. Who was she to believe these days when so many around her were self-seeking, hypocritical, and untrustworthy? She would not open old wounds by asking her mother, and Molly was not the one with whom to discuss such a private matter even if she had known about it, for Molly would not speak about Lady Agnes's affairs to her daughter, though she had been expected to report Ginny's affairs to her. But Maeve would know, almost certainly.

They left Elvetham Hall at first light, refusing the invitation to stay there again on the return journey on the pretext that she would be calling at D'Arvall Hall instead, now that the days were lengthening.

Her arrival at Lea Magna, though unexpected, was heart-warming and calming after

the disturbed night just past. With Molly to take
charge of the accommodation and her mistress's
creature comforts, Ginny's first call was on her
stepdaughter and a reception that made the tra-
vails of the previous day worth while. The child
was ecstatic, not only remembering Ginny's
name but eager to show her what else she had
learned in her absence, new words, using a
spoon and pusher, hiding from her nurse, the
names of some early flowers and birds, and
how to dress her puppet, if somewhat roughly.
Ginny spent most of her time with Etta in the
large garden where crocuses and daffodils were
pushing through the soil, where spiders hung
their dewy webs and ducks and swans came
to be fed on the lake. And Ginny felt both the
contentment and longing of having a child and
wanting one, too.

Breaking all her father's rules, Etta was
allowed to spend two whole days, dressed
warmly, in the spring sunshine, exploring every
part of the house both outside and in, with no
less than four guardians in attendance and her
bedtime rituals watched over until sleep came
with sweet exhaustion. Not once did the child
mention her father, and although Ginny introduced the name whenever she found the op-

portunity, there was no response other than a thumb tucked into the little triangular mouth.

But when Etta was asleep, Ginny and Molly took a candle to the upper room under the sloping roof that no one used, where a stack of old portraits leaned against one wall as if waiting to be hung. 'There's sure to be one somewhere,' Ginny said, 'because Master Holbein told me she sat for him soon after their marriage. He put her name and date on it, too, so we can't mistake it.'

'Are we looking for a fair-haired woman, do you suppose?' Molly said, placing the candle on a dusty table. 'Judging by Etta's, that would make sense.'

'I should have asked Master Holbein while I had the chance. But what interests me, Molly, is how no one seems able to say anything much about her except that she was wealthy and popular, and that she spent more time at court than she did here. I want to know how beautiful she was.' *And why my husband finds it so difficult to let her go.* 'I think I deserve to know more about the competition. Bring the candle up closer. There's one here that looks quite new. This is it, here's the name above. Lady Magdalen Raemon, AD 1537. So *this* is her, Molly. Look!'

'But this one is not fair haired, my lady. She's as dark as Sir Jon.'

'Is it the light? Let's move it out. Lift!'

They sat the heavy gilded frame on the table and placed the candle nearby, moving their heads from side to side to avoid the shine, to study the colours, the marvellous detail of reality, of texture and tone, as only Holbein could do. The face of a voluptuously lovely woman stared out over their shoulders, gowned in deep red shining silk and rich, golden, fur-edged sleeves, a small French hood perched at the back of her head showing the sheen of black hair swept from her forehead, stopped by the crescent-shaped biliment of pearls and diamonds, then the heavy fall of velvet over one shoulder and down the back, wealth showing in every facet. Black eyebrows curved like delicate bows over lustrous dark-brown eyes hinting of the excitement of being studied at length by a man. She was quite magnificent. Any man would have fallen in love with her for her beauty alone.

Ginny stared, then the truth stole upon her like a sudden storm cloud on a summer's day, wiping out every other explanation but one and chilling her heart with the sting of it. 'Put it away,' she whispered. 'I've seen enough.' Trembling with sudden realisation, she covered her face with her hands and stood there while Molly complied, then put a gentle hand on her shoulder.

'It might not mean what you think,' she said. 'There may be another explanation. Come now. Come away. You're tired and not thinking straight.'

Ginny could not speak. Molly was mistaken. She was thinking very straight. Dry-eyed and white with shock, she was glad then to have had Molly with her, a woman to whom she could speak in confidence about what she had just discovered, who would not try to pretend there had been nothing significant to see. A dark-haired beauty, as lovely as they'd said. Etta's mother. Etta, whose hair was as pale golden as the Princess Elizabeth's, with the true colouring of the Tudors. There was only one explanation. The king had used the first Lady Raemon in the same way he intended to use the second, the new wife of a man he could trust to oblige him in this most disgraceful royal habit. She had been willing to place some trust in Jon, at last, but how could she trust a man who owed his favour to this kind of betrayal? Poor little Etta. Was it any wonder Jon wanted so little to do with her? Another man's offspring.

In the comfort of her room, Molly wrapped a blanket round Ginny's shoulders as she sipped the hot posset that her maid had made for her, deciding what best to do, with or without Sir Jon's approval. 'He won't like it,' she said, 'but I'm going to take Etta to London. She will live with us there. We'll find extra rooms for her and her nurses at Whitehall, or we'll open up the house that Sir Jon has at Westminster and live there. If my sister Maeve can do it, so can I. Etta needs me and she needs her father, too. He cannot keep her hidden away like this as if she was not a part of his world. And I need her too, Molly. She's our family. She should be with us.'

'My lady, it's going to create the most enormous problems, isn't it?'

'No bigger than those that already exist, Molly. We'll find ways round them.'

'Is it worth Sir Jon's anger, my lady?'

'What can he do? He'll not take her back without me and I think I'd rather be with Etta than with him, if this is the kind of thing he's capable of.'

Molly did not need to ask what she meant by 'that kind of thing' when it was obvious that her mistress now disbelieved in her husband's protection from Henry's attention. He had allowed

it to happen to one wife and he had agreed to
let it happen to her. Or that was how it seemed.

*I am no more eager than any other man to
be cuckolded, even by the king,* he had told
Ginny, *nor do I particularly want my wife to
be his whore.* And she had believed him, agreeing against her will to put some kind of trust in
him. What was she supposed to believe, now
that she'd seen with her own eyes what he had
not the courage to tell her himself? Well, then,
she would take the child where he could see her
oftener than he wished, to remind him of the
perfidy that Lady Seymour had warned her of.
She would make him be more open about the
child's true parentage and count Etta as one of
the rewards the king had already bestowed, and
try to make amends, somehow, for the time he
had lost with her. Etta, short for Henrietta. Sir
Jon had probably chosen the name himself, but
as to whether he had grieved for the beautiful
wife who had never truly belonged to him, well,
that was still impossible for Ginny to know.
Had she, like herself, been coerced into a terrible situation and died as a result of it?

They stayed overnight at Hampton Court
Palace on the return journey before going on
to Maeve's spacious town house. This was not

a development either Maeve or her husband, George, had expected but, true to form, they understood why Ginny had brought the child with her, for they had known all along of the relationship between Etta's mother and the king, as well as Sir Jon's reasons for keeping the child at Lea Magna. To proclaim her identity in London would be to show the world how he had shared his wife, without disclosing the reasons. If Sir Jon chose not to tell Ginny what they were, then how could her sister and brother-in-law interfere in what was not their business? George, however, had reservations about the scheme, and he was not averse to saying so, after Ginny's departure. 'I know what I'd say if my wife took my child away from its home without my permission,' he said, pulling the willowy Maeve towards him.

'Whatever it was,' she whispered, 'I'd be able to handle you.'

'After a good beating?' he said, lapping at her lips.

'Before or after. No matter.' Their smile tangled into the kiss.

The arrangement, however, offered no problems to Maeve and her bevy of nurses who cared for the young Betterton family. Edwin was Etta's age; Aphra was two years older and as level-headed as her parents. In many respects, this was exactly what little Etta needed, though Ginny had not said exactly what had prompted this sudden decision, except that she needed the child with her, nor was there time to discuss with her sister the disturbing matter at which Lady Seymour had hinted. Ginny preferred not to talk about the portrait of Magdalen Osborn either, and her own mistrust of Sir Jon that had deepened so rapidly, for she knew she might have wept in the telling. The arrangement was only to be a temporary one, for as soon as Sir Jon opened up his grand house situated by the river only a few minutes' walk from where Etta was staying, they would settle in there as a family at last. In theory.

Enquiries at the palace of Whitehall revealed that the king and his entourage had returned from Greenwich at midday, though the first person she met there was not Sir Jon, but her brother Elion, with a look of a very proud man on his charming face. He hardly needed to be asked. 'A knighthood,' he said, modestly turning away from the groom who led Ginny's mare to the stables. 'Yes, for me.'

So the rewards had begun. Was she now at greater risk, or less?

'I'm so happy for you, dear one,' she said,

kissing his cheek. 'Sir Elion D'Arvall. Sounds good. And Father? Did he…?'

Elion's eyes twinkled, and she knew the answer. 'Sandrock,' he said. 'He's being allowed to buy it at a good price. It's his for the asking. He's as proud as a peacock.'

Ginny smiled at the analogy, but now the news that should have pleased her for Father Spenney and Ben's sakes had a sour taste. 'And Paul?' she said.

'No, not this time. Cromwell thinks Paul will have to wait a while longer.'

'Cromwell? What does he have to do with it?'

'Don't be naive, Ginny. He has everything to do with it. He's the one who suggests who is to be promoted and which properties they'll be given. His lists are as long as my arm, lass. And he's at the top of it. He's been made Earl of Essex.'

Ginny didn't mind being called naive, but felt she would not be the only one to show astonishment at this sudden rise into the high aristocracy by a commoner, even one with the talents of Sir Thomas Cromwell. 'Earl of…? But I thought he was in disgrace over the latest marriage problems. Isn't he?'

'Apparently not, love. Rewards are usually for services given. They don't grow on trees, you know. That's why Paul doesn't qualify. Well, not in Cromwell's book anyway. Father qualifies for his services to the household department.'

'But I thought it was for...well, you know.'

'That's what he wants you to think,' Elion said, pulling her arm through his as they walked towards the steps. 'But he was in line for this well before the king saw you. I suppose he thought it might come quicker if he had a daughter in the king's bed, but he hasn't, has he? Not yet. Or am I wrong?'

'No,' she said, watching their feet on the stone stairway, climbing...climbing. 'You're not wrong. And now it looks as if I might get away without having to, doesn't it, while Kat Howard is keeping him occupied?'

'She's not in his bed, Ginny. Be on your guard. You know what he's like.'

Yes, she knew what he was like by now, and the thought made her shudder.

Elion's warning came not a moment too soon when the king's page brought her a message requesting her presence in the king's room that same night, after which Ginny could only assume that Mistress Howard was indisposed. Frantic with worry, she tried to find her husband to discuss with him what to do, with no great hopes of cooperation after her recent findings, but to no avail. Sir Jon was not to be found, nor had he come to see her since her return, so there had been no chance to tell him about Etta. Elion, she recalled, had not asked where she'd been either, and her father would be overjoyed rather than helpful. Molly was the one to offer her the benefit of some well-tried practical assistance.

'Valerian root and hops,' she said prosaically, 'with a few other things. It always works. With that dreadful wound on his leg hurting him, he won't need any persuading to drink deeply before he tries anything. Now, you just keep talking about his favourite things and keep his goblet topped up, and slip this powder into it as soon as you can. It dissolves quickly. And it won't taste of anything in the wine. He'll be asleep before you know it, then you can go and tell Thomas Culpeper with a smile to get him into bed. Now, let me take a look at you. Yes, it's your hair he'll want to see. They always do, don't they?'

Ginny had not wanted to smile, but Molly's motherly concern, as well as her apparent knowledge of lusty men, brought a gurgle of nervous laughter to the surface. She wore a nightgown of soft white lawn with embroidery round the neck under a robe of fur-lined brown velvet, her long white-gold hair making a cape around her shoulders, its paleness almost equalled by Ginny's pallor. 'I never thought it would come to this, Molly,' she said, trembling.

'It won't,' said Molly. 'You'll be back here inside the hour.'

'I thought Sir Jon might have come to see me, after his return.'

Molly embraced her lovingly, holding her close, like a mother. 'There'll be a very good reason,' she whispered. 'I know your feelings are all over the place, my lady, but there are some times when you'll have to give him the benefit of the doubt. There's usually an explanation for most things.'

'It's the explanations I'm afraid of,' said Ginny ruefully.

But it was not the valerian and hops, with a few other things, that prevented Ginny from fulfilling the king's hopes that evening, for her long march through the corridors of Whitehall behind the royal page was intercepted by the one she had, in her thoughts at least, been maligning since leaving his home at Lea Magna. She recognised his lone silhouette and hurried stride from some distance away and felt her anger and disappointment in him waver before she remembered the reasons for it.

His single glance at his wife switched to the page, who hesitated. 'Go back to the king,' Sir Jon told him. 'Lady Raemon won't be needed.'

'But, sir,' the man said, 'His Grace will—'

'No, he won't. His Grace is asleep. He's been put to bed. Go.'

The page hurried off, leaving Ginny speechless with surprise and relief. With a sob, she covered her face with her hands and stood shaking like an aspen leaf as his arms went round her, holding her tight against his body. 'You didn't come,' she cried into the front of his doublet. 'I couldn't find you. This isn't a hoax, is it, like last time?' The hard strength of his arms was almost too sweet to bear, after the past few hours.

'It's no hoax,' he said. 'He's out like a light. Even that short journey tires him.'

'But why…?'

'Shh! I'll tell you later. Come on, let's get out of this draughty passage. Shall I carry you?'

'No, I can walk. Just.'

Since yesterday, her thoughts on what she might say to him had been dark and vitriolic, and probably wounding, too. To them both.

Now it was only his presence she cared about more than the why and the wherefore. Whatever else had been put to the test, her trust in him, his motives, his past, were now less important than being here with him and the knowledge that he had appeared at the last moment like a knight in shining armour to keep her from the king. He wanted her for himself. Surely that was why he'd come for her.

Molly had not expected to see her mistress quite so soon and could not refrain from an astonished, 'My, that was quick!' Hastily, she took her leave, though not too fast to see the tears of joy running down her mistress's cheeks and the hungry look in Sir Jon's eyes as the candlelight set a metallic sheen upon his wife's hair.

Despair, disappointment, and bitterness had raged so strongly through Ginny since their last meeting that she could never have believed how contrary her body could be and how easily it could turn against her thoughts, making her do what she'd sworn in her heart not to do willingly, ever again. Nor would she have believed how fast the turnabout could be from anger and humiliation to a desire as fierce as his. Mindless with a hunger that had seethed and been ignored for days, she cradled his head in her arms for the taste of his face in the shadowy

chamber, exploring him with her lips as if to
see and hear him was not enough after so long
a starving. Wet with tears, her face was mopped
by his fingers and the broad mouth that laughed
with audacity and relief. 'Mine,' he whispered.
'Mine tonight, my lady. Did you think I'd let
you go to him?'

His words washed over her, needing no answer. It mattered nothing what she'd thought,
for that would have spoiled their moment of re-
union, which, in different circumstances, might
have been bitter indeed. Besides, she could
scarcely remember what her thoughts had been,
for her fur mantle was now a pool around her
feet and she was being lifted and swung round
to the bed that Molly had been preparing. His
hands were comforting, as though they knew
what other caresses her body might have en-
dured, and though Ginny sensed his eagerness,
she delighted in his skill that brought every surface to life at her pace, for her enjoyment, for
the comfort she had not thought to find else-
where that night.

He had littered the floor with his clothes before she even noticed that he was as naked as
she. Then he took her slowly through every lesson she had learned with him, and some others that were new, making up time spent apart

when both had wanted only each other's comfort and the intimate acquaintance of bodies
that had been rushed into a marriage for all
the wrong reasons. There were still matters to
be resolved, but in this unexpected coupling,
they knew to put everything else aside, to give
unstintingly, and to take whatever was offered
without question.

Intending to make it last as long as possible, he explored the silken folds of her body
with careful hands, smoothing and stroking
over every surface, feeling the responses that
told him of her desires, the sighs of ecstasy, the
moans that rose up from the deepest awareness
of her needs. She trembled and gasped as his
mouth teased and touched her breasts, reminding her in some faraway place of her childless-
ness, her longing to suckle, to mother and to
bear his child. Etta had sat before her on the
saddle for most of the way, asleep and nestling
into her body at times, fuelling the wordless
longings to be fruitful that now tugged at her
womb as his lips tugged at her nipples, causing her to cry out with each surge of pleasure.
'Now, Jon... Now, please...now!' she moaned,
opening herself to him like a flower.

He had waited so long to hear it, his name
spoken in desire from the one he had never

thought to possess during all the tribulations of the past years. This beautiful creature, this angry, resentful, haughty woman who had almost escaped capture until fate had finally shown him the way. She had not liked it. He was not sure she liked it yet, but this was one way she would follow him willingly. So now he took what she was offering with all the generosity of a careful lover, gently overpowering her with his hard, muscular physique over which her hands played to complete the mental picture of him through her fingertips. Her deep sighs spurred him on to play every variation on that one theme and, when he held himself above her, she became once more aware of the change of pace, deeper and faster, like a sudden storm. Now, for the first time, Ginny discovered the final element that had escaped her on previous occasions, the all-consuming wave of bliss that held her breath deep in her lungs, surging through her body like a tide before releasing it on a long sweep of languor. That part of him she held inside her continued to pulse softly, its energy dissipating along with hers, dissolving all those bitter thoughts she had brought from Lea Magna and leaving her awash with the kind of fulfilment that, before this, had stayed just beyond her reach. Whatever he had done in the past, nothing could now convince her that he had wanted it, and, lying close in his arms, she thought briefly of what she had to tell him that would wait until tomorrow and of how she would do it so as not to cloud all the bright loving they had just shared. But she was asleep before reaching any conclusion, and it was only in the early hours, when she turned in his arms, that the plan began to take shape.

'Was he really exhausted?' she asked him as they dressed. 'Greenwich is not so very far, is it?'

His grin was boyish and heartbreakingly handsome. 'No, my sweet, it isn't, but he had a little help, one might say.' His head was bent as he tied his breeches. 'A little liquid help.'

'You got him *drunk*, when you knew he'd sent for me?'

'No. But his leg was painful after that ride and I thought he'd be better off asleep than with my wife. So I gave him a double dose of the stuff his physician left for him, for his pain. No harm done. Much better for him to leave a man's work to a man, eh?' Tucking in his shirt, he looked at her with a smile that melted her knees.

'That was dangerous,' she whispered. 'That was *very* risky.'

He came to where she was standing in front of the mirror, putting his arms around her waist, his lips to her neck. 'Yes,' he murmured. 'It was. And that's what I shall do to keep you to myself, my lady.'

'I'm glad you did, Jon, but *please* be careful. Don't let anyone see you do it.'

'They won't. But now I have to go. He'll expect me to be there.'

'Will you return when he's up and about? I have something to show you.'

'Something nice?' he said, caressing her arms. 'Pink and soft, is it?'

'Yes. I brought your daughter from Lea Magna. Yesterday.'

The hands hesitated and dropped away as he stood back apace, his reflection in the mirror suddenly clouded by disbelief. 'You've *what*?' he said. 'You've...?'

Ginny turned to face him, sure she could manage his surprise. But it was more than surprise she saw in his face. 'Yes. While you were away. I went to see Etta and I've brought her back here. I want you to see her, Jon. We could...'

In her eagerness, she had not thought that he

would place any other construction on her act than the one she had intended, which was to bring them all together. But now his attention turned towards the rumpled bed where they had spent the night in each other's arms, his expression not of surprise, but of dawning realisation. 'So,' he said, 'we seem to be covering the same ground, my lady, do we not? A night of sweetness in return for—'

'*No!*' Ginny cried. 'No...no! That's not so! How can you believe that, after what we've just shared? How *can* you?' She took fistfuls of his doublet to shake him, her voice rising in despair. She could see now how it must have looked.

'Then what *am* I to believe, woman?' he snapped. 'You go off to Lea Magna without telling me, without permission, and bring back the child when you know full well I do not want her to be here, of all places? You spend a night of passion with me and then you present me with this? Not a request, even, but already done. Well, you can take her straight back, Ginny. I won't have her here at court.'

What am I to believe? How many more times must they say that to each other?

'Listen to me, Jon. She's *not* at court. She's at my sister's house. We can live together, all three of us, in your house at Westminster. Isn't it time, now? *Please?*'

'No, it isn't. And you should not have involved Sir George and Lady Betterton in this escapade without my knowing of it, either. That puts us all in an intolerable position, aiding one partner against the other. She goes straight back. *Today.*'

He would have turned away, but Ginny caught at his arm and pulled him back to her, determined to make him discuss the matter reasonably. 'I know,' she said, wrapping herself round him so that he could not escape, her head tucked beneath his chin. 'You're quite right. It was wrong of me to go without permission and to bring her back without asking. But I went on the spur of the moment, not waiting for your absence, and I had no intention at the time of removing Etta, nor did I ask Maeve and George beforehand. They knew nothing of it until yesterday. But I could not leave her there, dearest one. I could not.' Her voice became husky with emotion as the mothering ache filled her breast again and he felt her tremble against him. 'I could not. She needs me—both of us—and I need her, too. She's with Maeve's children and you should have seen her with them. She's never seen others like herself before. It was magical. She ought to have brothers and sisters. We should make some for her. Could we not make some, Jon? You and I? And live as Maeve and George do, partly in Westminster and partly at Lea Magna? Their children don't come to court.'

'I'm not giving in, Ginny. You are disobedient.'

'Yes, I know,' she croaked as tears dripped off her chin.

'She will have to return. Your duties with the queen will demand all your time.'

'But will you come with me this morning and see her? Will you, Jon? For my sake? Before we take her back?'

He took her arms and eased her away from him. 'Expect me later on when His Majesty is in council. Does the queen not expect you?' He spoke curtly.

'Not until after noon. And you'll come with me?'

'I'll come, but don't think I shall change my mind. I shall not.'

'My loving was not about wanting to change your mind, Jon. It was because I wanted you. I think I have always wanted you.' She looked down at her hands as she spoke, not trusting herself to accept what she might see in his eyes.

She felt his fingers beneath her chin, lifting her head for him to study, showing her his dark, liquid irises that intentionally gave her no clue about his response, only the anger that had been there before. She stood, trying to control the trembling in her legs as he closed the door quietly behind him. In the night, she had not seen it happen quite like that.

They rode to Maeve's house in Westminster, although it was only very close to the palace of Whitehall, taking with them a wagon for Etta's things to be returned to Lea Magna. Sir Jon, still determined not to give way by as much as an inch, cast a cool but appreciative eye over the soft green gown that Ginny wore, with its hanging sleeves of white fur. Over her hair, she wore a close-fitting bonnet of matching white fur that tied under her chin, and short boots of green kid on her feet, and she knew the outfit suited her well. She had no real hopes of persuading Sir Jon from his plan, but wondered if Maeve would help, somehow.

As it was, Sir George was there, too, in the large welcoming stone-built house so different from the sumptuous halls of Whitehall, and their arrival was welcomed by childish shouts from little Edwin, holding a small Etta by the

hand, and from Aphra, who followed like a
mother hen with her chicks. Behind them, Sir
George and Lady Betterton held out hands of
greeting to their visitors, whom they had half
expected. Smiling, they noted without comment
the sparks of anger in Sir Jon's eyes as well as
the uncertainty in Ginny's, and knew that diplomacy would be called for, if matters were to
be resolved to their liking.

Sir Jon was apologetic. 'Forgive this invasion,' he said, grasping Sir George by the arm.
Doffing his cap to Maeve, he apologised again
before Ginny could speak, and she knew he
was more concerned that it would look as if he
was not master in his own house than that they
had come unannounced. His new wife, he told
them, had made decisions about his child without consultation. It was a mistake. Etta would
have to return to Lea Magna.

Etta, smiling broadly, was being held by each
hand, obviously the centre of attention, adored
by everyone for her striking good looks and
sunny nature, her curiosity and her speech,
which was not as advanced as it might have
been if she'd had the company of others. With
arms up, she rushed to meet Ginny to be lifted
and cuddled, and carried in to the large parlour
where the aroma of new bread wafted across

beams of sunshine. A large biscuit was shoved into her hands and from there into her mouth without a second look except at her father, who came in for some serious study by two nut-brown eyes.

Ale was poured and handed out, courtesies observed, apologies discounted. 'She's a beautiful child, Jon,' said Sir George. 'She's pert, too. Bright as a button. Do you not think she needs more than the company of her nurses? Would you not think of having her near you, now you have Ginny?'

Sir Jon did not answer directly. 'Are they allowed the run of the house?' he said, watching the young things chase after a hound puppy. 'Do they not get lost?'

George laughed. 'Did you, when you were a mite? 'Course not. They have their nurses with them. I can't imagine what life would be like without our two. Why not let her stay, Jon, and live with you and Ginny in the house down the road? Better than poky apartments at the palace, surely?'

'You know why not, George.' The reply was soft, but delivered with a sharpness that escaped none of them. 'I prefer to keep her at Lea Magna. And we both have duties to perform.'

'So does George, Sir Jon, but little ones need

a mother,' said Maeve gently, 'and Etta now has one. Can you still justify keeping them apart when they both need each other? Didn't you say you needed a stepmother for her? Well…'

Sir Jon stood abruptly, walking away from the argument he couldn't face.

Behind his back, Etta wriggled furiously on Ginny's lap, demanding to be put down with a squirm and a slither of skirts. Dropping the biscuit, she walked on sturdy legs over to where her father stood by the window, looking out across the shining river and, because she could reach no higher, grabbed him around one leg, her head just reaching his knee. 'Papa!' she said softly. 'Papa. Mine!'

The room became still and silent, waiting to see what Sir Jon would do. He looked across at Ginny. 'She's never said that before, has she?' Then he bent and picked his daughter up with large hands that spanned her middle, holding her to him, face-to-face at last, brown eyes regarding, assessing, reading the thoughts behind. She sat on his arm comfortably, touching his nose with one tender finger. 'Wha?' she said to him.

'Nose,' he said.

'Nose?'

'Yes, nose. That's right. Where's *your* nose?'

She thought, then touched her nose. 'Nose.'

'Good. Now mouth. Where is mouth?'

Her fingertips touched his face. 'Papa mouth,' she said. 'Mine.'

He smiled at the confusion. 'No, mine.'

Etta was not at all confused. 'No...*mine!*' she insisted. Then, flinging one little arm round his neck, she laid her chin on his shoulder with her fluffy, bright, copper hair next to his black jaw-line beard and stuck a thumb into her mouth, half-closing her eyes in contentment.

For a moment, Sir Jon's nose and mouth rested beside the downy head, and to some it might have looked as if he was quietly amused, though Ginny thought otherwise. Whatever the reason for this sudden emotion, it was quickly controlled before it overtook him, and just as suddenly he was himself again, commanding and wanting to be seen as the one to make decisions on domestic policy without persuasion. 'I could open up the house, I suppose,' he said. 'We both need more privacy and the space to spread out. We might even do some entertaining. Perhaps we'd better go and take a look, Ginny. Do I get a biscuit, too?'

It was Sir George who brought him one. 'You deserve more than a biscuit, Lord Raemon of

Risinglea,' he said. 'Congratulations. We should be having wine.'

Ginny caught her husband's quick guilty glance in her direction and she knew he would have told her had it not been for the argument over Etta that morning. 'I shall be embroidering coronets all over his shirts,' she said. 'And I shall expect a bit of bowing and scraping from my family, too, if you wouldn't mind.'

The smiles she received from Lord Raemon of Risinglea and his small daughter were conspiratorial and heartwarming.

Chapter Eight

Wd

While Lord Raemon's Westminster house was being prepared, it was decided that Etta would remain with Maeve and George, and to all intents and purposes, it looked as if that episode was over and Etta's future decided. The news of Sir Jon's new title, however, could not be allowed to slip away without comment, especially after the earlier misunderstanding when Ginny's motives had been doubted. 'Is this where I get to talk of rewards, my lord?' she said on the way to Tyburn House. 'You will forgive me if I do a little blaming of my own, I hope, but I think our scores are equal now, are they not?'

'You might think so, my lady,' said his lordship. 'But apparently it was the new Earl of Essex who put my name forwards to be rewarded with a title for services to His Most Gracious Majesty. Not for any domestic reasons.'

'Services? You mean in Cromwell's department? Cyphering?'

'Decoding cyphers, yes. You knew.'

'Of course. I assumed that…well…'

'Naturally. Now, can we close that chapter and move on? We have a house to look at, and arrangements to make. And a child to install, with all her belongings.'

'Yes, husband,' she said demurely. 'Thank you. As you say, we should move on.' Though ambiguous, the wish was genuine. Yet there were still matters unresolved between them and sensitive facts to be revealed that would slow down the pace unless she could discover more about the inexplicable resistance she had just witnessed regarding Etta's move to London. Obviously he did not particularly want the king to see her, but could this be because Jon's experience as a cuckolded husband was so very painful, when he had loved his beautiful wife? Was the shame of it still lingering, the reminders of it so terrible? And was that why he had decided not to share her, Ginny, with the king after all? Because he had lost his beloved first wife that way? Bearing the king's child? What other explanation could there be?

It was only a short distance to Tyburn House farther upriver from Westminster, kept open by a small staff for Jon's occasional use, though it was large enough to accommodate a growing family. Imposing, red roofed, part stone and part timber, it stood on the banks of the River Thames with gardens sloping down to the wooden retaining wall at the water's edge and a mass of smaller buildings built round a courtyard with an orchard beyond. 'I would rather be living here than at Whitehall,' Ginny said as they passed through the gatehouse an hour later. 'Didn't you think I might like to set up my household here, with a proper staff?'

'Not until recently. No,' said Lord Jon. 'I thought your duties with the queen would keep you at Whitehall for most of the time.'

'And with the king?' she said.

'That was always a possibility. Now I think there might be more advantages in living here than I'd thought, even if you'd not brought Etta to London. We'll see.'

'I shall enjoy setting up her nursery, my lord. Large enough for more than one, do you think?' She peeped sideways at him through her lashes. 'You're not...?'

'No, not yet. But we should not discount the possibility, should we?'

'Your lady mother managed four, so I see no reason why you should not do the same. It runs in families.'

'And is that one of the reasons why you agreed to marry me?'

'It was a consideration, I suppose, but not the deciding factor.'

'And am I allowed to ask what the deciding factor was? Clearly the new title was earned for reasons other than marriage to me, so if not for stepmother duties and as a breeder, what else is there? You were never short of bedmates, I believe.'

'You've been listening to the wrong people again, Lady Raemon. If you want to know more about why I married you, then you may have to wait a while longer.'

'Until…?'

'Until you've learned to trust me better,' he said, looking straight ahead.

She thought he might have said more, but a squealing pig ran across in front of them, followed by a yapping terrier and its owner, making the horses swerve dangerously and back into each other, and the thread of their fragile discussion was lost in quieting the mounts and resuming their short progress to Whitehall. The talk of trusting him, however, stirred some pangs of guilt, for she had not thought it was so obvious. It also did not explain why a man with a talent for encrypting cyphers and codes should be so obtuse when it came to explaining to his wife what was on his mind and finding out what was on hers.

The following weeks were filled with comings and goings to their new home, with the hiring of servants, and filling the rooms with homely things, with beautiful wares from Cheap Street and the merchants' warehouses clustering around the wharves. Her husband gave her permission to buy whatever they needed and, with Maeve to guide her, the experience was typically exhilarating and rewarding. Afterwards, when she had spent time with the children, Ginny would return to Whitehall to be with the queen, who, increasingly abandoned by her royal husband, was still optimistic of a happier outcome. Why else, she asked, would Sir Thomas Cromwell have been created Earl of Essex if not because he had found the king a loving wife? Sadly, it did not occur to her that it might be because Cromwell had suggested to the king a legal way to dispose of his loving wife and to take to his bed a woman who made him feel younger. Lord Raemon hinted at this to Ginny, but swore her to secrecy without realising that the knowledge made her even more uncertain of her own future. Would the king need her more during the lengthy negotiations? Or less? And what would happen to her dear friend Anna?

Although Ginny could sympathise, her own situation was being blessed by having daily access to little Etta, who soaked up the attention like a plant in sunshine. Not only that, but the relationship between the child and her father began to thrive in a way that no one could have foreseen only a few weeks ago as they watched the boats on the river, visited the horses and the litter of puppies in the stables. Taking each change of location in her stride, Etta seemed to revel in her new surroundings, the daily contact with her stepcousins teaching her new words and skills.

About her father's 'little fling' mentioned so ruthlessly by Lady Seymour, Ginny could find no evidence, for Maeve knew nothing. That she and George knew about Etta being Henry's child, however, was apparent, for as Hampshire neighbours of Sir Jon and Lady Raemon, they had seen that a copper-haired child was hardly likely to be the product of two dark-haired parents, though ginger-haired throwbacks were known now and then. They had not been surprised, but that was all Maeve would say, and Ginny stopped asking for more. When she confided that she had feelings of guilt about wanting a man she could not fully trust, and that neither of them had ever spoken of love, she was advised not to be concerned, to wait, be patient, and to let it grow naturally out of what had been a traumatic situation, none of her doing. And if she thought her sister's happy marriage to Sir George was typical, then she was mistaken. It was not. It was quite exceptional.

From Tyburn House, Ginny had seen the lights of the royal barge as it crossed the river to Lambeth under cover of darkness and knew that Anna would not see Henry again until the next day, if then. If she had been the queen, Ginny told her husband, she would have sighed with relief rather than with longing.

'And now?' he said, bending over her on one elbow. 'Tell me about these coded sighs. What do they mean? What, for instance, does this one say?' His hand drew from her a deep gasp of delight as it slid between her thighs into the warmth, caressing the soft folds contained there with the tenderest of fingertips, like a harpist.

'I don't know,' she whispered. 'Can you not decode it, my lord?'

'Give me time and I think I might,' he said, exploring further.

'Don't take too long.' She sighed.

'One should not hurry these things,' he said, purposely tantalising and teasing her body while stopping her protests with kisses too deeply satisfying to interrupt. There was, as it happened, no code that he did not know how to interpret, and soon her cries became sweet moans as she forgot the problems of the past few days and the trust that was not quite there. There, under him, claiming every moment of his attention, Ginny stopped thinking, stopped wondering and worrying, giving herself entirely to his pleasure and hers, for him to take into his heart and remember as her gift, not as a bribe. One day, she knew he would be convinced of her love, just as she would be able to trust him completely.

So she revelled in the closeness of his magnificent body, in the power of his hard, muscular arms as he lifted her closer to him, in the great shoulders and strong neck, the short black hair that capped his head, shaping it like a helmet. She recalled how she had watched him during her first month at court, wondering about him, about the women he pleasured and danced with, but rarely with her. Now she was where so many of them had hoped to be, receiving his kisses and attentions, learning how to please him after the misunderstandings that still lay so close to the surface. There would be times, she was sure, when she would need all her reserves of patience to help him through those days when his work with Cromwell weighed him down, for life in royal circles took a heavy toll.

As the May Day festivities drew closer, Lord Raemon spent his days practising at the rings in the new tilt yard at Whitehall, perfecting his jousting skills for the tournament. Whenever he was free from the king's duties, he would return to the house by the river with more bruises and contusions to be salved, more aches to be massaged, and with a hunger for victory that men possessed before a contest. Their infrequent nights together often dwindled into sleep too soon for loving, which Ginny accepted as part of the build-up that conserved her husband's energy in some way, and though he spoke laughingly of the friendly rivalry between him and his friends, she suspected that there was more to it in the case of Thomas Culpeper, whose admirers were mostly female.

A masque was being planned on the same evening as the jousting, for which Ginny was helping to design costumes for herself and seven maids. Unfortunately, Mistress Howard

was often absent in the evenings when she could
have been helping and, told that her costume
was to represent desire, took offence, stamp-
ing her feet in annoyance. 'I am *not* desire!'
she scolded. 'And I do not wear that dreadful
mulberry colour, either. I shall have virtue. The
green one. It goes better with my hair.'

'That's Ginny's,' said Anne Basset. 'It's been
made to fit her figure, not yours.'

'Then have it altered,' said the Howard girl.
'Where's the headdress?'

The masks, like the costumes, were elaborate affairs made of stiffened canvas painted
and stuck with sequins, completely covering
the face and rising high above the heads of the
wearers, the floating streamers partly disguis-
ing the hair and leaving only the figure to give
any clue about identity. Yet even the figure was
partly concealed by the rich ornament, and the
swathes of flimsy fabric were intended to both
conceal and reveal tantalising glimpses of body,
all young, and recognisable only to intimates.
Ginny had made sure that hers conformed to
her own personal requirements, nothing too revealing, while that she had designed for Kat
Howard was rather more exposed, the bodice
lower, the rippling mulberry tissue transpar-
ently violet and gold. The colour would have

been perfect for Kat's auburn hair, which would be seen later and, given the girl's boldness, Ginny had assumed she would like the style, too. But now her choice had backfired and it looked as if Ginny herself would have to wear it, leaving the pale green 'Virtue' to the Howard girl and the blue to Anne Basset and 'Gentleness'. They both said, when she'd gone, that she was behaving as if she were queen, with her demanding ways. Much more so than Anna.

On May Day, the whole court flocked in their finery to the purpose-built Whitehall tilt yard to sit cheek by jowl in the stands overlooking the sand-covered lists. Superb specimens of manhood would ride against their opponents wearing specially made jousting armour, one against one, while their horses were identified by gaudy caparisons that billowed like sails in the wind, the colours competing with those of the heralds in scarlet and gold, green, and white. Ginny had had very little time to wish Lord Jon anything more lengthy than good fortune in his contest that morning. He was good, she knew that, but so were the others. She had given him her favour, her best red silk scarf to tie round his arm with a prayer that he would emerge unscathed as well as victorious, and he had hurried off with his grooms, still briefing them on the details of how to pass him his next lance, where to stand to make the horse turn properly, to check every buckle and strap, how to decipher his instructions through the heavy metal helm with its narrow slit.

Ginny felt sick. She had seen the practice bruises, the reddened skin. She wished men would not do this, as Henry had not since his terrifying accident four years ago, but this was all for shows of bravery in front of the women who sat on the stands as deeply caring as she was, but better at hiding it. It served also as a useful tool for settling old scores, to reinforce the pecking order, and to establish the respect of one's peers. And Ginny had no doubts about her husband's target on this occasion. There was no choice, unless you were the king, about who would fight against whom, so it was fortunate for Lord Jon Raemon that he was drawn against Master Thomas Culpeper, who needed to learn his place as never before.

Seated near the royals in an open window of the gallery overlooking the tilt yard, Ginny had a perfect view of the proceedings, so was able to see how Kat Howard laid her green favour on the tip of Culpeper's lance while the king and his queen looked on, laughing at the harmless, chivalric fun between friends. Anna wore her newest gown of ivory silk threaded with gold that shimmered in the bright sunshine. Ginny, wearing tawny velvet and brocade to complement her creamy skin, blew her husband a kiss, wondering with dread how she would live if he were killed in this pointless fashion. Or any fashion.

Used to the limited view through the narrow slit in his helm, Jon knew to within an inch what to aim for, how to position the heavy lance and lock it under his arm, to lower the point at exactly the right moment and angle it across the four-foot-high barrier towards the target that came thundering towards him. It was time for Culpeper to be knocked off his high horse, but that, he was sure, was what *he* had in mind, too. Jon was under no illusions about Culpeper's skills.

The first shuddering crash was taken upon the small shield on Jon's left arm, and he heard the crack as his opponent's lance splintered, wrenching his shoulder. His own lance had done the same, and now he tossed the broken haft to his squire and received from him another as his horse pranced and reared from the shock. The noise inside his helm grew fainter as the crowd settled back to watch the next charge, and he could see Culpeper at the far end making his turn, the flash of green on his arm fluttering as he saluted towards the stands. So his mind was not on the job. What a conceited fool the man was.

The end of the contest came only after six lances had been broken, the last one hard enough to lift Culpeper out of his high saddle and fling him backwards as his horse fell, screaming with fright, landing in a tangle of flying legs and a cloud of dust. It had taken every last ounce of Jon's considerable strength to bring down both horse and rider, and now, as he galloped past, he rose in his stirrups to salute his waving wife with the broken haft of his lance. His body was numbed by the constant buffeting, but through the roar of blood in his ears, he heard the blare of the herald's trumpet and knew that, up in the stands, she would be weeping for him.

She came to his tent and he knew he'd been right about the weeping, for her smile blinked dewdrops from her lashes. Rubbing water from his head with a towel, his squire stopped to let him speak. 'Well, lass?' he said. 'Have I your favour at last? Will that pay him back for his nasty tricks, d'ye think?' Her red scarf had been used as a temporary bandage around his shoulder and he hoped she would not notice the dark patches, still wet.

'Oh, my Jon,' she said, half crying still, 'you were magnificent.' She placed her lips carefully on his grazed cheek that was already turning into a swollen bruise. 'But you are hurt. You *must* have been hurt by that. Let me…'

'No,' he said, catching her hand. 'The chirurgeon is here. It's nothing. He'll fix it. You must return to the stand.'

'You've sent for the chirurgeon? You *are* wounded. Do let me see it.'

His head swam and her voice came from far away. 'I'd rather you didn't,' he said weakly. His squire caught him as he swayed, laying him down like a child. 'Bring water,' somebody said, before he lost consciousness.

Determined not to allow Culpeper to know how bad the injury was to his shoulder, Jon would not be persuaded to let someone else take his place in the masque that night. His victory in the lists would be hollow indeed if he showed how much the effort had cost him, and Culpeper would gloat in spite of his defeat. Pride was at stake here and Jon felt it keenly. Consequently, in the rooms he and Ginny had recently vacated at Whitehall, he allowed himself to be strapped up tightly to staunch the flow of blood, then to be dressed in padded white satin with silver linings, in braids of gold, with dyed plumes in his extravagant cap. He was one of eight of the king's men, all similarly rigged out, meant to rescue and partner the female masked virtues after the mock-siege. Days ago, Ginny had told him that she would be wearing green as Virtue itself, a name he had promised to divest her of before the night was out.

'If you catch me, my lord,' Ginny had said.

'Oh, I shall catch you, my lady.'

Now his shoulder throbbed like a drum and, instead of food, he had relied on half a jug of wine to keep him upright until suppertime. Even from this distance, he could hear the musicians' pipes and the thud of tabors coming from the great hall, and he steeled himself for what was to come.

The lofty hall heaved with colour, with glitter, the rise and fall of laughter, the clatter of dishes, the aroma of spiced food, and the pungent smell of warm overdressed bodies. Still in her tawny velvet, Ginny was relieved to see Jon enter behind the king and she moved along the bench so that he could sit with her, smiling her concern. 'My lord,' she whispered. 'Are you recovered now? Is your wound paining you?'

'I'm perfectly well, my lady, I thank you. The wound is nothing.' He cast an eye admiringly over her, taking his place proudly by her side. 'You look ravishing. Don't let Henry see you.'

'He doesn't see anyone these days except the Howard girl. I'm quite safe now.'

'None of us is safe around Henry,' he whispered. 'Take care in the masque.'

'What…?' But her query was snatched away in the general conversation that allowed no topic to continue for long, and by the time the last course had been served, Ginny had quite forgotten to tell him that, in the masque, he must look for the woman in mulberry, not green. It was only when she began to don her costume that she remembered, but by then it was too late.

Jon saw her at once as she and the other maidens climbed up into the mock castle, ready for the siege to begin with the throwing of sweetmeats and flowers from the white-clad attackers and shouts to surrender. Screams of encouragement and laughter accompanied the nonsense as maidens were hit, yelling defiance and refusing to budge, the maid in the green gown, which Jon knew to be his wife, doing more than her fair share to attract the support of the onlookers. Dancing lights from the hundreds of candles created shadows that cavorted amongst the brilliant colours and jewels, deluding and confusing those who watched, and yet in the medley of disguises and the press of flimsily clad bodies, Jon's attention was drawn to the maid in the mulberry gauze whose gown was so diaphanous as to be almost transparent, low-cut over her bosom, barely covering the luscious curves of her beautiful body. No wonder, Jon thought, that Culpeper and Henry were both besotted with her if this was what she looked like underneath, though he had not thought the Howard girl to be so slender.

At last, breathless with shouting, the Virtues surrendered and came down, still disguised, to be claimed by the knights in white. Ginny made sure Jon was close enough to find her, but was dismayed when she saw him grab the arm of the girl in green and lead her into the dance. Then, before she could resist, her own arm was taken in a firm grip and she, too, was taken into a partnership she had no wish for. 'Master Culpeper,' she said, 'you have the wrong maiden, I fear. You must have meant to...'

'I am not mistaken, Mistress Desire,' he said, smiling benignly. 'I wish to dance with the one whose charms I can see most of. Do I not deserve that, at least, after my poor showing in the lists? You'd not deny me a closer look, surely, while we dance?'

Ginny was in no position to deny anything as the music drew them into the set where, lifting her hands and arms higher than was called for, Culpeper was able to gaze at everything the gauzy fabric revealed through its mulberry tissues where the skin beneath turned it to a sultry shade of pink, and the low, beaded neckline slipped ever farther down over a figure slenderer than Kat Howard's. She was quite sure he knew who she was just as, by now, Jon would have recognised his partner.

Mortified by the mistake, she would have moved away quickly at the end of the dance to where Jon was bowing over the hand of the green maiden, but again her arm was taken and, because her vision was restricted by the headdress, it was not until she almost bumped into the gross bulk of King Henry that she realised what was happening. Culpeper had done this on purpose, thrusting her into the king's arms before she could escape, knowing how quickly the royal lust could be redirected.

'Your Grace, 'tis time for the maidens to unmask,' a loud voice called over the top of the din. 'And as one of this afternoon's victors, I claim the hand of the one known as Desire.

Which one is she? Come, lady, you are mine for the rest of the evening.'

Relief flooded over Ginny. 'I'm here, my lord, but would you not be gallant and exchange *me* for the lady with *you*?' she said. 'That would be courtesy to His Majesty.' As she spoke, she lifted her mask and slid it over her shining hair while Jon untangled the prickly sequins, his expression resolute rather than kindly. Kat Howard was quick to slide into her place with a ravishing smile, but Culpeper was not pleased to see his plan misfire. Turning away from the sight of the king with his girl, he buffeted Jon on the shoulder with a fist that ordinarily would have had no effect.

'Well played, *my lord*,' he said with a wide smile that did not reach his eyes. 'In a winning mood today, are we not?' Sweeping a glance at Ginny's beautiful figure, he turned away with the words, 'I thought you'd be well used to giving up your woman to His Grace by now. Worth a try, though.'

Jon paled visibly, grabbing at Culpeper's arm to bring him round. 'Quite mistaken, Tom,' he said quietly. 'One never quite gets used to that, but it looks as if *you* might have to try. Come to me for advice.'

Culpeper heard the sound of truth and could

find no ready answer. Instead, he looked down
at Jon's hand on his arm until it was slowly removed. Ginny tugged at Jon's elbow to break
the hostilities. 'Come away, my lord. Come, we
need not stay.'

Jon collected himself. 'We must. We cannot
leave before the king,' he said.

But Ginny had seen the patch of bright red
seeping through his white doublet, as big as a
rose. 'You need attention,' she whispered. 'I
shall send a message. His Grace will understand.'

With willing hands to assist them, Ginny
and Jon were escorted back to Tyburn House
where, with the help of Jon's squire and Mistress Molly, they discarded the blood-soaked
costume and bandages, then washed and
tended him to the ungrateful accompaniment
of grumbles and protests. But by his unusual
pallor, Ginny saw that there was indeed some
urgency to treat both his wound and his exhaustion seriously and, taking charge of the
situation, decided that neither of them would attend the other festivities planned for that week.
Had they but known it, that day was the last
on which Henry and Anna were seen together
as man and wife. Nevertheless, Ginny had no
fears for her husband's recovery, for he was a

strong and healthy individual who for the past few months had been under the same kind of mental pressure that she had experienced, and still did, to come to terms with a new partner chosen by the king with all the implications and restrictions this imposed. Surely there were few marriages, even arranged ones, where so many barriers had been erected against their mutual happiness by a selfish man who liked to have more than one woman at his disposal. Added to this was the grief of losing the mother of his child, who must have been well used by Henry, according to the snide remark made by Culpeper. That Jon had been willing to go through this all over again with her was something of a mystery, especially now when she could no longer doubt that he was actually refusing to give the king access to her. Several times he had proved this, despite having bargained with Henry beforehand. Yet Henry had agreed to Jon's new title, as he had to her father's grant of property and Elion's knighthood, which she had been assured was for services to the crown, not specifically as rewards of a more personal nature. This was not what her father had led her to believe when his persuasions had been so brutal. So what was the truth, exactly? Would she ever discover it?

* * *

For the rest of that week in a reversal of roles, Ginny was closer to being in control than at any time since February, when she had felt that life was running away with her. She had assumed Jon would not have the energy to make love to her with the pain of a shoulder wound, but she had not realised the depth of his desire. Sitting in a garden filled with spring sunshine and nothing else to concern him but the waste of time, as he saw it, he watched her comings and goings and saw how much she relished the management of the house and its occupants. After a few days of this, he discovered that her determination to draw them together as a family had given him a sense of belonging and a purpose he'd been lacking except to defy the king in this one thing. This was something he'd not experienced before, and he found it suited him well to play games with Etta, to tell her stories, and to watch her daily progress.

At night, when the house was still, Ginny would climb quietly into bed so as not to disturb him, protesting only mildly when he reached out for her to snuggle into his side. 'Your shoulder...' she whispered. 'Don't make it bleed again.'

'It's almost healed, sweet lass,' he said. 'It's the rest of me that needs attention.'

She did not pretend not to know, for he had caressed her thigh when she stood close to him in the garden, thinking that no one would see. 'I cannot have my patients lacking attention,' she said, smoothing her palms over his chest. 'Will this do?'

'No. I can see I shall have to be more explicit.' Even with one shoulder strapped up, he was still able to spin out his loving into aeons of time and to bring cries of rapture to her lips, each caress bringing with it new delights of experience she had thought could not be bettered. His days of jousting practice had deprived him of this greatest of his pleasures, so now he shared his pent-up energies with Ginny, who had not deserved to wait, or to be grieved by this unnecessary injury. She was a remarkable lover, quick to learn and responsive to every touch, imaginative and exciting in her teasing ways that drove him wild with passion, urging him on to heights he'd never reached with any other woman. He would like to have whispered the words of love she deserved, too, but he knew that to do so would provoke a string of questions he was not yet prepared to answer. A declaration of his love would demand openness and trust and explanations too strange to make sense, and there would be a better time than this.

But at times like this, Ginny's mind dwelled in other places where sensation, not explanation, was everything, where the closeness of his well-toned body transported her into a world of heady pleasures that were in many ways still new to her. She could never have done this with any other man. It was only his hands she wanted on her breasts, tenderly moving the swelling nipples under his fingers, raking them into hard buds ripe for his mouth, cupping the fullness of each one to make her gasp with desire and melt her womb. It was only his mouth she wanted on hers, tasting her before unleashing a new surge of energy, barely under control, goading her to give still more of herself with abandon, to fight him, then to surrender. And it was only Jon she could have allowed to possess her in the way she had tried to dream of before their marriage, and failed. That had been nothing like this, for she had not known of the overpowering thrill of holding him inside her, pulsing, throbbing and alive, taking ownership with each move, deeper than desire.

And it was with a growing certainty that she knew no other man could have taken her to such a blaze of passion where something inside her scattered into fragments and made her cry out and cling to him while trying to hold the moment before it was lost to them. Then, she felt that nothing else mattered except that she loved him and wanted to be everything to him the way she imagined his first wife had been, so that he would grieve for her, too, if she were to go away. No other man could have made her feel like that. How she had hated him for his rejection and how she loved him now for accepting her, however controversial the reasons.

As the month of May wore on and the king's involvement with his queen became less, his passion for Katherine Howard grew daily until it became obvious to everyone at court that something would have to be resolved, one way or another. The only person not to see this was Anna herself, whose good nature always found an excuse for other's failings, even the Howard girl's frequent absences from duty. Ginny could not pretend to be unaffected by this development when she was rarely seen by the king. In her case, too, out of sight meant out of mind. It was to her advantage.

Her father, having received what he wanted

most, dropped his belligerent manner towards her and became almost pleasant, hardly noticing his daughter's coolness and lack of interest in his new property. Eventually, Ben and Father Spenney would return to their own home and she would see even less of them than before, but she lost no sleep over that. Only Paul was disgruntled, having been overlooked for any reward, and she had not needed Elion's warning to beware of him as a troublemaker. A letter from her mother had said how excited she was to be the mistress of Sandrock at last, and how she intended to restore it to a fabulous mansion on par with any of the king's palaces. Which she had not seen. No mention was made of Ginny's failure to reach the king's bed, but that could hardly matter now, nor did it appear to matter whether she had found happiness. So the only ones to notice any change in Ginny were her husband, Maeve and George, Elion, her brother, and Molly, who knew that the spells she had planted in the garden at D'Arvall Hall had had some effect. Sharing her time between her own home and that of her adopted cousins, little Etta had never been happier.

Eventually, Jon returned to duties with the king and spent less time at home, and it began to look as if he and Ginny had reached some kind of understanding that would have to rely on her patience and his timing. It was not the best of foundations on which to base an arranged marriage, but until the king's marital affairs were sorted out and they were both released from their obligations once and for all, Jon believed, quite wrongly as it happened, that there would be enough emotional crises to deal with from the royals in the near future, without adding to them in any way.

With simmering heat by day and fiery skies every sunset, May moved into June without a sign of rain, though there were fears of plague and talk of crops failing dismally, village ponds beginning to stagnate and more than usual vagabonds turning up at the gates of Whitehall Palace for daily handouts of food. It was as if London waited for something dramatic to happen. By June 24, everyone had heard the incredible news of the arrest of the Earl of Essex, the man who had risen from plain Thomas Cromwell to be the king's chief advisor. Jon had hurried round to tell Ginny while she was still in the queen's apartments, his face pale and shocked by the suddenness of the arrest and the brutality of it. But with the royal infatuation for the Duke of Norfolk's niece, the duke's influence with the king was on the rise again, and he had been waiting for this moment to pounce upon Cromwell with some ridiculous charge of treason. Jon's position as one of his assistants was now uncertain, and perhaps dangerous, for he, too, had been given a title very recently, like his employer. Who was safe these days?

'But, Jon,' said Ginny, 'you cannot think you'd be in any danger, surely? If you do, then you must not return. You have a family to think of.'

'So has Cromwell. And he relies on his staff at such times to keep the office going and to do what has to be done. Someone else will be given his job and I'm supposed to be there to help. I must go back.' Jon's tone was terse and uncompromising. His duty was to both masters and he could not be seen to fail either of them.

'So what happens to me and Etta if you're arrested?'

'Nothing, Ginny. Nothing will happen to you. Go home and stay with Etta.'

'Jon, be careful. I thought you'd have stayed with us, too. For safety.'

But he was already halfway through the door and all she heard was the sound of his

hard boots on the floorboards growing fainter.
Holding back the angry tears in her eyes, she
slammed the door after him. He had not even
remembered a last kiss.

Chapter Nine

Two shocks in one day might have seemed excessive, even in those troubled times, but the news of Cromwell's arrest did not require immediate action, whereas that delivered to Queen Anna did. Her face, usually so composed, reflected hurt and bewilderment as she stared at the royal messenger. 'What…now?' she said. 'Today?'

'For your health, Your Grace. Immediately. The king fears the plague, as you know. He believes you'll be safer at Richmond.' The page had the grace to look shamefaced. 'It's very pleasant at Richmond,' he said. 'More peaceful than here. And it's only eight miles away.'

'So what's all this about, do you think?' she said to Ginny when the page had gone. 'If His Grace is so afeared of the plague, then why is he not going to this…Reeshmond…too? He's sending me away, isn't he? Will he be sending the Howard girl there, too?'

Her line of questioning suggested to Ginny that she had more than an inkling of what was happening and that this might be only the beginning of something that could affect the woman for the rest of her life. Ginny hoped that whatever it was, it would not humiliate Anna any more than she had been, and that her usual good sense and composure would sustain her through the days ahead. It was inconceivable that Ginny should desert the queen at this time when her star was on the wane, when not only had she been told to remove herself from Whitehall, but reduce her household from one hundred and twenty-six to fifteen. If that wasn't the beginning of the end, then what was?

Obedient to the letter, Queen Anna packed her belongings and left her servants to continue the process over the next few days in a fleet of barges that would be rowed upriver to the palace of Richmond, the beautiful waterside residence that neither Anna nor Ginny had ever visited. Leaving Etta with her nurses had been the hardest thing, but Maeve was close by and Jon not far away, and she herself within easy reach. Her real fears were for Jon, whose loyalty to the disgraced Earl of Essex, now in the

Tower, conflicted with his loyalty to the king, whose wrath, it seemed, could fall on friend and foe alike at the drop of a hat. The earl had been Henry's closest and most loyal advisor, only recently rewarded with a title. One could be excused, Ginny thought, for thinking that the king had turned into a monster. Jon's hasty and abrupt departure appeared to reflect her anxiety about his own future, for he knew more than most about the king's strenuous efforts to uncouple himself from an unpleasant situation, added to the fact that Henry was willing to sacrifice his most devoted subjects on any pretext that suited him.

Richmond Palace stood like a fairy-tale castle on the edge of the Thames where the queen's heavily laden barge reached it through a water gate leading to the stairs and a system of elegant chambers and courtyards. Leaning her head towards Ginny as the barge moored, Anna said brightly, 'I think I might like to live here. This is my kind of place. Did you see those domes and flags, and the gardens?'

They had been silent as the barge approached, but Ginny had noted with some amusement how Anna's eyes widened at the sight of the many towers with domes of burnished gold, each with its own chattering weathervane. Set within walled gardens and orchards with green hills beyond, the high walls reminded Ginny of her white openwork embroidery that made row upon row of windows. The neglected opulence of the halls within led them to the queen's own privy chambers overlooking the river, and Ginny felt that Anna would eventually find both peace and pleasure in such a magnificent setting. Confidentially, Anna had told of her fears that she might be sent home to Cleves to face her brother's fury and the disgrace of rejection. But in answer to Anna's earlier query about young Kat Howard, the girl's absence indicated that they had probably seen the last of her, although, even then, Anna's charity forbade her from making harsh judgements. 'She's very young' was all she would say, as if to excuse her rudeness.

The problem of Anna's future was solved sooner than any of them could have anticipated when a deputation from the king, including the Archbishop of Canterbury, arrived the next day to speak in private with the queen. Closeted with four men for the best part of an hour, Anna emerged white-faced and desolate. Her voice, usually so firm, shook with the effort of control. 'I am no longer to be His Grace's wife,' she whispered, sitting down heavily on a clothes chest in her room. 'I am to be annulled, Ginny. Already they have decided it in your House of Common, ten days ago. Why...*why* could he not have told me himself? I am not married. Never have been.'

Like sisters, they moved towards each other to place arms around shoulders to still the trembling. 'I'm so sorry,' Ginny said. 'So sorry. Did they tell you what's to happen next? He's not sending you back to Cleves, is he?'

'No, His Grace is kind,' she said, contradicting what Ginny thought. 'He gives me a generous allowance. More than enough. He allows me to keep all I have and this palace to live in, and another at Hever, and one somewhere else, I cannot remember. He wishes to call me his sister, Ginny.' The sweet, sad face suddenly broke into a sobbing laugh as the ludicrous request shaped their lips. 'His sister?' they said in chorus. 'His *sister*?'

Anna's acceptance of the king's propositions, especially after the humiliations of the past months, was humbling to Ginny, who would have protested violently. It was not only Anna's phlegmatic nature she envied, however, but her dignity and intelligence, too; her wit and prag-

matism that had turned the whole ugly episode
into a bargain whereby she remained in possession of all she owned, and more, in return for
her compliance. She was to be allowed complete
freedom, with precedence over all the ladies
of England after the queen and the king's own
daughters as long as she did not embarrass him
by making a fuss, as his previous wives would
certainly have done. That was what Henry was
most anxious to avoid. And although Ginny
could not know for certain, she suspected that,
once the shock had abated, Anna would secretly
be relieved to be free of him and his monstrous
ego. How different, she thought, from her own
situation in which she had learned to acknowledge her love for the man *she* had been told
to marry and how broken-hearted she would
have been if he had sent her away, like Henry
with Anna.

Over the week that followed, while Ginny
heard nothing from Jon, Henry sent his councillors back again to Anna to make sure she
understood what was involved, insisting on
signed letters of agreement to him and one to
her brother, the Duke of Cleves, spelling out
his generosity in no uncertain terms. To everything they asked, Anna wisely agreed, car-

ing only that she was to be allowed to remain in England. It was no great surprise to them to hear that the Earl of Essex, the man who had risen to great heights as Thomas Cromwell, had been executed and that Henry had married silly young Kat Howard on the very same day. Henry's crass insensitivity was almost unbelievable.

Lord Jon Raemon rode to Richmond after the terrible event, giving away in every line of his body and in the sadly drawn face how deeply the shock had hurt him. Cromwell, he said, had always been good to him, but with enemies like the Duke of Norfolk, the Howard girl's uncle, his power over the king could not be allowed to continue. The Howards were on the rise again and Cromwell had had to go.

'Can you stay awhile?' Ginny said. 'You look as if you need some rest.'

'Henry is away with his new wife,' he said, 'but I have to return to my lord's office to help go through his belongings and papers. I promised him I would, before the Howard rats get at them. I can stay a night, perhaps, but no more.'

'Have you seen anything of Etta?'

'I called in yesterday. She'd been to your sister's all day. Sir George tells me that Paul visited them in a bit of a stew.'

'My brother? I'm surprised he even knows where they live. What has he done this time?'

They walked in the garden beside the palace where gardeners had been set to work on the plots, littering the paths with tools, clippings, and wheelbarrows. Others had been set to repaint the heraldic beasts on top of striped poles at each corner. 'Nothing, yet,' Jon said. 'He's concerned that Tom Culpeper is trying to involve him in his affair with Kat Howard. He's discovered just how dangerous it could be. This latest execution has scared everyone. If Henry can do it to Cromwell, who'll be next? And if Culpeper is caught getting too close to Henry's newest toy, he'll bring his pals down with him, unless they get out of the way before it happens.'

Ginny waited until they had passed the nearest gardener before answering, 'How is Culpeper involving him, exactly? Lying for him, you mean?'

'Giving him notes for her. Messages. Trinkets. Culpeper will use anybody, and he'll have no qualms about using Paul.'

'So what does he think Maeve and George can do about it?'

'Shelter him. He's asked to be allowed to stay with them where Culpeper can't reach him. They think he's beginning to come to his senses, at last.'

'Hah! When *he's* in danger. *I'm* not convinced and I wouldn't want Paul anywhere near Etta. He's not to be trusted. I know him better than you do.'

'Don't be foolish, Ginny. How can he harm her when she's never alone? She's not at Maeve's house every day.'

Jon's tone surprised her. He had never sided with Paul before. 'But the next thing we know,' she said, 'he'll be at our house, too. Heaven's above, have you forgotten how irresponsible he is?'

'Of course he won't! How can you think so, when your sister is willing to help him out of a corner? Have you so little faith in him? Are you not willing to shelter your own family when they need it?'

'Shelter him my *foot*!' Ginny retorted. 'All he has to do is to refuse Culpeper's requests. Stand up to him. He could always go home to D'Arvall Hall.'

Jon stopped as they reached the arbour where the tunnel of trelliswork supported rosebuds on the point of opening. Ginny could see by the haggard lines on his face how much the past few days had upset him. He had been at the execution of his friend, the man who had recommended him for promotion. The horrific events had taken their toll of him and now, when he had come to find comfort, she had provoked an argument about something and nothing. His expression was far from lover-like. 'I think I can be trusted to know what's best to do, while you stay out of danger with the queen,' he snapped. 'I had not thought you to be so unhelpful to your own kith and kin, my lady. If you're like this with your brother, then heaven help the rest of us.'

'I only...' Ginny began, realising the danger too late.

'Do excuse me. I have to get back.'

'My lord...don't go...*please*! You said you could stay...'

But Jon was already striding along the gravel pathway through the stone arch into the courtyard and, before she could catch him, the clatter of his horse's hooves was echoing through the gatehouse. A hot lump rose in her throat, burning, making her gasp with pain. He had ridden eight miles to see her, hoping to find some kind of normality in a world that had turned upside down, and she had failed him miserably. How could she have been so clumsy?

* * *

That night, she wept herself to sleep, longing for his arms, exaggerating the damage she had done, berating herself for not putting his needs first and wondering what she could do to make amends. The light of the new day was no more than a faint wash of colour that brought with it the first song of the blackbird. The door of her chamber opened very slowly. 'Molly?' she said, sitting up with a start.

'No. Me,' the familiar deep voice said. He closed the door without a sound, shedding his clothes and dropping them to the floor, and Ginny caught the aroma from his heated body, the familiar smell of leather and horse that told her he had ridden hard to reach her. He had returned. He wanted her still. Even through a quarrel, he needed her.

Stifling her cry of joy, she held out her arms, drawing him to her side, still drowsy and limp with tears. 'Oh, my love, you came back to me. Rest…there…in my…' But although he had ridden back to Richmond, it was not to rest that he'd come, but for the loving he had forfeited for no very good reason except to make someone, her, suffer for his pain. Even now, he could show her little of the tenderness she had been used to expect. He had not come for tenderness.

For the next hour or so, while the household began to stir into life, the distress he had been forced to contain under the guise of efficiency was released in a storm of passion he doubted would be understood, lacking any kind of explanation. It was not only Cromwell's death that had disturbed him, but also the insecurity of his own position and the newest arrangements that had removed Ginny from him, which everyone knew had nothing to do with avoidance of the plague. Pulling her warm, pliant body close to him, he smothered her invitation with kisses over her face and breasts that left her with no breath for pleasantries or teasing, and with nothing to do but act as a vehicle for his pent-up emotions. Only in this way could he blot out the memory of the barbarous events of the past few days.

There had been time, since his last abrupt leave-taking, for Ginny to realise what was the cause of his unusual black mood. The king could cut a swathe through anyone's life without losing any sleep over it, but it was those closest to him who bore the brunt of his brutal decisions, those with feelings not dulled by constant adulation. They were the ones, like discarded unloved wives, councillors, daughters, and loyal servants who suffered most. Like

Jon, who was having to pick up the pieces of Henry's petty revenge.

So, making what she could of her husband's darker side, Ginny gave herself unreservedly without taking anything in return except the satisfaction of knowing him better than she had before. When he took her quickly, she made no complaint, sensing his urgency to spend himself in the oblivion of her body. His first climax came with a ferocity she had not experienced before, but that was not to be the end of it, for the next time was long, self-indulgent and beautiful in its purpose, which was for nothing more than comfort and the mind-numbing rhythms of desire. She could not deny him what he needed so badly, having ridden to be with her when he could easily have made use of any of the willing courtiers at Whitehall.

At last, exhausted and sated, he fell asleep in her arms with her hand smoothing his brow, her lips touching his face like the wings of a butterfly, her satisfaction of a different order from the usual, her body tired and aching. He was still soundly asleep when Ginny washed herself down and dressed, giving Molly the task of folding his clothes ready for when he awoke. But when they returned from taking breakfast with the Lady Anna, as she was now to be known, Jon had gone, leaving no sign that he had been there except the rumpled sheets on the bed. Again, Ginny felt the sad emptiness of his too-hasty departure, though now she understood more about the patience and acceptance of married women. Lurking like a spectre at the back of her mind were questions concerning the first Lady Raemon and how she would have dealt with the crisis, whether she would have known not to cross him at such a time, whether she would have placated him with sweet words and sympathy for his distress, whether she would have abandoned Anna in favour of the husband who needed her more. Until he chose to tell her, she would have to make her own assumptions.

Weeks passed, taking them through the burning days of August when the wells started to dry up for lack of rain and fears of approaching plague were in everyone's mind. The Princess Mary, now a young woman of beauty, and her younger sister, Elizabeth, came to stay with the Lady Anna at Richmond where they found that her kind of fun was very much to their taste and, in the long hot days, they almost lived out of doors in the gardens and on the river. Master Holbein came regularly to be with the Lady

Anna and Ginny felt that she herself would not be much missed if she went to visit her step-daughter.

At Tyburn House, where the grass was parched to a straw colour, she found her brother Paul and sister Maeve romping with the children, which provoked an angry reaction in Ginny after the first welcomes were over. Carrying little Etta in her arms, she followed Maeve into the cool hall where she voiced her concerns. 'What are you thinking of?' she scolded her sister. 'Letting *him* loose with the little ones. My lord must have told you how I feel about Paul being here.'

'He did, love,' said Maeve, pouring out beakers of ale. 'But he also said he had no objection if George and I were convinced he means what he says about reforming. That seemed to us quite genuine, Ginny, and he's been wonderful with the children. They adore him.'

Out in the orchard, Ginny had seen how they held his hands and clung to his legs, and listened to him as he showed them the spirals of a snail shell. They had chased him on their hobby-horses as he darted away like a hare, then allowed himself to be caught. She did not want to be persuaded. 'Yes…well, two swallows don't make a summer, Maeve,' she said, holding her beaker out of range of Etta's hands. 'You don't know what he's capable of, as I do.'

'Ginny…stop it! Sit down and listen to me for a minute. I do know what you're referring to.'

'How do you know?' Ginny said, lowering Etta to the floor. She sat, wiping her forehead with the back of her hand. 'This heat!'

'I know,' Maeve said, 'because Paul talked to me and George about it, and about you seeming to believe that he was as guilty as the others. He's upset that you should think so.'

'Hah! Upset? So how d'ye think the park keeper's wife felt, Maeve? He was there. He didn't deny it.'

'He *was* there, but he swears he tried to stop it, but he couldn't. They killed the other man who tried to help her, and they're all older than Paul. They swore him to secrecy, but news of it got to Henry and he dismissed it as a game men play. Paul was *not* one of the offenders.'

'You believe that?'

'Yes, I do. So does George. He may be immature and irresponsible, Ginny, but he's never been vicious. And what's more, he's concerned that you should think so ill of him that you could believe it without giving him the chance to explain. He would have told you more, but you walked away, didn't you?'

'He blushed like a girl, Maeve. I took that as guilt.'

'Because you wanted to believe it.'

'Because of the nasty trick he played before, at home. And the remarks.'

'Which he regrets. He's trying to make amends.'

'By ingratiating himself with you and George. And with Jon, too, through Etta.'

'Well, then, you might remember this, love,' said Maeve, coming to sit beside her. 'We're all reasonably worldly. George is not easily duped and neither is your Jon. They've both known Paul for some time and they've always thought that if Culpeper had not drawn him into his set, he'd not have run so wild and tried to keep up. Paul has always listened to George, and he's very aware of how others have gained good positions, like Jon, for instance, while Father would never recommend *him* for anything. Jon has told George that he thinks it's time somebody gave Paul a break and that it ought to come from family first. I think your Jon would have given quite a lot to have a family to support him and a father he could have relied on for help. You and we are the only ones Paul can turn to, Ginny, and I'm well able to judge for myself when an apology for bad behaviour is genuine. Father has given Paul a hard time over the years for some reason best known to himself, as if Paul could never please him. Which is probably why our mother tried to adjust the balance by appearing to spoil him. That's what mothers do. I'm not at all surprised that Paul fell in with the wrong crowd. They were the only crowd that would have him, when Father wouldn't employ him as he had Elion. So George has taken him on at the Wardrobe.'

'Was that wise?'

'George thinks so. He's already proved his worth in getting the best deals from the mercers in town. He knows more than you'd think about fabrics and what's going to be fashionable.'

Feeling exhausted by the heat after the ride from Richmond, Ginny let the matter drop, but kept a close eye on Paul until he left with Maeve. She didn't want to think the worst of her brother, nor did she have any grounds for pursuing her fears in the face of their belief in him. Perhaps they were right. Perhaps Paul, too, had been made to feel insecure and threatened by Henry's volatile tendencies, by his father's early disapproval, and by Culpeper's unfair demands on his loyalty. Perhaps he *was* seeing sense at last, and perhaps Jon was displaying more understanding than she, after Paul's immature pranks.

* * *

It was the beginning of September when Lord Jon Raemon came home to his wife and daughter at Tyburn House, when Ginny's determination not to go and seek him out was beginning to falter. She regretted her obstinacy as soon as he came through the door, silhouetted against the red evening sky that set the satin river on fire, his great frame almost filling the space. She sensed the change in him, too, when he did not return her cry of greeting but held her in his arms as if more for support than welcome. She saw how his hair covered his head like a thick layer of silk that slid through his fingers as he raked it back wearily. That was how it had been when they'd first met at Sandrock when she was sixteen. Now he was not so arrogant.

'What are *you* doing here?' he said, unsmiling.

'I live here,' Ginny replied.

'Oh? I thought you lived at Richmond.'

She could have countered that with a similar remark, but held her tongue. He was here and that was all that mattered, not personal scores or accusations. 'How long can you stay, my lord? Come, sit… Let me take off your boots. You look weary.'

'Thank you. I am. But I shall not be staying

more than a night. I'm going to Lea Magna for a while.' He sat on a stool, sticking out his feet, too weary to lift them up, his attempts at an explanation foundering.

From his dull, brief replies, Ginny could tell that he was exhausted and in no mood to supply her with the information she would have liked. But more than exhaustion was a deeper reason, she suspected, for this uncharacteristic surliness that threatened to spoil the warmth that had once begun to flourish between them. Something like despair seeped through Ginny's veins and washed around her heart, constricting her throat at the thought of never holding him, never having his love, never discovering how to be more to him than his first wife had been. 'Yes, stay overnight,' she said. 'The king has released you from duty?'

He nodded. 'And my lord of Ess…Cromwell,' he whispered. 'I've finished there, too. It's all done.'

The sickly smell of hot unwashed feet nearly turned her stomach as she placed the boots to one side. 'Good,' she said. 'Now I shall send for a bath to be prepared up in your room and clean clothes, and then you shall eat. Then some sleep, I think.'

She caught his look of desire before his eyelids drooped. 'There is something else I need before sleep,' he said, 'which any dutiful wife would have thought of, my lady. Is that on your list, too, I wonder?'

'My lord,' Ginny said, trying to ignore the pettishness, 'what you have in mind is not on my list of duties any more than preparing your bath is. Nor has it ever been. I thought you had understood that.'

Jon sighed and looked away, dropping his head between his shoulders. 'Forgive me, lass,' he said to the floor between his feet. 'I am not myself. This business has...'

'Hush, my lord. There will be time to talk after you've rested.'

She went to him as he bathed, and it was then that she saw how the wound he'd received at the joust had opened up again, how inflamed around the edges and obviously causing him great pain. This, his tiredness, and his distress needed instant attention, and she knew of the best people to give it. So in spite of his intention to make love to his wife after the long abstinence, sleep overcame him well before she climbed into the big curtained bed and lay on top of the coverlet, where the air from the river could cool her skin. Early tomorrow, she would pack her own and Etta's clothes and go with Jon

to Lea Magna, and she would send a messenger
to Father Spenney at D'Arvall Hall. There was
no one who knew more about the treatment of
wounds than he, for as well as being the prior,
he had also been the apothecary at Sandrock.
Before she fell asleep, she decided to send a letter to Lady Anna at Richmond asking for an ex-
tended absence. She could not allow Jon to go
on his own when they had already been apart
for far too long. The effects of their enforced
separation were becoming all too evident.

The protests came, but not prolonged enough
to make any difference, and perhaps it was
Ginny's reminder of the encroaching plague
that finally won him over. They would all be
safer at Lea Magna. Taken in two stages for
Etta's sake, the journey was hot and uncomfortable with attempts at conversation more for the
child's entertainment than their own. There was
no grumbling or whining from her; everything
was an adventure, even when they watched the
blacksmith replace a shoe on Ginny's mare and
caught up with a crowd of pilgrims at the inn
where they had to sleep five to a room. As Lea
Magna appeared through the trees, the relief
washed over Ginny like a warm tide. Here was
home, at last.

'Home, my lord,' she said to Jon, reaching out to take his hand. 'Are you not pleased to be here again? Shall we stay longer this time?'

Wearily, he turned his head to look at her, his skin sallow, with dark circles beneath the eyes. 'You'd like that?' he said. His voice, usually so deeply vibrant, had paled like his skin.

'With you, my lord, yes. The danger has passed. It's time for us now.' She thought he would fall from his horse with weakness, but he clutched at the pommel and merely nodded his agreement as they rode through the gatehouse into the courtyard. Men came running and eager hands lifted them down. 'Tend my lord,' Ginny commanded. 'Lift him gently. Carry him to our chamber.... Send for Father Spenney, one of you.'

'He's already here, my lady,' someone said.

Even after long absences, the household fell quickly into the routine of care and service honed by years of practice. Etta's nurses reestablished her nursery as if they'd never been away and, ignoring her own fatigue, Ginny soon had the place buzzing like a hive to respond to the invasion they'd had such short notice of. It said much for her mother's training that she was able to take charge so efficiently, seamlessly transposing her skills from the town house in London to this huge mansion in the Hampshire countryside with all the differences of quantity and the allocation of space. It was then that Ginny was glad she had insisted on accompanying her husband, for now all protests had stopped as he was half-carried to the beautiful panelled chamber they had shared so briefly and put to bed between clean linen sheets.

Father Spenney stood beside her as the bloodied bandages were removed, partly stuck to the suppurating wound. 'What in heaven's name is this all about?' he said, washing his hands in the basin. 'Why did he not have it stitched? How long ago was it? Who tended him? The king's doctor? That old fool.' Answers to his questions were easy enough to supply, but to the question of why a man as fit and resilient as Lord Jon should still be suffering from a wound inflicted four months ago, the answer was more obscure. Some time later, stirring a whitish potion to help Jon to sleep, he shared his theory with Ginny. Speaking softly, he said, 'I've seen it before. The body, although seemingly strong, is unable to fight the ill humours that invade it when the mind is out of tune. Oh, don't look alarmed, Ginny. I don't mean to say he's deranged. Not at all. But for all his size and energy, it's his mind that will cry enough first, and delay the body in its mending. You did well to bring him back home. He needs time to come to terms with what's happened.'

So do I, she would like to have said, but the kindly monk was more used to dealing with men's minds and bodies than women's, and she was taking good care to conceal the fact that she would have appreciated a similar concern. 'So you knew about Cromwell?' she said.

'Oh, everyone knows by now, Ginny,' he whispered. 'News like that sweeps through the country like wildfire. Most men rejoiced, but your husband admired him not for his ruthlessness, but for his sheer brilliance and loyalty to the king. They all must have known what would happen after the latest marriage fiasco, and it must have hit Lord Jon very hard, being so close to the man.'

'But surely it isn't that alone, is it?'

'Probably not, Ginny. We'll talk tomorrow, when he wakes. I've done what I can to start the wound healing. The stitches will help. But a lot has happened to him and now he needs to sleep.'

Ginny could hardly disagree about the need for Jon to talk, for it was that same lack of communication that had come between them from the beginning. Having started marriage on the wrong foot, only explanations could provide the complete trust that was essential to them both, after the interference, one way or another, of almost everyone they were close to.

She was both surprised and pleased to find that Ben had come with Father Spenney to Lea Magna, and to hear that he was learning the arts of the physician, initially as his uncle's assistant. This, he told her proudly, after a few years at the University of Oxford, would fit him for a place in the world where physicians were always sure of employment. In the darkening chamber where Lord Jon slept like a child, she and Ben held a low-voiced conversation by the open window beyond which bats skimmed the apricot sky and the gardens were awash with pink and mauve. It was then that Ginny noticed for the first time how the low light caught the smooth planes of his nose and chin and how, in some indefinite way, he resembled her brother Paul, who in turn resembled his father more than Elion, Maeve and herself. Those three had always had Lady Agnes's looks. She dismissed it at once as a trick of the light. Neither of them noticed Father Spenney's discreet presence in the doorway, nor the frown of concern on his forehead as he turned away.

That night, Ginny had slept alone, restless with the heat and the strange sounds from the nearby woodland. At first light she rose and went to Jon, where she found him already awake and deep in whispered conversation with Father Spenney. The talking stopped abruptly as she entered. 'Looking better, my lord,' Ginny said, kissing his forehead. 'Are you pleased with your patient, Father?' The furtive glances between the two men, the uncomfortable silence, warned her that all was not well. Sitting on the bed beside Jon's feet, she prepared herself for bad news. 'Now tell me what's wrong, if you please. The wound is infected?'

'The wound is healing nicely, my lady,' said Father Spenney. 'Our patient is making an excellent recovery already. Nothing's wrong.'

She would have expected Jon to confirm this, but he preferred to examine his gold signet ring. 'Something is,' she insisted. 'May I not know what it is? I'm sure it can be put right.'

Father Spenney seated himself on a joined stool and she knew then that he would explain the matter, even if Jon didn't. He spoke, however, to his patient. 'This is for you to say, my lord. But my advice would be—'

'Yes Father,' Jon said, 'I know what your advice would be. What concerns me is *how* to tell my beloved wife without upsetting her. She's been upset so many times these past few months, and for the life of me I cannot—'

'For pity's sake!' Ginny said. 'What is it? Obviously something I ought to know. Is it Etta? My mother? Is it Paul? Just tell me.'

'Ginny, sweetheart. None of that, thank God, but nothing we can do anything about now. You remember how you and Ben were sitting over there by the window last night, in the last of the light?'

'It's Ben! What's happened to him?'

'Nothing, love. Only, you see, I was not asleep, as you thought.'

'Jon, our talk was innocent, I swear it. Ask Ben, if you will. There has never been anything but friendship between us. Ever.'

'Ginny,' said Father Spenney, 'your husband knows that, but what you and I know is that Ben's feelings for you have always been more than friendly.' He raised a hand to prevent her cry of protest. 'Just listen to me awhile. Your husband saw what I could not, that Ben and your brother Paul look so alike that it's hard for anyone to believe that they're not related.'

She had seen it, too, last night, for the first time.

'It happens, Ginny,' Jon said quietly, reaching out for her hand. 'These things happen. Men away at court, wives left alone, arranged marriages, the need for love as well as duty.'

Ginny shook her head in bewilderment. 'I'm sorry, you're going to have to spell it out for me. You're telling me that Ben and Paul may be related, but how? Surely that would involve Father... Oh!' Both young men had Sir Walter's looks. She had noticed that, too. 'Oh, no! That's quite impossible. Sir Walter has always been uncompromising when it comes to infidelity. Except in the king's case, of course.'

'Unfortunately, infidelity is common enough even in those who swear they're against it, Ginny. Your father suffered the same temptations as most other men, as I know only too well, and this happened when he was young and vulnerable.'

'This happened? *What* did?'

'Ginny,' Jon said, 'I looked across to the window and thought it was Paul you were talking to until I saw the habit. That's why I spoke to Father Spenney about it. They're both your father's sons, but not your mother's. Sweetheart, don't judge him too harshly.'

'Harshly? The hypocrite! What a damned *hypocrite*!'

'He's just a man like the rest of us,' said Father Spenney. 'His marriage to your mother was arranged in exchange for property, as is so often the case, and then men look outside marriage for love. Unfortunately, your father found it in the wrong place, in St Clare's Priory. The prioress was one of his tenants.'

'The *prioress*?' she whispered. 'Did...did my mother know?'

'Yes, she knew. She loves him, you see.'

Ginny freed her hands to cover her face and she spoke through her fingers. 'Tell me,' she said, 'about this woman. St Clare's Priory was closed down four years ago by Cromwell's men. So where is she now?' Unable to mask the accusing tone, she saw the shadow of pain pass over Father Spenney's lined face. St. Clare's had been closed down, they said, for lax behaviour by the nuns. That was the excuse they needed, used often and unjustly, but not in this case.

'She was my sister, Ginny. She died four years after the birth of Ben.'

'So Ben...is my *brother*?'

'Half-brother. He came to me at Sandrock

at that time. And now perhaps you'll begin to understand why Sir Walter was so keen to buy Sandrock when we were closed down, too. He wanted to pass it on to Ben as the inheritance he would not otherwise be entitled to. Younger sons traditionally do rather badly when their fathers die, don't they? And illegitimate sons can be ignored, unless their fathers make provision for them.'

Ginny dropped her hands despairingly and looked up at the rafters with a sigh. When she spoke, it was as if she was speaking to herself. 'Unbelievable! So Father used *me* to make sure of getting Sandrock for Ben. He couldn't simply rely on his own merit. He had to drag me into it, too, just to remind the king of his services. That's beyond hypocritical, Father. That's immoral. He didn't spare a thought for my feelings, did he? He actually *bullied* me into being the king's mistress when he believed he might be allowed to buy Sandrock anyway.'

'I'm afraid that's true. And I think it was partly for my sister's sake, too.'

'She must have meant a great deal to him.'

'She did. She was a wonderful woman, but not the right material for holy orders, even though she was elected prioress.'

'So how long had the affair been going on? Years? Paul is older than Ben.'

'Your sister Maeve was only four when Paul was born. Elion was two. They were too young to be surprised when Paul appeared from nowhere. Your father asked Lady Agnes to accept him as her own and she agreed.'

'As she would. She agrees to everything Father wants, but he had no right to ask that of her.'

'She took Paul in from birth and he became part of your family. It's not unknown, Ginny.'

'Huh!'

'Then when Ben came along, Sir Walter would have brought him home, too, but Lady Agnes was expecting you at the time and the pretence could not have been maintained. She was upset. She refused.'

'That must have been the first and only time. And no wonder.'

'So my sister kept the child with her, as two other nuns had also done and, when she died, Ben came to me at Sandrock. He was four. We took young children occasionally, if their parents could help us with the fees, which your father did, most generously.'

'So Paul and Ben never shared a home. That's why they're so different.'

'Hardly surprising, considering their up-bringing. Lady Agnes tended to overindulge Paul to compensate him for his illegitimacy and the loss of his natural mother. I do believe she felt sorry for my sister, in some way. That kind of compassion is a rare thing, Ginny. She is a good woman, your mother.'

'Is that what you'd call it? I'd say she was weak to spoil Paul so.'

'As I said, she loves your father. That's what women do when they love. Your father took advantage of that, but as long as Paul was there with them, he was reminded of his own weakness, and perhaps that's why he found it difficult to approve of anything Paul did. He saw so much of himself in Paul, you see, and he didn't like what he saw. He never saw very much of Ben.'

'You noticed it, too?'

'Whenever I was there, it was glaringly obvious. It made me sad for my sister, but Ben had four years of her love. I do not break any confidences in telling you this, Ginny. I was never your mother's confessor, or your father's, not even recently as chaplain at D'Arvall Hall. I tell you these things as uncle to your father's two sons, that's all, and because your husband and I believe you have a right to know the truth.'

'Shall you tell Ben what you've told me?'

'Yes, he must be given the facts, too. Every man has a right to know who his parents are. He must also be told not to worship you as he does.'

'Oh!' Again, Ginny's hands covered her face, but this time it was to conceal the awful contortions of grief. If only Jon had worshipped her instead.

Jon leaned forwards to pull her gently into his arms, rocking her like a child to the soft sound of his endearments, while the prior moved away to comfort his own grief in the presence of his nephew. 'Dear heart,' Jon whispered into her hair. 'Dearest love, don't weep. This cannot affect our love. It happened long ago. We have something your parents never had. Hush, love. Let it go now.'

Chapter Ten

The weeping abated. 'This is not like you, little wildcat,' Jon said with concern. 'I'd have expected anger. Some very un-Christian words, at least. You knew this kind of thing happened, my love.'

'Not in my family, it doesn't,' she croaked.

'Beloved, it happens, one way or another, in most families.'

Carefully she drew herself away and took one of his hands upon her knee to examine it. 'Your nails need trimming. And your hair...tch!' Her change of subject was not entirely successful.

'Thank you, wife. And you look as achingly lovely as a summer morning. And I'm getting up.'

'No, you're not, you're staying put. You need rest.'

'That's not what I need.' His hand left hers to

smooth the underside of her breasts, unconfined by boned bodice and stiffened fabric.

Ginny caught at his hand before it could explore further. Her breasts were tender and swollen, and she knew he would be able to tell that she was with child, even at this early stage. She had rehearsed, more than once, how she would tell him, how his face would light up, and how he might at last begin to share with her the love he'd borne his first wife. Now, after hearing of her father's treachery, her emotions were raw and confused, and she was no longer sure how Jon would react to yet another change of circumstances when she would be obliged to leave court. What had he just said about leaving wives at home? About temptations. Could she bear it? Against all her efforts to control them, the tears gathered again and dripped off the long sweep of her lashes onto Jon's hand.

'Ginny…my dearest, darling girl! Whatever is it? Have these revelations shocked you so much? Oh, my love, tell me.' Taking hold of both her shoulders, Jon turned her to face him.

'You…you called me…beloved,' she whispered, choking on the words. 'You said we had love. I may have misheard, but you see, I love you, Jon. I always have. And I've so longed to hear you say…'

'Ah…sweetheart, you did not mishear me. You *are* my love and I adore you. Could it be that we both fell in love that day at Sandrock? I thought it was only me.'

'You didn't, Jon. You were horrid and arrogant.'

'I adored you the moment I saw you, little scold. Even when you berated me for my duties. I told your father I wanted you at the time.'

'But he said you'd think about it.'

'Oh, beloved, what a dreadful tangle. Were you so very angry with me?'

'You broke my heart, Jon. But I could hardly blame you for choosing a lovelier, wealthier wife. Well, I *did* blame you. I think I hated you for it.'

'And I never stopped loving you. Wanting you. I've loved you every moment since then.'

'Then why…?'

'Listen, sweetheart. You have to know what happened then. I've kept things to myself for far too long. Will you let me tell you, so that you might understand?'

'If you wish, Jon. But you see, I know Etta is not your child. I can see who fathered her. That must have hurt you so much, but then I was in exactly the same position, wasn't I? You knew it.'

'I knew it, yes, but there's more to it than that, my darling.'

'You told me once that things are rarely as clear-cut as they appear to be. This is going to be one of those times, isn't it?'

'Never more so, Ginny, darling. Come here into my arms.'

Nestling into him on the bed, it seemed to Ginny that the dream she had chased for so long was within reach at last. Jon loved her. Her head rose and fell on his deep sigh while she used the linen sheet to mop her damp cheeks. 'What are these things you could not share with me, Jon? I'm listening,' she whispered.

'Things that happened since my father died that I am not proud of, which I didn't intend you to know because I thought that, once you did, you'd hate me for forcing you into a marriage without giving you a chance to back out. I had reasons that I told myself were excuses, but they're not. I treated you shamefully, but I could not take the risk of losing you again, not after what had happened. I knew your pride had been hurt. I could see it when you came to court. You'd not have accepted me then, so I intended to wait and perhaps to court you a little. But then I had not known of Henry's interest, that he'd invited you there for a purpose that had nothing to do with his new queen's needs, but his. He offered me the chance to have you and I took it, even though you were unwilling. Since then, Ginny, darling, I've never been quite sure of you.'

Ginny spoke to the soft warm side of his chest where she could feel the vibrant rumble of his voice telling her things she had never thought to hear. She sensed he was skirting round the edge of some explanation, something deeply hurtful that he'd kept hidden until now. 'If I tell you,' she said, 'how I've loved you since that first time we met when you were so superior, would you begin to feel sure of me? Would you believe me if I said you were in all my dreams and that I'd built my entire future on being your wife, even at sixteen? Can you begin to imagine how I felt when Father said you were to marry a wealthy heiress instead of me? She must have occupied your thoughts, surely?'

'She did, but not in the way you think.'

'What are you saying? Did you not love her?'

'Love? *Hah!*' His voice was hoarse, indignant with loathing. 'No, sweetheart, love was never one of the ingredients of our sham marriage, I'm afraid. But I'll begin with my father, when he was imprisoned in France. He died just days after his ransom was paid in the autumn of '36, and it left his estate completely without funds. Henry felt partly responsible for that situation because he'd said he would contribute to the ransom and then he kept on delaying until I paid it myself in the end. So when I inherited, which was soon after you and I met, I found myself in debt to the tune of over fifty thousand pounds. The estate had been allowed to run down during Father's absence while I was at court, and our steward and bailiff had not been doing their jobs, and I was left with the option of selling Lea Magna and all its land. I told the king and he then offered to help me out.'

'Oh, dear,' Ginny said softly. 'That usually comes at a price.'

'It did. He offered me a bride, an heiress in his wardship wealthy enough to cover all my debts and much more. Magdalen Osborn, newly come to court and looking for a titled husband from an ancient family. I was not in a position to refuse if I wanted to keep the estate intact. I was torn, Ginny. I'd just been offered your hand and I was smitten by you.'

'But everyone I've asked tells me how beautiful and clever and witty she was.'

'She was, but, as you say, Henry's gifts are

costly. He was quite open with me about his motives. He wanted her for himself.'

'But hadn't he just married Jane Seymour?'

'He had, but he expected to get her pregnant almost immediately, and then he would take a mistress. And you know from experience that he prefers them to be married. She was to be his mistress-in-waiting.'

'Did *she* know that?'

'Oh, yes. And, being the kind of woman she was, she found the idea very appealing. Mistresses have power. But she was also the most promiscuous woman I've ever known, and if I'd told Henry what I had discovered about her, he would have been less keen. She looked virginal, but she was a whore. Henry offered me more lands and to pay for my father's funeral, and he set me up with a wealthy wife so that he could use me as insurance. I was to be the passive husband. Oh, he made no secret of it. That was the price of his aid, take it or leave it. So I took it. I couldn't afford not to. We were married in January, 1537.

'She knew the situation, and so as soon as Queen Jane's pregnancy was announced that May, my eager wife took up her duties. It was a wonder she'd not become pregnant herself before then, because she was never faithful to me in the short time we were married. I thought I wouldn't care, Ginny, but she was boastful, taunting me with her lovers and what they did to pleasure her. Culpeper was one of them. That first night you came to me here, I was stricken by memories of what I might have had with you, Ginny. And I couldn't tell you.'

'Oh, my love. I'm so sorry. I knew you were lonely. I wanted to comfort you. What a way to live.'

'I ought never to have agreed. But it was not long before she became pregnant. After only eight months, she gave birth to Henrietta the following January. She died a week later, just as Queen Jane had done the year before when she gave birth to Prince Edward. But then I was free of her, master of my own estate, wealthy and in debt to the king.'

'And a father.'

'Little innocent Etta. The image of Henry.'

'But I thought your wife must have been caught in the same net as I was, in love with you and you with her, but part of Henry's scheme. And I assumed you couldn't bear to see Etta because she reminded you of how you lost a beloved wife.'

'On the contrary, I couldn't bear to be reminded of an evil woman who took lovers with such willingness. I felt demeaned and worthless. Cheated of a wife and marriage. I felt that half the court was laughing at me and the other half sympathising. It's you who reminded me just how innocent little Etta is and how she needs us both. You have been an angel, showing me the way to go, and I love you.'

'But, Jon, you did it all again with me.'

'Can you forgive me? I still longed for the beautiful pure young woman I'd fallen in love with, and when Henry suggested—again—that I might take another wife...'

'For him to borrow whenever he felt like it...'

'Yes, and then there was young Mistress Virginia D'Arvall, whose father was greedy and eager to agree to it. Henry had seen you at home, and he knew your father would cooperate.'

'So you agreed. Just like that.'

'Ginny, darling, I knew that if I didn't agree, he'd marry you off to somebody else. It's as simple as that. So I agreed, having not the slightest intention of letting him anywhere near you. I never intended to honour the bargain.'

'What *bargain*?'

'I owed him, remember? For lands. His generosity. For rescuing me. What I had *not* bargained for was the conflict it caused when I tried my hardest to push Kat Howard under his nose instead of you, when I knew that would result in putting the Howard family in a position of power and my friend and master in danger.'

'Thomas Cromwell, Earl of Essex.'

'Yes. You know how Thomas Howard, the third Duke of Norfolk, and Cromwell were sworn enemies, even though they had to work together for Henry? Well, although I was successful in one respect, Cromwell had to pay for it when, as soon as Henry announced that his marriage to Anna of Cleves was over and his marriage to Kat Howard was on, the Howards rose to the top perch and found a way of committing my master to the Tower. And that was the end of him, as he and I both knew it would be. I had to watch them kill him. These past few weeks have not been easy for me, Ginny. Forgive me for neglecting you. I've been hard on you, sweetheart.'

She turned round to look up into the eyes so full of anguish, eyes that searched hers for signs of understanding. 'There's nothing to forgive, my love,' she said. 'It was just unfortunate that she is one of the Howards and that they had it in for the man you admired. Had he been born an aristocrat instead of the son of a brewer, he might not have been so despised. But they don't like men who work their way to the top, do they? They prefer them to be born there.'

'Apart from that, Norfolk never forgave Cromwell for closing down Thetford Abbey in Norfolk where his parents were interred in a magnificent tomb. Of course, it was wrecked and that forced them to transfer their bones to Suffolk instead. It's a sad story, my love, that has dragged innocent people into it.'

'But, Jon, we don't have to stay at court, do we?'

With surprising energy, he flipped her over to change positions and she saw how his face reflected the love and desire she had sometimes misread. He had loved her from the beginning and Fate had taken a hand against them, causing Jon to suffer conflicts of loyalty and love, and herself to suffer the ambiguous pangs of rejection and longing. He had coerced her into marriage with him against her pride, not knowing whether she could begin to love him, or whether he could trust in her after his first unhappy experience. If only she had known the full story, she could have helped him more, instead of reaching so many wrong conclusions. 'Jon, my love. Let's stay here at Lea Magna. Let's start again, from the beginning. I have another, very small reason for wanting it.' She felt Jon's stillness as her words found a niche in his mind, his dark eyes probing hers to find the merest hint of laughter behind the tears remaining on her lashes.

Slowly, he turned her towards him and gently pulled at the drawstring round the neck of her chemise, baring first one beautiful full breast and then the other, showing him what he expected to see in the darkened skin around the nipples, usually a dainty pink. He stared, then tenderly fondled, stroking the blue-veined skin to soothe the sensitive heaviness. 'Is this it, sweetheart?' he whispered. 'Is this what made you weep? And all this time you've been waiting on me hand and foot, riding all this way to nurse me at home and keeping it to yourself? Did you think...?'

'You were unwell, Jon. I had to get you better first. I wasn't even sure you'd want it, though I hoped you might like a brother for our Etta.'

'Beloved...dearest, most wonderful wife. Ah...sweetness.' Closing his arms around her, his kisses were in answer to all her uncertainties. 'We'll do whatever you wish. We'll have sisters and brothers for Etta, wild, beautiful creatures like their mother and big lads like me. We'll make the rafters ring with their laughter, shall we?' His arms gathered her up as his kisses roamed over her tear-stained face, the question of leaving court hardly warranting a reply. 'Damn Henry' was all he said.

Freed from the duties of court life, Ginny and Jon spent every part of the day together with Etta, watching her progress, teaching her new words, playing ball games of every kind, even football with the help of their guest, Lady Agnes, and with Ben, Molly, and Father Spenney. Cheating was all part of the fun. At night, with all the windows open to catch any breeze, the adults lingered on the parched lawn to watch the moon rise into the indigo sky, finally yawning their goodnights and leaving Ginny and Jon alone, hand in hand, happier and more content than either of them had ever thought to be.

She lay her head on his shoulder. 'I don't know what I've done to deserve this,' she whispered. 'You've been part of my dreams for so long, I think that one day I might wake up and find myself back in my own bed, crying myself to sleep and listening to the rain beat on the windows.'

'Sweetheart,' he said, gathering her up closer, 'this is no dream. It's real. This is me with you in my arms and that's how it will stay until we're old and toothless. We shared the same dream, but we were made to wait, perhaps to test our love, to see if it would last. Ours grew stronger.'

'But I couldn't tell love from hate, Jon.'

'Ah, Fate nearly had you there, didn't she? She plays that trick on lovers. But she brought us back together again and you were spitting fire. Little dragon.'

Her body shook with laughter in his arms. 'Did ever lovers go through such trials? Do you remember the first night we spent together?'

'Determined not to let me near you.'

'And the masque, when…'

'When you wore the wrong outfit.'

'And you shoved Kat Howard at Henry?'

Laughter made them speechless for a while as they clung and kissed, and felt the fierce rise of passion lift their banter to a different level. Jon's hands were still careful as Ginny took the lead. 'I think, dear heart, we should continue this in bed. I don't want to wait any longer. I want you,' she said, 'tonight.'

'Let's go up,' he said. 'I shall be the gentlest father-in-waiting ever.'

In the warm darkness of their room with only a large silver moon to see past the open bed curtains, they lingered over the loving while he drew from her cries of rapture as her body responded to his touch, as he used every artifice and caress to give her the joy they had perfected with a deeper understanding. At last, unfettered by any outside influence, they soared freely into oblivion where only they existed, in tune, with words of love as the perfect accompaniment. 'You are my heart's desire,' Jon said, taking his hand slowly down the length of her body. 'I loved you from that first moment I saw you standing in a pool of sunlight and I could think of no gallant words to say. All I wanted was to take you in my arms and kiss you and make you say you'd be mine. I thought I'd lost you for ever, my love.'

'Oh, Jon, and I thought you couldn't possibly care, even when you were free again. So much has happened to you. It was unfair.'

'What matters now is that we have no more secrets, no more shameful admissions, nothing to hold us back. You are mine, woman. I won you and I shall hold you for ever. Shall I claim you now?'

'Yes, take me, beloved. I have always been yours.' She guided him into her, feeling his warm hardness push against her with a sweetness that made her gasp with excitement. She held her breath, as if to breathe would somehow cause her to miss that first deep, gentle, slow plunge that rippled across every nerve like wavelets before they break on the shore. Her breath finally emerged as a whimper.

'Did I hurt you, sweetheart? Was that too rough?'

'No…no, Jon. It's just…too wonderful.'

He smiled and kissed her without breaking his rhythm, then talking stopped as they allowed the sensation to overwhelm them and to carry them on into a time-stopping place of sheer ecstasy where Jon's passion urged him on still further to a conclusion more sublime than anything either of them had experienced before. Earth-shattering. The aftershock left them both reeling from the intensity, mindless and sated.

'What happened?' Ginny whispered as Jon withdrew from her.

He took her hand and held it between them, and she felt that he was on the verge of laughter. 'I think,' he said, 'we might just have moved the earth between us. Lie still, my darling.'

She did not, of course, do what she was told, and soon the white-gold hair was spread across his arm as she slept in the crook of his shoulder with one hand trapped upon his chest.

Convinced that the terrible drought would soon have to end, they accompanied Lady

Agnes, Ben, and Father Spenney back to D'Arvall Hall before going on to Richmond Palace to visit the Lady Anna. The ex-queen was in the garden playing a game of skittles with Master Holbein, the Princesses Mary and Elizabeth, and several of their ladies. They had never seen her looking so happy, so fresh-faced and contented after her disastrous start earlier that year, and the laughter that echoed across the pristine lawns made even the dour-faced gardener smile.

Entertaining them all to supper that evening, Anna gave them the chance to see how well her household was organised and to meet some of the many guests who flocked to her doors. Although she was reluctant to accept Ginny's decision to spend more time at home, she could see how much it meant to her to make up for lost time and to raise a family. 'But who shall I have to advise me now, Ginny?' she said.

'My lady, that was months ago. Now you have no need of advice. You have style and grace, and all the things Henry's new queen does not.'

The compliment obviously pleased her and, when they left the next morning, she threw her arms around Ginny like a sister. 'Visit me often,' she said. 'I shall want to know as soon as the baby is due. And write to me? Promise?'

Ginny promised. 'And what about Master Holbein?' she said. 'Does he stay here with you?' The question was intentionally ambiguous.

Anna turned a little pink. 'For the moment. He's painting Princess Elizabeth's portrait here at Richmond. After that, perhaps another one.' She smiled impishly.

'Marriage, perhaps?'

'Oh, no. Master Holbein has a wife and children in Germany. But we are good friends. Henry visits me quite often nowadays, too. He finds it peaceful here.'

They embraced again. It had all been said. Anna was an example to them all.

Ginny, Jon, and Etta stayed at Tyburn House in Westminster for two weeks, entertaining Maeve and George and their family, giving them the good news and observing the astonishing changes in Ginny's brother Paul. From irresponsible rogue, he was now a shrewd buyer working in the royal wardrobe department. His former delinquencies had not been repeated and no one had a harsh word to say about him, not even the merchants who had tried, and failed, to swindle him. As for his relationship with the younger ones, it only took little Etta's yelp of joy to convince her parents that there was genuine affection on both sides. Had he not been taken up by Culpeper's cronies, they said, he would not have been led astray so easily, but when Ginny told her sister about the possible reason for Sir Walter's different treatment of Paul since childhood, she found herself in agreement.

As for their father's behaviour, Maeve's opinion was that it accounted for much that had previously been something of an enigma. Their mother's unswerving obedience to him, for one thing. For her, loyalty was absolute. Elion, who had listened to the sad story, agreed that Paul had always been treated rather differently. As boys together, he had seen more of it than the others.

Jon, who had also been listening to the discussion, voiced a dramatic sigh. 'Well,' he said, 'I don't see *my* wife offering me any of that unswerving obedience in the near future. It's all she can do to stitch me some new aglets on the ends of my laces. Look here,' he said, waving one of his doublet laces at them where the spearheaded gold stopper was missing. 'She sends me out like this.'

'Disgraceful!' agreed George. 'But my wife is just the same.'

Retaliating at full volume, the two sisters set about reconstructing the truth of the matter and so drowning out the first distant rumbles of thunder.

Epilogue

The weather finally broke at the end of October, causing floods and more hardship, washing away roads and drowning livestock. But by this time Jon, Ginny, and Etta were safely back at Lea Magna, beginning their new life together as landowners and dedicated parents. Occasional visits to their London home gave them a chance to see old friends and to catch up with the news, and to spend time with Sir George and Lady Betterton and the young ones. They went regularly to see the Lady Anna at Richmond, too, though Master Holbein died of the plague exactly three years after the end of this story. Anna remained single all her life.

Molly predicted, correctly, that twin boys would be born on Saint Valentine's Day to her lord and his lady. They had masses of dark hair like their father, and the christening was conducted at D'Arvall Hall by Father Spenney.

Paul's conversion became even more convincing when he found a well brought-up young woman to love, the daughter of a silk merchant. Sir Elion, still footloose, went abroad for a while, but always remained in touch with his family.

Ben continued to study medicine as his uncle's assistant while Sandrock Priory was being restored and adapted for domestic use. He then went abroad to Leyden to continue his studies and graduated with an MA in 1547, qualifying with the College of Physicians, whose offices were on Knightrider Street in London. Father Spenney died at D'Arvall Hall in 1550, being nursed to the end by the devoted Lady Agnes, though he was buried at Sandrock Priory, the home of Dr Ben Spenney.

* * * * *

Author Note

England in 1540 was an unsettled time for those who lived and worked within the orbit of Henry VIII, when his marriage to Anna of Cleves, his fourth wife, was annulled after only five months. Marriage to his third wife, Jane Seymour, had ended abruptly with her death after the birth of Prince Edward and, although Henry now had a son to succeed him—and several illegitimate ones—it was essential for a king to have more than one son, for safety's sake. Plague and other ailments carried off so many people in the days before reliable medication.

The getting of another heir became an obsession with Henry and, for once, his choice of bride in 1539 was not conducted in the usual way, but by attraction to a portrait commissioned from that most superb of all portraitists,

Hans Holbein, who saw in the lady qualities Henry could not. In the end, she had the wisdom to react exactly as Henry wanted a woman to react when she was told that her marriage was over; that is, with a meekness and complete obedience that might even have ruffled his vanity when he was told there had been no tears. Not even one. If Anna was upset, she had the sense not to make a fuss. She fared best of all six wives by being afforded high status, making herself a very popular hostess and enjoying her freedom enough to remain friends with all the royals, including Henry himself. As an author, I have the greatest fondness and respect for this woman, which is why I chose to make her one of the characters in Ginny's story. As for Henry calling her 'a Flemish mare', there is no evidence for this insult, which comes from a later historian, although Henry's juvenile behaviour at their first meeting is difficult for us to comprehend. Much nonsense has been written about Anna's appearance, but one only has to look at the portraits of her to see that, although perceptions of beauty change over the years, she is certainly neither fat nor ugly. Nor do I believe she smelled unclean, as Henry petulantly stated. Anna soon adapted to English fashions and habits, and was much loved by everyone, living out the rest of her life in the countryside at Richmond, Hever, and Bletchingly. She died in 1557 at the age of forty-two, outliving the king by ten years.

The terrible and catastrophic enmity between Thomas Cromwell and Thomas Howard, third Duke of Norfolk, is well documented and actually much worse than I have made it sound. Henry's second wife, Anne Boleyn, was also a Howard on her mother's side, her mother being the duke's sister, who married Thomas Boleyn, whereas Katherine Howard was the daughter of the duke's younger brother, but orphaned. So getting anywhere near the throne, either as a mistress or a wife, was a sure way of tipping the influence of power in that family's direction. The Boleyn family, and therefore the Howards, took a fall when Queen Anne lost her head on trumped-up charges partly engineered by Cromwell, and the Howards were desperate to return to favour. As the possibility of Katherine Howard becoming wife number five became a reality, Cromwell had the Duke of Norfolk kept out of London, knowing that, once he returned, Cromwell's days would be numbered. It is a sad indictment of Henry's loyalty to his faithful servants that he should not only have allowed, but encouraged the feuds between them to colour his own judgement. But that was what he did. Cromwell, the friend for whom Jon deciphered coded letters, was brutally beheaded. Some time later, Henry bitterly regretted it, but by then it was too late. He had lost his ablest minister and gained a wife, Katherine Howard, who turned out to be as foolish as anyone could have imagined. Her affair with Culpeper, the courtier in the story, caused her death on the block, as well as his. He is portrayed here as he was, and sadly the incident of the park keeper's wife is true, as is Henry's 'forgiveness' of his favourite. Which serves to illustrate the status of women in sixteenth-century England.

The practice adopted by the king of allowing personal friends to buy the monasteries that were closed down and destroyed between 1535 and 1540 is quite true. Some he gave away as gifts with all the land and property they owned, which was usually considerable. Sandrock Priory and St Clare's Priory in Hampshire, however, are fictitious, although some of the more fortunate priors and abbots were given positions as chaplains and clergy in parish churches. And although Henry VIII made himself head of the church in England, taking the place of the pope, he remained staunchly Catholic in his devotions to the end of his days. Nothing changed suddenly except the acknowledgement that the pope had no influence over the English church, but the loss of abbey treasures, like the Sandrock library, was quite unforgivable.

The severe drought of 1540 is true also, causing crop failure, food shortages, and many deaths. It broke suddenly in October, causing floods. There was plague in London, too, so Henry took his new wife on progress to the southern counties.

Elvetham Hall in Hampshire is now an hotel, but the original building on the same site was the residence of Sir Edward Seymour, Jane's elder brother, whose sad story of paternal deceit is also true. Hampton Court Palace is still open to visitors and, although Whitehall Palace is much changed, its history is well documented. Richmond Palace has long gone, although its gatehouse is still intact, and there is an excellent model of it as it was in Tudor times in Richmond Museum. D'Arvall Hall, Lea Magna, and Tyburn House are all fictitious, but there were houses of wealthy people lining the Thames in both directions from Westminster Abbey, and the use of the river for travel was more common than it is today.

Bibliography

For information on the life and times of the Tudor Court, I have relied heavily on the following books:

Henry VIII: King and Court Alison Weir
The Six Wives of Henry VIII Alison Weir
The Six Wives of Henry VIII Antonia Fraser
The Other Tudors Philippa Jones
Henry VIII Lacey Baldwin Smith
Life in a Tudor Palace Christopher Gidlow
House of Treason: The Rise and Fall of a Tudor Dynasty (for the Howard family) Robert Hutchinson
Thomas Cromwell Robert Hutchinson
The Tudor Age Jasper Ridley
Henry VIII and His Court Neville Williams
The Tudor Housewife Alison Sim

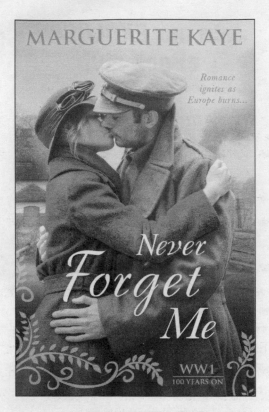

As a war blazes across Europe, three couples find a love
that is powerful enough to overcome all the odds.
Travel with the characters on their journey of
passion and drama during World War I.

**Three wonderful books in one from top
historical author Marguerite Kaye.**

**Get your copy today at:
www.millsandboon.co.uk**

The World of Mills & Boon

There's a Mills & Boon® series that's perfect for you. There are ten different series to choose from and new titles every month, so whether you're looking for glamorous seduction, Regency rakes, homespun heroes or sizzling erotica, we'll give you plenty of inspiration for your next read.

By Request

Relive the romance with the best of the best
12 stories every month

Cherish™

Experience the ultimate rush of falling in love.
12 new stories every month

INTRIGUE...

A seductive combination of danger and desire...
7 new stories every month

Desire™

Passionate and dramatic love stories
6 new stories every month

n o c t u r n e™

An exhilarating underworld of dark desires
3 new stories every month

For exclusive member offers go to
millsandboon.co.uk/subscribe

WORLD_M&Ba